WILSHIRE POINTE

P. MITTRA

DEDICATION

To my firstborn, Parisha.

Your excitement and enthusiasm
for this book were the fuel that kept me going.

No matter where it takes us,
we have created something for future generations to experience.

Love you.

PROLOGUE

*T*ick tock.

The sound of an invisible clock looms over a hollow cave; its echo bounces off slick stone walls. The location is unrecognizable. Somewhere she'd never been before, yet she's standing there.

A faint light from the lantern she clutches tightly in her hand illuminates her immediate surroundings. It's aged, made of iron, and powered by animal fat. The flames grow stronger as she approaches the cave, casting elongated shadows that twist along the cave walls.

A thick, viscous substance dribbles down the stone walls and pools at her feet.

A sharp crack breaks the silence, like the snapping of a bone.

She spins around.

Nothing.

The lantern light falls on her body, and confusion clouds her mind. She's wearing a Victorian nightgown—one she's never seen before. It hangs loosely from her shoulders, flowing to just above her ankles, trimmed with once-white lace, now yellowed with time. On the sleeve, embroidered in delicate thread, are the initials: J.C.

The shadows begin to change.

The flame's movements contort into human shapes—arms and legs bent backward at impossible angles. The shadows merge into the cave. They stretch, and they extend their limbs, reaching for her hair with evil intentions.

As she turns her head, she lets out a scream. Her body is frozen, paralyzed with fear. No sound can come out. Her mouth is open, and the evil energy pours in until the extensions vanish.

With caution, she opens her eyes, afraid of what's to come.

By her feet is a note, written on tea-stained paper. She looks around to the left, then to the right, but is too afraid to look back at the cave. With trembling fingers, she bends down to pick up the note. Before her hands can reach it, the note crumbles to dust.

She jolts awake, drenched in sweat.

Her heart pounds violently against her ribs as she lunges for the bedside lamp and flicks it on. Light floods the room.

Safety. Familiarity.

She grabs the glass of water and drains it in one gulp, her hands shaking. Slowly, her breathing steadies. Her gaze drifts downward.

She's wearing it. The same Victorian nightgown.

The same lace. The same fabric.

On the pillow beside her lies a folded piece of paper, stained brown at the edges.

Her fingers tremble as she picks it up and slowly unfolds it, fearful of what it might say.

Elegantly written in calligraphy:

"Shelby Jones. You're not who you think you are. Your entire life is a lie."

TABLE OF CONTENTS

CHAPTER 1

WILSHIRE POINTE UNIVERSITY

1978

"Why do you suppose architects of the past placed these hideous gargoyles on buildings? Any guesses? No?"

The tour guide seems quite pleased with himself as he continues, "Well, my inquisitive friends, their purpose was to collect rainwater from the roof and direct it away from the building's walls and foundation, preventing water from seeping into the stone. The word gargoyle is derived from the French word *gargouille*, meaning *throat*, reflecting the gargling sound of water draining through a spout. He lowers his voice. "They also served another purpose." He pauses. "To ward off evil spirits." A faint gasp ripples through the group, appearing to be slightly thrilled by the thought of evil lurking.

"And here, at the entrance of Wilshire Pointe University," he says, gesturing grandly, "two oversized, eighteenth-century gargoyles welcome you. Their grotesque appearance can assure you that no evil can pass through here." The group chuckles politely.

"This beautiful university, built in 1725 atop Wilshire Hill, boasts Gothic-style architecture with stained-glass windows and enormous pointed arches. It is one of the great landmarks of Wilshire Pointe, Massachusetts."

A few courteous acknowledgements follow as the group trails behind him along the original cobblestone path, worn smooth by centuries of footsteps. Gas lamps line the walkway, dormant in the daylight, waiting for nightfall. His voice fades as they ascend Wilshire Hill, swallowed by the sprawl of Gothic stone.

Students lounge across the campus courtyard, soaking in the last generous days of September before the cold creeps in. The midday sun moves like a spotlight, illuminating scenes as though flipping through television channels.

Channel 1: *The animated tour guide with a cluster of awestruck tourists. The Visitors.*

Channel 2: *Giddy couples sprawled on the grass, whispering sweet nothings through smoke-tinged laughter. The Lovebirds.*

Channel 3: *Bookworms with thick-framed glasses poring over syllabi, determined to make the right first impression. The Geeks.*

Channel 4: *Some students tossed frisbees; others, seated cross-legged on crochet blankets, strummed a guitar and played folk tunes by Bob Dylan or Cat Stevens, while their friends passed around a thermos containing "coffee." The Stoners.*

The overall mood is relaxed, charged with youth and quiet rebellion. Anything feels possible. However, nothing in this small New England town has to make sense just yet.

Channel 5: *This channel is the most interesting of all.*

It's the precise moment Shelby Jones enters the scene—oversized, paint-splattered overalls, books tucked under one arm, and a protest sign dangling from the other. She doesn't see the frisbee on the ground until it's too late. She trips, going down hard, face-planting into the lawn. The sign, the books, and her bag scatter in different directions, as if angry with one another.

The Freak.

"Aw, shit," she mutters, pants now torn at her throbbing knee. "I just bought these." A smeared grass stain and a small hole are new additions to her appearance.

No one rushes to help her up. Some stare. Some snicker. Others whisper, anticipating her next move. Shelby brushes grass from her knees and keeps walking as if nothing happened. The sign she made protesting the Shah's regime in Iran is bent at the corner; just another inconvenience on a long list. She's grown used to moments like this. Her waddling gait, with feet slightly turned outward, only adds to the spectacle.

"Quack! Quack!" two boys yell.

Shelby keeps her eyes on the ground. She has always been the odd one. Unapologetically herself. And that, more than anything, makes people uneasy. Everyone else seems busy rehearsing acceptance, blending seamlessly into expectations.

She watches the girls in knee-high platform boots and short dresses— feathered hair and practiced laughter—and feels a familiar wave of relief that she isn't one of them, yet a part of her was drawn to them, wondering if she could ever walk a day in their shoes. Wondering what it would feel like to be noticed.

Their conversations orbit hairstyles, boys, and the next party. Nothing that feels real or meaningful to her. But something in her wants to be a part of those conversations. Something in her wants to belong.

In her head, *she's* given *them* a name. *The Phonies.* She secretly laughs while thinking of it, her own little inside joke, with herself.

Shelby thought she'd left all of this behind in high school. But the university has turned out to be just a smaller version of the same town, full of people who never left and never wanted anyone else to either. "College will be different," everyone used to say. Turns out, it *was* different. It was actually *worse.*

And then there's Alice Whitman, the epitome of the phonies, at least in Shelby's book.

Alice looks at herself in a compact mirror, fixing her hair, powdering her nose, dragging her tongue across her teeth to check for any trace of lunch. A coordinating cloth headband holds her blonde hair neatly in place. Her flared jeans, embroidered with flowers, ride high up on her waist, and a bright orange blouse is neatly tucked in, showing off her small figure. White platform sandals lift her just enough to command attention. The ends of her perfectly styled hair flip outward, stiff and deliberate, as though trained to behave exactly as she wants them to.

Alice Whitman moves through the courtyard like someone who has never been told *no*—and never expects to hear it. Students react instinctively, stepping aside as she passes. They're not afraid of her in the way they are afraid of Shelby; they are intimidated by Alice's confidence and charm. Shelby doesn't need to know Alice well to understand her. If she's kind, it's calculated. If she's cruel, it's deliberate, and if she decides you don't belong, you don't.

Students clear a path as Alice sashays past. Shelby watches from a distance, already certain of one thing: Nothing good ever comes from girls like Alice Whitman.

****

Apparently satisfied with her reflection, Alice snaps the compact shut and clears her throat loudly. "She's going to be my project this semester."

"Who?" The voice behind her feigns interest.

"Who do you *think,* you bonehead?"

He stares blankly ahead, confused. Alice pivots on her heel, books tucked under her arm, and kicks his foot. He winces. "Oww. What the hell was *that* for?"

She tips her chin toward the girl across the courtyard. "Shelby Jones?!" he blurts.

"Shhhhh!" Alice clamps a hand over his mouth.

"What? Why are you shushing me?" he whispers once she lets go. "And why the hell do you always need a project? Don't you have enough to do—being head of the university social club?" He squints toward Shelby, studying her. "Why bother with *her*? She's clearly fine with herself. Have you noticed? She doesn't *care* what you or I think. She totally owns her weirdness. That's pretty rad, actually."

Alice rolls her eyes and snaps her bubblegum. "I could glamorize her," she says. "Shelby Jones has a face and a head of hair I can work with. She just doesn't know it yet." She pauses, lips curling. "And besides, I have a bet going on with River. I'm not letting him win."

Jared stiffens. "There it is," he says. "That's your problem. Not everyone wants to be like you. Just accept it and move on." He slings his backpack over his shoulder. "And I don't even want to know about this bet. Spare me the details." He pretends to rummage through his bag, avoiding her glaring eyes. Jared is aware that his comments didn't sit well with Alice. Before she can fire back, he takes off toward the parking lot. "Asshole!" she shouts after him. She flings a pencil in his direction, missing him by nearly ten inches and hitting the next person over. Jared doesn't slow. He flips her the bird without looking back and breaks into a jog, weaving through campus like it's a minefield; dodging conversations, ducking invitations before they can land. He cuts through a cluster of girls, with his eyes locked on his van. They straighten their shoulders, toss their hair, and offer smiles he doesn't return. He doesn't notice. *No time for girlfriends. They feel like prison guards in disguise.* It's a thought he repeats often enough to make it stick.

At last, he reaches the van. His sanctuary. Kicking open the door, the familiar scent of vinyl records greets him. Moody's clings to his clothes no matter how long he's been gone. The job pays enough to help his mom with everyday expenses, but more than that, it gives him somewhere to disappear when the world gets too loud.

If Jared could show up to his own wedding wearing high-top Chuck Taylors, he would—olive green or black. Corduroy bell-bottoms. A graphic T-shirt, usually a band or a brand. Today it's the Rolling Stones. Sometimes he lets his mustache grow out of sheer laziness, lending him a more seasoned look than his years suggest. Wavy, dirty blonde hair frames his high cheekbones with dimples that others pour over. With blue eyes sharp enough to unsettle, he never tries, never has to, and hates every bit of attention it earns him. Compliments make his skin crawl. The only girl who ever catches his attention is Shelby—not romantically, but protectively. They both come from one-parent households, a quiet rarity in Wilshire Pointe. That's why Alice calling her a *project* lodged so uncomfortably in his chest. If Jared has one redeeming quality, it's loyalty. Once you're his friend, you're his for life.

"Hey! Shelby! He calls out to her from inside the van with its window rolled down. She turns slowly toward the van, startled not just by the voice but by the fact that someone knows her name.

"Listen, I gotta get to work, so I'll be quick." He scratches the back of his neck. "Just a heads-up. Alice has some plan to, I don't know, make you up or something. Whatever you girls do." He shrugs. "She's gonna approach you. Just wanted you to know so you're not caught off guard."

"Um...ok?" She sheepishly replies with her eyes moving between him and anyone else who may be witnessing the conversation. He gives a brief wave and rolls the window back up. Shelby stands there, hovering between confusion and irritation. *That's the first time he's ever spoken to me, and I barely got one word in.* She exhales, grateful for the warning, but the irritation flares hotter.

A *project.* As if she's unfinished, as if she's *broken.*

"Shelby! Hey—Shelby, wait!" Alice's voice is sharp with a hint of desperation. Shelby closes her eyes. She keeps walking, lengthening her stride, pretending she doesn't hear. It never works. No matter how hard she tries to stay invisible, she somehow entangles herself in a web of drama.

Footsteps close in behind her. The relentless predator has struck.

"You're a tough one to track down!" Alice is out of breath. "Hey, wait.

Would you hold on and listen to me? I had an idea. I think it would really benefit you, Shelby. I was thinking—"

"No, Alice." Shelby spins around. "I'm not going to let you turn me into a joke. I am not like you, and I don't want to be like you. Why are you so obsessed?"

Alice's smile tightens. "Damn Jared and his big mouth! He got to you first, didn't he? I swear I'm gonna rip him apart." Shelby steps across the carpet of fallen leaves, books clutched tight against her chest. She blows a strand of hair out of her eyes, refusing to look back.

"Oh, c'mon, Shelby. You could absolutely use a makeover." Alice's voice floats beside her. "I could turn you into the grooviest girl in town, after me, of course. And I mean that in the nicest way possible."

Shelby scoffs. "Yeah, so kind of you. I'm not some dumb charity act you can put on display."

Alice shifts tactics, her voice dropping into something more measured. For a moment, it appeared as if Alice had left the scene. She was gone from Shelby's sight, but Alice wasn't one to give up easily. Once Alice Whitman had a plan in mind, she would see it to the end. She had taken a detour and found her way back to Shelby, jumping in front of her from a cluster of tall bushes. Caught between Alice and a stream running behind her, there was no place for Shelby to escape.

"Face it, if you wanna move up in this world, you have to make a good first impression." Alice's eyes scan Shelby from head to toe. "You don't get a second chance. Jobs. Dating. Life." She gestures vaguely at Shelby. "Look at you. You're...forgettable."

As she says this, Alice lifts a clump of Shelby's oily hair, then recoils slightly and crinkles her nose. She wipes her hand on her jeans.

"Honestly," Alice says, almost gently, "you leave no impression. And when people do notice you, it's because you're awkward. I know this sounds harsh." She pauses. "I feel awful saying it." She lets out a sigh. "But no one else is going to tell you the truth, because no one else cares."

Shelby takes deep breaths, controlling her anger as her grip tightens on her books. *The words burn, sharp, and humiliating. Who does she think she is?*

Somewhere deep inside, something in her subconscious stirs. It wasn't sadness, nor was it shame. It was recognition.

Shelby stares down at her oversized overalls; the hems are frayed. The fabric hangs straight and shapeless. Dirty white Chuck Taylors peer out from the cuffs. Instead of a purse, she carries a canvas bag slung over one shoulder, splattered with paint she never bothered to clean. Her long straight hair is parted down the middle, falling on either side of her face, dragging her features downward. There isn't a speck of makeup on her skin; something she refuses to wear. Freckles lightly dust her nose and cheeks, impossible to hide even if she wanted to. Jewelry is out of the question. She doesn't have any. Her fingernails are always short and chewed, and the skin around her fingers is red, bitten so far up it hurts to write or use her hands for any small task, such as tying her shoelaces. Anxiety lives in her hands, her jaw, her chest. It's constant and unexplained. It has always been there, like background noise she can't turn off.

Papa had always emphasized education, independence, and fighting for causes that mattered. He taught her how to stand her ground. He always told her to walk in the opposite direction from the majority. That most people didn't know what they were doing. But there were times, a lot of times, she just wanted to fit in.

"Education is power," he'd shout, fists up in the air—something Shelby would chant with him since she was three years old, mimicking him by raising her tiny fists in the air. What he couldn't teach her was how to be a woman. And that wasn't his fault. He wanted her to be independent—socially and economically. Free from ever having to rely on a man. In this world, nothing felt more dangerous to him than ignorance.

"I like my clothes," Shelby snaps at Alice. "They're comfortable! I'm not like you and all the other phony girls." There, she said it, and she couldn't take it back. She knows she crossed a fine line. An awkward silence hovers over them.

For a brief moment, color flashes across Alice's face and disappears. She has somehow mastered the art of self-control, especially when pursuing a desirable outcome. Some may call it wicked. Others...calculated.

Shelby immediately regrets the words that slipped out. Alice doesn't lash out. She doesn't raise her voice. She does nothing, and somehow, that's worse. Calm has always been Alice's sharpest weapon.

"Yes," she says lightly, "they definitely *look* comfortable, but it's not always about comfort, Shel."

She circles Shelby once, slow and deliberate, without moving her eyes from the target. "You have to present yourself to society, and honestly, no one is going to give you a job if you carry yourself like an absolute mess of a human." She waves her hand in front of Shelby, from top to bottom, as if Shelby is living proof of her theory. "You take care of your father, right?" Shelby cannot look her in the eyes. She plays with the cuff of her sleeve, almost absorbing the words spoken by Alice. *How does she know so much about my life?*

"Right now, your part-time job covers the medications," Alice continues her lecture, "but eventually, you'll want other things. Travel. Clubs. Art collections. Concerts. Movies." She smiles and touches Shelby's shoulder. "A life that's not just about surviving." Alice leans in slightly. "That takes money. And money requires a good job."

She ties her scarf dramatically around her head, slides her 'old Hollywood' sunglasses down her nose, and lifts her chin. "So, Shelby Jones, you're going to listen to me. Follow my lead. I shall be your stylist." Shelby laughs. For a moment, she forgets she's talking to Alice Whitman.

Shelby, a skeptic at heart, is not one to fall prey so easily. "Alice, just the other day, you and your friends were laughing at me when I asked the professor a question. I heard you snicker. I saw you pointing at me. And now, you wanna invest your time and effort to turn me into a glam girl?" Shelby meets her gaze. "What gives? Why are you doing this?" She pauses. "And don't tell me it's out of the goodness of your heart." Alice exhales and looks down. "Okay, fine," she admits. "You're too smart to be fooled by anyone." She hesitates, then continues. "River and I were joking around one day. I told him I could turn any girl in this university into a glam girl. He didn't believe me, so I made a bet with him." Shelby adjusts her shoulders slightly and clears her throat, already feeling humiliated by what Alice has to say. Alice, with eyes like daggers, doesn't waver once as she explains to Shelby why she has been chosen for the bet. "River pointed at you, without giving it a second thought. At that very moment, you confirmed his pick as you spilled your drink all over some boy in the courtyard."

Shelby looks away, knowing exactly what moment Alice was referring to. "Your timing couldn't have been better. River noticed you and said there was no way I could pull it off." Alice's voice trails off slowly, adopting a staged, guilty tone, and she lifts her chin again. "Forget the bet. I'm just sick of River swaggering around campus like he owns this place." Shelby looks at her straight in the eyes, and with unwavering confidence, states, "Alice Whitman, you really are something else. He's the male version of you." They both burst out laughing. Shelby knows she *should* be angry. Someone reduced her existence to a challenge—a joke. But instead, something else stirs inside of her. Defiance.

Who does he think he is? I may be clumsy. I may not be beautiful by their standards. But Papa raised me to hold my head high, and that kind of resilience doesn't fade. Alice thinks she's using me? She has it all backwards.

"So, all the talk about making a good first impression was bullshit?" Shelby inquires as she studies Alice. "It was all about the bet?"

"Actually, no, Shelby. I still stand by everything I said. No one takes you seriously if you don't look the part. That's just a fact of life."

Shelby considers. Then nods once. "Okay." She raises her eyebrows. "I'm in." A slow smile spreads across her face. "Let's give River Smyth a taste of humble pie."

CHAPTER 2

THE HOUSE THAT NEVER SLEEPS

The Whitman house barely slept.

There was always someone from the staff looming around like a ghost in the night—the guards, pacing back and forth in front of the tall iron gate, or the housemaid, Mrs. Robbins, fluffing the living room pillows for the next morning, the way Mr. and Mrs. Whitman preferred.

Precision.

Alice lay awake at night, in her childhood bedroom, staring at the ornate ceiling medallion. Imported silk drapes cascaded from the bedposts, puddling like liquid onto the cold, marble floor. Her parents were gone again. France, this time. Or maybe it was Italy. It didn't matter.

A soft knock came at her door. "Alice," Mrs. Robbins whispered. "Your parents asked me to tell you they love you, dear. They'll be returning by the end of the week." She lingered a moment longer before retreating to her sleep quarters. Alice pretended she was asleep as a tear escaped her eye, ran down her cheek, and pooled on the pillow. She angrily flipped it over. A feather escaped and landed near her nose.

The house demanded order. The hall lights went off exactly at 10 p.m., as they did every night. Even silence had its schedule.

The week before, there was a small party. New friends from town. The useful kind. Those who would connect her parents to a top real estate agent. A beautiful property overlooking the water. In the Whitman house, friendship always came with an agenda. There was always something to be gained. Her father played tunes on the piano while her mother sang, her melodic voice slipping through the cracks. Always in perfect harmony. Alice turned up the volume on her record player, pressing the needle down harder than necessary. She was used to seeing them live dual lives, one for the public and one behind closed doors. The feeling of disgust crawled up her skin and tingled her every nerve in the worst way possible. Her parents lovingly laughed and put their arms around one another until the last guest left. Once the party ended, so did their affection. The show was over, and they both retreated to separate rooms for the night.

Tonight, the house was quiet. The staff disappeared into their quarters. She lay there in bed, unable to sleep, softly counting the flowers printed on her wallpaper. The stillness was interrupted by dull piano notes, drifting up through the floorboards from the living room below.

She sat up. "Hello?" Her voice sounded small and childish. A misfit in a home so large.

The music stopped.

Click. The hall light outside her door flickered on, disobeying the house rules. Her stomach tightened as she clenched her blanket and threw it off. Alice stepped into the hallway, barefoot against the cold floor. Portraits of her parents lined the walls; their painted eyes fixed on her with no expression, no emotion. The walls seemed to hold secrets she would never know.

You are alone. You always have been. And you always will be. The warmth. The affection. The love. The concern. It has all been an illusion.

CHAPTER 3

FROM BOGUS TO BOUGIE

"Our first plan of attack is your hair, Shelby. We need to do something with it." Alice doesn't wait for my response. She drags me to the most prestigious and expensive salon in town. The kind where expensive fragrances greet your nose, and everyone speaks in hushed tones while tasting imported chocolates from crystal glassware placed at each station.

I've always worn my hair long and straight, parted down the middle. I brushed it *when I remembered* and washed it with whatever soap happened to be sitting by the bathtub. It was obvious. I didn't belong here.

The stylist gestures for me to take a seat, as if I were an alien who accidentally wandered into the salon and didn't speak the language. A server glides over with a tray of Harrods teas. My fingers twitch. For a split second, I considered grabbing a handful and slipping them into my bag for later, but Alice's commanding voice appeared, uninvited, into my mind.

Etiquette, Shelby.

She had trained me quickly, almost aggressively, not to look amazed when presented with luxury. The trick, according to Alice, was to behave as if you *belonged* at the table. Ask for what you want, casually. Don't gawk. Don't gush. If you act impressed, people can smell it, and they'll place you as an outsider. They'll treat you accordingly. Maybe that was her secret. She behaved like she owned the world, and the world responded in her favor.

Luca steps in. Luca, the highly fashionable stylist, wears all black, mostly leather. His clothes mirror his personality: dramatic. Black leather pants. Black vest. Black V-neck. Black boots. His hair is tucked neatly behind both ears, a thick mustache perched above his slender lips. He spent two years in Paris and apparently never allows anyone to forget it. He somehow acquired an accent during that time. Alice had told me all about him on the ride over to the salon. Luca lifts sections of my hair, examining me like a sculpture in progress. "With her oval-shaped face," he murmurs to Alice, loudly enough for me to hear, "a layered, feathered style would be absolutely divine."

"Yes!" Alice exclaims like an excited toddler, bringing her hands together in a silent clap. I knew she had forgotten where she was, as she immediately toned down her excitement. She continues with Luca, "Like Farrah Fawcett. What about color? Do we keep the strawberry blonde or go darker?" Luca puckers his lips, closes his eyes, and inhales deeply, as if summoning divine intervention. I interrupt. "That's where I draw the line. I want my original color." Luca opens one eye, then the other. He raises a single eyebrow and snaps his fingers, impressed that I actually have a voice. "Yes, madam," he says smoothly. "At your service."

Ninety minutes later—after washing, conditioning, cutting, blow drying, and styling—Luca slowly turns my chair toward the mirror.

Alice stares. I stare. Luca stares.

For a horrifying second, I think something is wrong. Something is on my face. Something that isn't supposed to be there. My hair looked like something out of *Vogue Magazine*. It was bouncy, weightless, and framed my face to perfection. Beautiful. A word I've never used to describe myself. A word no one has ever used to describe me. It's unfamiliar ground. Startling, to say the least. And something warm settles in my chest—a feeling that's foreign—but I want it to stay there forever.

"The boys are going to *freak* when they see you tomorrow," Alice says. "I can't believe what a haircut can do." She bumps hips with Luca, celebrating their creation. "We're just scratching the surface," Alice admires my appearance through the mirror. She slips Luca a tip, one that was a lot more than I could afford.

I give her a nod with a forced smile, slightly afraid of what's to come.

CHAPTER 4

THE MASK

Alice's bedroom looks like it was ripped straight out of a glossy magazine.

Purple silk sheets. Are you serious?

A velvet, tufted headboard. A white shag rug. Framed posters of the Beatles, Pink Floyd, and Queen line the walls. Some are even signed. On the opposite side of the room sits a dresser with a lighted mirror, clearly intended for daily glam rituals. A writing desk, untouched, is positioned by the window with a lava lamp on top. In the corner, an oversized beanbag chair swallows fashion magazines. Her wardrobe is already laid out across the bed. We're the same size, which delights her.

Before I can fully process what's happening, I'm zipped into a short dress, shoved into tall platform boots, and layered with makeup I've never owned in my life. Liner snakes across my eyelids and gently flips up at the ends. Alice holds the instruments lightly and brushes my cheeks with a warm, rosy glow. She's truly an artist. In full concentration. Creating. Coral gloss softens my mouth. I barely recognize myself. But I felt safe behind my new mask, and somehow through this process. I like her. I like Alice Whitman. Who knew this day would come? She circles me, inspecting her work, equal parts proud and possessive. She wants to help me, but she also wants to *display* me, her very own wind-up doll. Her ego is on the line. She never loses. I owe her. I never could have done this on my own. "So," I say casually, "what was the bet?"

"Huh?" Alice blinks, snapping out of her artistry. "The bet. You and River. The reason why we're here." I asked her while staring at my new face. "Oh. Right." Alice smirks, leaning against my chair. My eyes shift to her from my reflection in the mirror. "I've been having a blast creating a masterpiece here," she gestures to me, "I almost forgot about the bet! So, if the whole university notices you, River Smyth has to ask you out. Publicly. In the courtyard." I swallow hard, knowing this question may sting. But I ask anyway. "And if you lose?"

Alice stares blankly at the wall, quietly contemplating the dreadful words about to exit her lips. "I show up to campus in oversized overalls. No makeup." She shudders at the thought. "Absolutely not. That's definitely not going to happen, because there is no way in hell you will go unnoticed."

I laugh, picturing it—secretly hoping she loses. In the worst case, she can always borrow my overalls.

CHAPTER 5

HUMBLE PIE

It was the day of my debut as an irresistible woman. *Why am I doing this? Yes, the goal is to humiliate River.* I keep reminding myself. This is just temporary.

I practiced for hours, walking in three-inch, ridiculous platform shoes, rehearsing my posture, my dialogue, my expressions, my *nonchalance*. Nonchalant, Alice explained, meant cool, calm, and relaxed. Effortless. I'd never heard of that word before, and now I was supposed to *embody it*.

Alice had her driver pick me up from home. She sat in the back seat, bouncing with anticipation. She could be so childlike at times. Her eyes were on me, scanning her creation, and she appeared completely satisfied. Letting out a squeal, she cupped her face with her manicured hands, admiring me from head to toe. I have never seen anyone so delighted with their creation. Her parents must have raised her on a steady diet of affirmation, because Alice possessed an almost alarming level of confidence. She constantly celebrated herself, and I couldn't decide whether it was admirable or terrifying. A part of me wanted to borrow just a fraction of it.

As we exit the car and head toward campus, the stares begin, the jaws open. The boys follow me with their eyes, and the girls scan my entire body. With their concerned expressions, I could almost see how threatened they felt—holding on even tighter to their ogling boyfriends. The reaction was immediate. Alice's face beamed with victory. But we weren't at the finish line. Not just yet.

We passed by groups of students and the chattering stopped mid-sentence; I could feel their lingering stares follow me. The same young men who had quacked at me just days before now whistled behind my back. They probably thought I was a new girl on campus. I started to slouch a little, suddenly self-conscious. "*Posture.*" Alice nudged me sharply with her gaze to the front. Immediately, I corrected myself. My feet kept moving. I counted steps, pretending to balance a book on my head the way she'd taught me.

Stomach in. Arms loose at my sides. Long strides. Project confidence. Don't look at your feet. A hint of a smile, but not too much.

Her instructions play on repeat in my mind. This was exhausting. How did women do this every single day?

River approached us and elbowed Alice playfully. "Hey, aren't you going to introduce me to your *new friend*?" Alice took him far too seriously and launched into a formal introduction. River and I exchanged a look. He'd seen me on campus at least a hundred times—but now, for the first time, he was actually seeing me. He looped his arm through mine and strutted into the university with me.

With me. River Smyth. Campus royalty. Star quarterback. Wanted to be seen with me.

Papa's voice, the one that preached independence and resilience, began to shrink in the back of my mind as River was leading me around. Jared was walking in our direction from across the way. He shifted uncomfortably once he saw my new look, his eyes narrowing in suspicion before he masked it with a poker face and jumped into a conversation with River about the upcoming game. I couldn't tell whether he was disappointed in me for ignoring his warning or didn't care. He gave me a half-smile—something between confusion and concern.

I couldn't read him.

River laughed. "See, Jared? This is exactly why you don't have a foxy babe like Shelby yet. You don't know how to compliment a queen when you see one." Jared rolled his eyes and fled to class. This was exactly the reaction Alice wanted—and she got it. But she played it cool. *Nonchalant.* As if she expected it all along.

I opened up the pink, glittery case of my compact mirror for a quick check- hair in place, teeth clean, lipstick intact, and no smudged eye make-up. What I hadn't paid any attention to before became second nature in a span of twenty-four hours. I wasn't quite sure about the person who was staring back at me, but I was ready to get to know her. I pressed the compact together, making a loud clicking sound, and threw it into my new leather handbag, courtesy of Alice. It felt like Halloween, and I was dressed up as someone else. But it was working. Just as planned.

Later, in the courtyard, I sat on a bench rereading my history notes, though I already knew them by heart. Across the lawn, River's silhouette grew larger as he made his way toward me. I felt his eyes examining every inch of my body, and it took every ounce of my energy to sit still and appear comfortable in my own skin. My heart picked up speed. My hands left damp imprints on the shiny cover of my book as I closed it. I swallowed hard and took a deep breath. This was the moment. I couldn't let Alice down. She had positioned herself perfectly on the steps near the fountain—front row seat secured, peering above an opened science magazine of no interest to her. She gave me a 'you can do this' nod. She had already won the bet. The entire university noticed me. But now it was time for the humiliation. The part she was anxiously waiting for.

I kept my eyes on my handwritten notes as his presence closed in. A breeze carried the scent of his cologne—Ralph Lauren Polo—that smell. I could have drowned in it.

Focus, Shelby. It's a trap.

Black Adidas sneakers crept into my peripheral vision. He hovered beside me, self-assured, like a bee circling a flower. I pretended to rearrange items in my bag, not wanting to give him importance. I took my time, then looked up and tilted my head to the side, slightly squinting as the sun hit my eyes. I knew it was the most flattering position as the rays hit my hair and make-up quite perfectly. I had checked it with my pink compact. With smug confidence, I asked, "Is there something I can help you with?" He dropped onto the bench—too close. I liked it but pretended to be irritated. He then draped his heavy, muscular arm around my shoulders.

"I dig this new look you got goin' on, Shel."

Shel. Yesterday, he barely knew my name.

"You free Friday night?" he continued, staring straight into the horizon, chewing on a toothpick. "Pizza Noli's, maybe a movie after?" The audacity of being asked out without eye contact was almost impressive. His confidence was so inflated, I imagined his head floating skyward like a runaway balloon. I stood up all too quickly. It happened so fast. My ankle twisted. Gravity took over. I fell straight onto him. His arms caught me. I swiftly glance over at Alice. She dropped her magazine and was now shaking her head from side to side. I wasn't sure whether she felt sorry for me or was just being entertained. For one brief, mortifying second, it looked exactly like one of those romantic movie scenes I always scoffed at. The ones that seem so unrealistic. Where one can only wish those juicy moments happened in real life. Apparently, yes, this *did* happen in real life. I recover quickly, clear my throat, and step back, regaining control of my dignity. My perfectly manicured hands brush my skirt, and I recover my balance, standing tall. "It's a shame you never noticed me before," I said evenly. "I'm busy this Friday. And the next. And the one after."

The courtyard went silent.

"But don't worry," I added, "I'm sure there are plenty of girls who'd love to go out with you." I met his eyes. "I'm not one of them."

River blinked, stunned. Then, desperate to save face, he laughed and called out, "What about Saturday?"

Alice's mouth was still open. And at that moment, we both knew.

River Smyth had just taken the biggest bite of humble pie, served by yours truly.

CHAPTER 6

THE NIGHTLY PRAYER

My social life had completely changed. I actually had one now. Somehow, without meaning to, I crossed over. I was one of the Phonies.

Not just an ordinary one. I'd moved up. Next in line to Alice—her right hand. I was seen with her everywhere. Across campus and in town, the movie theater, the mall, you name it. I was friends with Alice Whitman. The realization took me by surprise. Not because it wasn't true, but the speed at which it all transpired. One day, I was invisible. The next, I was invited. People wanted me at their events. I'm almost embarrassed to admit I was addicted to the rush. My face lit up when someone smiled at me or called out my name. The feeling of being appreciated became a natural high, one I easily embraced. It felt good to be acknowledged by people who *mattered*. Yes, that made me shallow. I knew that. But it was easier than being a freak. Easier than pretending I didn't care.

Still, no matter how much had changed on the outside, one thing remained constant. I had a secret. Not the kind you tell after midnight or whisper to a friend you trust. This was bigger. Heavier. A secret that lived in my body, not my mouth. It followed me into sleep and hovered at the edges of my thoughts during the day. No matter how polished my appearance became, no matter how full my calendar looked, something inside me stayed relentless, tugging at me and clinging to my being like a relentless toddler. There were questions buried deep in my subconscious, but I didn't know what to ask. Behind this new lifestyle lived an uneasy dread of something about to unfold, and no amount of temporary glamour could mask it.

Only one feeling remained. That this life, my life, was incomplete. There was more to it than what I'd been told. More than what I remembered. More than what made sense. Something from my past was inching into my core through my anxiety, through the sleepless nights. Nights, I would wake up in a sweat. Calling out, but there was no name to call. Every night, before bed, I asked to be shown.

"Dear Lord," I whispered into the darkness, "show me what I need to see. Guide me toward the truth. Free me from this constant pull into the unknown." I kissed the small cross hanging at my neck and pulled the covers up to my chin.

Night after night, I rehearsed the same prayer with complete faith, with the hope that something somewhere was out there, listening, and would eventually answer my call.

CHAPTER 7

MY SWEET MOSES

It's a normal morning at my home.

I like my breakfast with a side of coffee and silence. The newspaper sprawls across the table and the television is off, along with the radio. Even the drip from the faucet feels too loud in the stillness.

Papa is still asleep. These hours are mine: no questions to answer, no explanations to be given, just me with my own thoughts. I circle job listings with a pen that barely works. Secretarial positions. Medical offices. Places where I can be seen. I'm not afraid to be seen anymore. I'm pretty. And I want the world to know it.

Ugh, stupid pen. I toss it into the trash. Dead pens don't belong in cups. Empty boxes don't belong in pantries.

A whisper brushes my left ear, interrupting my mental rant. *"And you, wretched girl, do not belong in this world."* I swivel around.

There's no one there—only the sharp scent of whiskey lingering where the voice had been.

What the hell was that?

Coffee steams in my mug. I breathe in the bitterness, closing my eyes.

A shriek tears through the morning. My back jolts upright as coffee sloshes over the rim, burning my wrist. Outside, tires screech. A yelp gets cut short.

Moses. My cat. I had left the screen door of the kitchen open- the one that leads to the next-door neighbor's front yard. I ran barefoot. I didn't feel the nail on the driveway wedge its way into my foot until the blood left footprints on the concrete.

Moses' lifeless body lay in pieces on their driveway, the last link to my childhood.

The neighbor stands frozen beside his car, staring at the carnage, face pale. He is horrified, sympathetic, helpless and cannot find the right words. His mouth moves, but nothing reaches me. All I can hear is a faint ringing in my ears. Heat rises to my face. I dropped to my knees. My shaking hands reach for his collar. I can't breathe.

His collar no longer says Moses. It now reads: LIES.

I jerk upright in bed. My eyes fly to the bench at the foot of the mattress.

Moses, my light-tan American Shorthair with coffee-bean stripes, lies there. He's licking his paws.

My hand presses to my chest. *He's alive.*

My quick movements are contagious, causing him to jump to his feet—eyes sharp and alert, suspicious of my next move. Moses has always had an intense stare, but now it's different.

I scooped him up and gently stroke his fur, grounding myself. Usually, he purrs and rubs his head against me. This time, his back arches, and a hiss rips from his throat.

Not a normal hiss, but something darker. Something I had never heard before.

CHAPTER 8

THE CLUMP OF FUR

I place Moses gently back on the bench and begin pacing the floor, desperate for a distraction strong enough to shake the nightmare. Nothing works.

I grabbed the phone to call River, suggesting we see the new slasher film, *Halloween,* later that evening. He agrees immediately, probably excited by the thought of me jumping into his arms each time a scary scene flashes on the screen. By the time I arrive at the theatre, he's already invited nearly ten people, including Jared, Alice, and the orbit of wannabes that always trail behind us. He always had to have a crowd around him.

The movie starts, and we all sink into darkness, absorbed by the carnage on the screen. I wonder why I chose an anxiety-inducing film when I'm already drowning in it. Maybe I'm drawn to the feeling now like a drug addict.

During a quiet scene, a faint ringing creeps into my ear. I ignore it at first, assuming it'll fade, until it grows louder, drowning out the sound of Alice chomping on popcorn beside me.

The ringing sharpens and then changes pitch to something intolerable. It becomes the sound from my nightmare. That awful shriek. The screech from the tires. The screech that crushed Moses. Pressure slowly builds against the bones of my skull. I clamp my hands over my ears and bolt from my seat. The scent of River's Ralph Lauren Polo Cologne follows me as I sprint out of the theatre. The sound cuts off the instant my face hits the cold night air. I lean against the glass doors, breath ragged, hands braced on my hips, staring down at the pavement.

Should I wait it out, or go home? There's no way I can sit through the rest of the movie.

Sweat beads along my hairline. I wipe my forehead with my sleeve, shaking my head. What was supposed to distract me has become another episode of terror.

And then the thought creeps in. The one that haunts me. The one that always sits in the back of my mind, like a bully, pointing fingers and laughing at me. The one I can never run away from. Because it's inside of me.

What if I end up like my father?

He was once a respected man who slowly lost his grip on reality. The medical term was "mentally disturbed."

"What's going on?" River asks, catching up to me, interrupting my spiraling thoughts. His tone was concerned, but I could tell he was annoyed about missing the movie. "This was your idea. Are you okay?"

"No, I'm not," I answer honestly.

He waits.

"I have a terrible headache. I'm just gonna call it a night, take something, and sleep it off. You should go back in." He studies me for a moment, then nods. "Okay. I won't call later. I don't want to wake you. Call me tomorrow." He walks me to my car and kisses my forehead. I close my eyes, letting myself feel it. Each day, I found myself growing closer to River, more than I expected. But the feeling is buried beneath unease, something I can't remember living without anymore. It follows me everywhere like an uninvited roommate. It's nearly midnight. Moonlight slips through feathery clouds as a breeze lifts my bangs, brushing them into my eyes, like something doesn't want me to see what's ahead.

My hands search for the car keys. They must have slipped to the bottom of the oversized purse that Alice loaned to me. My fingers brush against something soft and furry, which I don't recognize. I pulled it out. It's a clump of cat hair, the same color as Moses.

"Ew. Gross," I mutter, tossing it onto the pavement as I hurry to my car, still keyless.

Panic flares. I dump my bag onto the hood. The keys finally jingle free. Pens and lipstick scatter across the asphalt, but I don't stop to collect them. My head was pounding too hard, and I couldn't bend down to pick it up. I jump into the car and drive off, leaving the flickering streetlights behind. Turning into my neighborhood, I slam on the brakes. My leather bag flies forward, hitting the windshield. In a hurry, I forgot to zip it up. Whatever is left inside spills onto the seat and some onto the floorboard.

My eyes meet a cat, the one I almost hit before my feet hit the brake pedal. It was standing in the road, staring straight at me, before disappearing into the trees. I exhale shakily and drive forward. A sigh escapes my lips as I see all the items scattered: my ChapStick, wallet, sunglasses, makeup—

And the clump of fur. It's back.

Moses waits for me at the bay window. The sight calms me, but only for a moment. I keep the lights off, my migraine pounding, and use a flashlight to find water and an Excedrin. The sleepless nights are catching up to me.

"Come on," I whisper, nudging him toward the stairs.

Moses rises slowly, slinking upward. Turning his head slightly in my direction, he pauses, blinks, and continues up the steps. His movements are deliberate, like he's trying to show me something.

And there it was, right in front of me. I had missed it somehow. A large bald patch on his side. I reach over to touch the spot. He spins, hissing sharply, forcing me back.

Instead of following me upstairs, Moses turns and pads down the steps. He stops at the small door that leads to the storage room beneath the staircase, clawing at it, purring insistently. He presses his head against the wood, listening.

When I reach for him again, he lashes out, scratching my arm.

That night, lying awake, I whispered frantic prayers.

I beg whatever I've awakened to stop.

I don't want signs. I don't want to know anything anymore. I want my life back. I asked to be shown. And something, somewhere, is listening.

CHAPTER 9

THE BIRDS

It's Sunday morning. Two days after my nightmare.

A sense of doom clings to me, inexplicable. My head still throbs as I shuffle downstairs to make coffee, hoping caffeine will dull this feeling. It doesn't. I had planned to spend the afternoon at the library, since I'm already behind on my research for a midterm paper. Being ahead of my class was always a point of pride.

"Winners always get a head start," Papa used to say. "If someone starts today, you start yesterday." His voice passes through my mind as I pour the coffee. He had a stash of these cliché one-liners he kept in a mental basket, ready to use when the time was right. Now I'm behind, scrambling to write this paper, which is worth half of my semester grade. Anything less than an A feels unacceptable.

The library is only a short walk away. I lace up my sneakers, sling my backpack over my shoulder, and grab an umbrella as clouds rumble overhead. I pull my ponytail out as it catches underneath the straps of my backpack. "Dad, I'm leaving!"

"Okay! Be safe!" he calls back. Then, quieter, absurdity spouts from him. "Don't let him get you. He's out there. Believe you me. He's coming for you, Shel. He's coming." I shake my head and slam the door behind me. It's been two years since I've had a normal conversation with my father.

Once, Benson Jones had been charismatic—brilliant, articulate, and worldly—a respected partner at a prestigious law firm. Everything changed on my sixteenth birthday. He didn't come home that night.

I'd returned from school expecting balloons, cake, and tacky streamers draped around the kitchen table. My favorite songs would be playing on the record, welcoming me home. I imagined gifts with colorful bows arranged around the cake table. I hoped to see him arrive early from work, pulling me into a hug. Hours passed. Nothing. I waited, convincing myself something had come up at work. Or he was planning something grand, tricking me into believing he had forgotten. After three hours, I called the police. They told me a man was found sitting alone on a park bench, talking to himself. Laughing and arguing with no one. He didn't know where he lived. He had no identification.

They offered me a ride to the station. Part of me prayed it wasn't him. Another part wished it was—safe and alive, at least.

I reluctantly got into the police car for the very first time. The officer sensed my anxiety as I twisted the cuffs of my sweater until they were almost torn. He tried to make small talk. School. Hobbies. I answered in single syllables, my heart pounding the entire way.

The station smelled of old coffee and disinfectants. Metal chairs lined the wall. A cluttered desk sat in the center. Behind it stood a woman with a cigarette dangling from her mouth, her voice raspy from years of smoking.

"Who ya here for, hun?" she asked, eyeing me. "You don't look like you belong in a place like this." As she tossed an empty Dunkin' Donuts cup into the trash, her cheap perfume hit me so hard it made my stomach turn. I pointed toward the corner. Shame, sympathy, and guilt flooded me all at once. The guilt was the worst. I never understood why it clung to me so fiercely. In that moment, a "normal" teenage life was what I craved most.

My father barely resembled the man I knew. In the corner, he sat on a metal chair, with his head leaning against the wall. Dirt and oil matted his hair. He wore suit pants and a ripped white undershirt. One shoe was missing. Stubble had grown along his chin, and his eyes were sunken, with large bags beneath them, a thick layer of grime collected underneath his fingernails, which needed a trimming. A flask of whiskey was clenched in his left hand. He looked at me like a child caught doing something unforgivable. I had been so consumed in my own world that I barely saw him at home. I left before he woke up and came home after he retreated to his room.

"I'm here for my father," I said.

While I filled out forms for his release, he muttered nonsense—about whiskey, about a night shift at a distillery.

Then, he stopped. He looked straight at me. "This is all your fault," he said. "You're a wretched little girl. That's all you are. That's all you'll ever be." The words cut through me and permanently stained my memory.

My fault? For what?

Should I even try to understand him? It was all senseless. Or was it?

The room spun. I collapsed into a chair, nauseous and dizzy, wishing desperately for ordinary problems: boy drama, gossip. I'd even take bad grades. But not this. Anything but this. Something in him had changed. His voice. His eyes. It was like listening to a stranger wearing my father's face.

There's one thing I didn't realize at that moment. It was my first glimpse of *him*. I just didn't know it yet.

And that was how I would always remember my sixteenth birthday.

They drove us home that night. Social services intervened. Monthly check-ins and warnings were administered. If Papa deteriorated further, he'd be institutionalized. I'd be sent to relatives I didn't know or—worse—end up in the system. I promised myself I would do everything to stay in that house. Over time, the roles reversed. I fed him. Managed his medications. Reminded him to bathe. To brush his teeth. The father I once admired was gone.

I blink and pull myself back into the present. Before leaving, I check on Moses. He's curled on the sofa, a patch of fur missing from his side.

"Focus, Shelby," I mutter. "No distractions. I need this A."

I step out through the side door into the short brick driveway. Autumn has settled in, and crunchy leaves blanket the yard. The neighbor's son was supposed to rake them, but he never does. Sometimes, I envy Alice, with all her luxuries. All her freedom. She never has to worry about the mundane stuff. It's always taken care of. I walk forward, the weight in my chest heavier than my backpack. Something felt off. The driveway looked unfamiliar. Leaves arranged themselves to create a perfect circle, framing the asphalt. I couldn't understand how the circle formed. From a distance, small shapes dot the exposed asphalt in distinct rows. Pinecones, I think. The spacing was almost measured. I step closer and lean forward.

They aren't pinecones. They're birds. Dead birds. Dozens of them. Their feathers were scattered, and their tiny bodies still. A man walking his dog slows and stares. He looks at the birds. Then at me. Then back at the birds. He quickens his pace, his expression twisting into fear and disgust.

"This isn't—" I stutter. "I didn't... I just found them here."

The sound returns. The shriek. It claws through my head, rising in pitch until it's intolerable. I clamp my hands over my ears and force my head to the bay window. Moses is staring at me. His eyes almost squint. Knowing. Challenging.

There is no warmth. There is no recognition. *Try me,* his gaze seems to taunt.

CHAPTER 10

THE THREE DAY MARK

Monday came after what felt like an eternal weekend. It was always meant to happen. There was no confusion. No chaos. No moment when I thought I could change anything. Something in me just knew. The dread hovered, mocked, gave me signs, until one day, it finally happened, unfolding like a story being retold. A story I had already heard.

From the quiet of my morning coffee to the shriek of the car brakes.

Moses was gone. This time, it was real.

I knew it the second I grabbed the dead pen from the cup. What began as a nightmare took three long, unbearable days to become real. The taunting and torture were just part of the game.

The dead birds cleared the driveway along with Moses. There had been at least thirty of them. I counted each one. The neighbor had seen them too. Had someone come and removed them? It didn't matter. Moses was dead, now a distant memory.

Moses. My birthday present. Papa had poked holes in a cardboard box and tied a big purple bow on top. He carried it into my bedroom the morning I turned ten and placed it gently on my bed, singing Happy Birthday to me. I still remember the way the box shifted its weight and the way my heart raced as I lifted the lid. I named him after my favorite book, *Moses the Cat* by James Herriot. It was the story Papa used to read to me about an abandoned kitten who survived with the help of his new family. Moses had been the last real thread tying me to my childhood, the last living link to my father, when he was stable.

A loud crash from the cellar snapped me out of my thoughts.

Whiskey dripped from the shelves onto the cabinets, pooling into a dark puddle on the floor. The smell was especially sharp and pungent, the way wasabi hits the senses the instant it touches your tongue. Shards of glass littered the tile: one of my father's collector's bottles, the kind he kept on the highest shelf. It hadn't been on the edge, and the windows were shut, preventing any draft from causing it to slide off the shelf. Moses was no longer there to stir up any trouble. I was too tired to make sense of it.

I grabbed the mop and Pine-Sol from the closet. By the time I returned, everything was gone. No broken glass. No whiskey dripping down the cabinet. The puddle on the floor had disappeared. The bottle was back on the top shelf, where it belonged, upright and untouched. I concentrated on the spot where the spill had been, thinking I could bring back the puddle, hoping I was not hallucinating.

Have I lost my mind?

The ringing slammed into my ears without warning. I cupped my hands over them. "Stop!" I shouted. The sound vanished. Silence rushed in, thick, almost too quiet. I was able to turn the noise off. That was comforting—for a brief moment, until I heard the laughter.

Muffled laughter. Evil laughter. It echoed through the walls, low and distorted, seeping from the storage space beneath the stairs.

CHAPTER 11

WESLEY

I stood there, staring at the door of the storage room under the stairway. The laughter had subsided, but my fear grew as the minutes went by.

The doorbell rang, unusually loud, echoing throughout the house. I could feel it in my brain, like it was part of my pulse, making me jump. Who could that be? It was too late in the day for any deliveries. I hesitated, not wanting to check but also desperate for proof there were still sane people in the world. I wanted to have a meaningless conversation about the weather, the new store around the corner, anything to drag my mind away from here.

I crept toward the side window and peeked out. Damn it. It was that new neighbor. The one who'd shot me dirty looks when he saw the birds while walking his dog. What did he want now? I hope he didn't report me.

He stood on the porch with his hands shoved into his pockets, eyes down, one foot tapping against the steps. It was that awkward moment when someone is waiting for a door to open and doesn't quite know what to do with their body.

I imagined him rehearsing what he was going to say. Paranoid, I created his opening sentence in my own mind. *"Hi, Shelby, I've reported you to the police regarding the suspicious activity I saw while on my walk the other day. I know you killed those birds while performing some ritual. They are coming to investigate you. They mentioned something about your ill father and taking him away to an institution, and you might be next."*

The doorbell rang again and awakened me from my anxiety-driven daydream. I stayed still, debating whether to open the door or leave him standing there in the cool fall air. He'd probably already heard my footsteps anyway. This might be my one chance to redeem myself. To prove I wasn't some bird-killing psycho.

I opened the door. His demeanor was overly friendly, almost jovial, like a baseball pitched too fast, before I was ready for it. "Hi, there!" he said brightly, beaming. "My name's Wesley. I live just down the street. I wanted to introduce myself. I'm new to the neighborhood and figured I should get to know everyone around." He was younger than my father, I guessed, maybe by a few years. Dressed casually, but in a way that suggested old money. Nothing flashy, just timeless. Chinos. A crisp white polo, freshly ironed. Brown leather loafers slipped on narrow feet. A misfit in this neighborhood. A ring with a colored gemstone hugged his right ring finger. He extended his hand. I looked at it for a second too long before realizing I was supposed to shake it. "Hello?" he said gently. "Are you alright?"

"I saw you the other morning," I said, flatly, shifting my feet uncomfortably. "You were walking past my house. You seemed disturbed. And rightfully so, seeing all those dead birds. Do you remember?" He blinked and looked at me with a puzzled expression, shaking his head. Lifting his eyebrows, as though slightly amused, he responded, "Well, that would be impossible. I drove in from New York last night. You must be mistaking me for someone else. Glad I missed those dead birds, though." He chuckled, as if it were nothing more than neighborhood gossip.

I didn't laugh.

"Either way," he continued, unfazed, "it's great to meet you, neighbor. I brought over some apple turnovers. I can't take any credit. The new bakery in town is all the rage, and I was able to get the freshest batch, so please, I would love for you to have them." He hands over a box tied with a blue ribbon. "Well, I'll let you enjoy the rest of your day." With that, he turned around, almost skipping down the porch steps, and headed back to the house three doors down on the right. I watched him fade into his house and shut the door behind him. I didn't remember seeing any moving trucks. No vans. No activity over the past few days. A cloud of Old Spice cologne lingered on the porch after he was gone.

There was no mistake. I will never forget his face. It was him. The man who had slowed his pace that morning, who had stared at the birds with disgust before looking straight at me.

My thoughts tangled, refusing to line up. Nothing made sense anymore.

CHAPTER 12

THE BURIAL

I can't risk accusations of lunacy, particularly with my father's condition. Not a word to anyone. Not a soul. It's just a strange coincidence, that's all, I tell myself again and again. It's easier to label it that way. Easier to move forward and carry on with my life.

Focus, Shelby. You're the star now. Everyone likes you. Boys want to be with you. Girls emulate you. They want to share their secrets. Don't ruin your reputation with something that's not even real.

I give myself pep talks every hour, especially when thoughts of Moses creep in, uninvited and sharp. Moses was buried in the backyard, along with his favorite toy, a plush mouse with one ear nearly chewed off. I barely remember carrying his limp, fragile body behind the small patio. The memory feels distant and unreal, like a phantom memory.

I dug.

At first, it was gentle and careful. Then it turned frantic. Furious. I stabbed the earth with the shovel, angry at the ground, at the world, at the cruelty of losing the last piece of my childhood so suddenly. Angry at how unfair life had been so far. Tears streamed down my face as I dug and dug, carving a hole large enough to hold him. I knew Moses would die someday, just not like this. He wasn't even sick.

When it was over, I placed a small cross onto the dirt near the grave. On a smooth rock, I wrote: RIP Moses Jones

I placed it beside the cross and pressed the soil down with shaking hands. After that day, I forced myself to move on. I returned to my carefully constructed social life, fully aware that it existed only because of how I looked now, not who I was. And that scared me more than I wanted to admit. *Who am I?* The question follows me everywhere. I ask it silently, over and over, never actually getting answers.

Sometimes, when I feel a gaze linger longer than it should, I look up and catch Jared from a distance. This version of me unsettles him. I can tell. His eyes dart away from me when he's caught staring, and his legs shift from side to side.

And for reasons I don't understand, it feels like he's watching out for me. Protecting me.

CHAPTER 13

THE NIGHT AT THE DOUBLE O

Music blared through the Obsidian Order frat house, *the Double O,* as they called it. A brotherhood River had joined in his first year: Zeppelin, Aerosmith, Black Sabbath, the Rolling Stones. The playlist rolled on into the early morning hours.

Smoke hung thick in the air as joints were passed hand to hand lazily, some guys dipping into the happy dust. The night belonged to them, unraveling and reckless. The overcrowded house reeked of defiant youth and untamed desire.

"So what's the story?" Jared asked casually, leaning against the wall with one thumb hooked into the pocket of his torn jeans, one knee bent, beer dangling loosely in his hand. "You and Shelby? Are you two, uh...a thing?" He avoided any eye contact with River while inquiring about his relationship status. Jared nodded along to a Rolling Stones track, his favorite band, eyes half-lidded, staring at the wall across the room. "You don't expect anyone to really believe you dig her, do you?" Jared added. "Dude, she's not even your type." River scoffed. "Nah. Not my type at all," he said quickly. "Too brainy. Doesn't have that supermodel bod either. She's cool, but I'm not into her. It was just a bet. That stupid bet with Alice." He took a swig of beer and added, "I want a *real* woman like Margaret Hudson. She's perfect. Everything about her." Jared wasn't convinced. Something about River's tone felt off, like it was too rehearsed. But Jared backed off. The last thing he wanted was for River to think *he* was interested in Shelby.

"By the way," Jared muttered, scanning the room, "what the hell are we even doing here? This place sucks. I'd rather be home watching TV or something. All these space cadets." He shook his head. This wasn't his scene. Jared had always kept people at arm's length. It wasn't something he talked about. It was just how he operated. Feelings made things messy. Dangerous. Every move he made was calculated, every interaction measured. That was why he never drank too much. Never smoked too much. Losing control wasn't an option. He'd learned that early. Jared had learned how to stay guarded by watching his mother. She didn't throw potlucks. Didn't host brunches or game nights like the other women. There was no time for that kind of life. And after her husband's disappearance, she withdrew even further, her warmth slowly draining away until survival became routine—wake up, work, repeat.

His attention snapped to Shelby. She was dancing, or attempting to, near the corner of the room. Completely uncoordinated. Arms flapping wildly, something between the Hustle and a chicken impersonation. Jared tried to hold it in. So did River. Eventually, they lost it. Both doubled over, clutching their sides, barking with laughter, gasping for air like two idiots who'd lost all sense of control. When they finally straightened up, heads pounding, the room felt dizzy and warped. The corner was now empty. Shelby was gone.

Jared pushed off the wall, scanning the crowd. They knew the mentality of the men there all too well. There were plenty of guys around here lurking, in search of a girl who was not quite in her senses. "Have you seen Shelby Jones?" River shouted at no one in particular. "Did anyone see her leave?"

From the corner, a stocky young man emerged with a beer in each hand, wearing a fitted shirt and bell-bottoms that covered his shoes. "I saw her," Preston Scott, the frat president, slurred as he staggered into the main hall. He made a crude gesture, and a smirk appeared confidently across his face. River snapped. Jared barely had time to register the shift before River's fist met fiercely with Preston's jaw. A tooth flew. Preston hit the floor hard, groaning, too drunk and stunned to fight back. Jared stared at River. "Not Interested, huh?" he said quietly. "That's one hell of a way to show it."

A cool breeze brushed the back of Jared's neck. The patio door stood open. From inside, the deck looked empty. But when they stepped into the night, they saw her huddled on the cold, wooden floor, knees pulled tightly to her chest. Moonlight reflected off her plastic platform shoes. Her head was tucked between her knees, and her teeth chattered in the brisk air. "Hey," River said softly, crouching. "Shelby. Wake up. Let's get you out of here."

"River," she loosely spoke, lifting her head, "I'm not the one sleeping. You are. And so is Jared." The boys look at one another, confused. She continues, "There is too much you don't know. You're living a lie. And so am I. And so is Jared. See that black crow?" She pointed into the darkness. There was nothing there. Jared felt his insides twist. "It whispered it to me." Her eyes flicked upward. "All the lies we live...and one day, the truth's gonna find us. The joke is gonna be on us. All of Wilshire Pointe. We are all doomed." A giggle burst from her mouth while she covered it with both hands. Then she stopped. Her face went serious.

"We're all connected. We just don't know it, yet. But we're going to find out—the hard way."

Jared swallowed. "Man," he said quietly to River, suddenly sober, shifting his weight from foot to foot, hands buried deep in his pockets. "We gotta get her out of here. She's had too much of...everything."

River nodded. "On three," he said. "You grab one arm. I'll get the other."

"One. Two. Three."

They lifted her and headed down the deck stairs, leaving the chaos, and the music, behind.

CHAPTER 14

DRUNKEN AFTERMATH

I groan, the pain in my temples radiates down into my neck and face. The damn light from the window shines brightly in my eyes, nature's alarm clock. A rather rude awakening. I grab the pillow and slam it against my face, using it as a shield against the invading rays. It must be Sunday, around noon. Something in me didn't want to check the clock, which would only confirm the fact that I was spiraling into the person I didn't want to be.

I need to get up. Be productive. Where was I last night? Oh. Right. For God's sake. That dreadful party at the Double O. I've become one of those pathetic losers. The Phonies. How did I stoop so low?

Get up, Shelby. Do something with your life.

Navy blue bed sheets?

These aren't my sheets.

This isn't my bed.

Where the hell am I?

Whose room is this?

A long men's shirt with a paisley print hangs off my shoulders, brushing just above my knees. It smells like Ralph Lauren Polo. My stomach drops. That's River's signature scent. No. It can't be.

Before my thoughts descend any further, he strolls out of the bathroom, casually brushing his teeth, wearing nothing but his boxers.

"Good morning, sweetheart," he says around a mouthful of toothpaste, spit flying dangerously too close to my cheek.

"River!" I bolt upright. "What the hell! What happened last night? Did you...did we...no!"

I wiped my face, horrified. "Shelby, would you just chill out?" he says calmly. "You passed out. You were like a toddler learning to walk, total jelly legs." He impersonates me, wobbling around the room. "Kinda cute, actually."

I threw a pillow at him.

"Jared and I saw you dancing alone in the corner, completely incoherent. We looked away for, like, two minutes and you were gone." His tone sharpens. "You need to be more careful."

I remain quiet, waiting for the speech to be over. I'm not used to anyone telling me what to do anymore.

"I'll save the lectures for later," he continues, "but there are a lot of gross guys out there. I brought you back to my place. And for the record, I slept on that sofa right there."

River motions with his chin to a brown couch against the wall. A pillow and blanket are tossed across it. His proof.

My lips form an inaudible "oh." I fold my arms across my chest, feeling like a child who had been taught a lesson. "Thanks..." I mutter. "I suppose."

His eyes held my gaze for a moment. "I would never want anyone taking advantage of you, Shelby." In that moment, there was a corner of my heart that felt something for him. Something more than friendship.

CHAPTER 15

ERODED IDENTITY

Alice slaps a page from the Wilshire Pointe University newsletter onto the table.

"Most exclusive couple on campus—*Shelby Jones and River Smyth!*" she squeals, pointing to the headline in the *Daily Wilshire*. "How stellar is this? You two are basically the university sweethearts. Thanks to me." She flips her hair away from her shoulder and bats her eyelashes, awaiting praise for being a catalyst for my relationship with River. I roll my eyes. All the hype feels ridiculous. I'd much rather read the political science section than the *Who's Who at WPU* page, which is the only reason Alice even bothers picking up a weekly copy. River smiles to himself, clearly pleased with the mention, even though his face already appears in the sports column nearly every week.

River Smyth. The guy all the other guys wish to be, except for Jared. And the one all the girls swoon over, unless Jared's nearby. He carries himself like applause is owed to him, like rooms should pause when he enters. His jawline looks sharp enough to slice an apple, and he never misses an opportunity to admire his reflection in a mirror or a window, sometimes even offering himself a wink. Star wide receiver, campus royalty, and my boyfriend. He's usually surrounded by teammates who inflate his ego even further, as if he needs the boost. "River hit the jackpot," people whisper. Some admire while others are bitter. I've heard the stories about him. Everyone has. He wasn't born into the Smyth family. He was adopted. Mr. and Mrs. Smyth were unmistakably Northern European:

fair-skinned, light-eyed. River's olive complexion and dark eyes told a different story. He was taller, leaner. The genetics didn't quite line up. Rumor had it his biological mother left him at the steps of an orphanage, too ashamed to leave a name or explanation. A devout woman of faith, they said, a mistake that would put her to shame.

The Smyths, wealthy and respected philanthropists, saw an opportunity. Adopting River was initially framed as charity, a gesture of generosity toward people with low incomes. The Smyths were afraid River would feel isolated, because he looked different than them. For this reason, they gave River everything he wanted, anything that would make him feel at home. If you were ever going to be adopted, landing in the Smyth household was about as lucky as it got. Smyth Jewelers. A Nantucket summer home. A perfectly curated future, complete with marriage, children, and legacy, mapped out with surgical precision. And from what I could tell, River hated every bit of it. A life built on someone else's expectations was the last thing he wanted.

My old self often tugs at me, ridiculing my sense of judgment, knowing this isn't my field to play in. But my *new* self enjoys the attention and the newfound popularity. I finally feel significant, through all the things I once believed were insignificant.

I obsess over my hair. My clothes. My shoes. My makeup. My reflection. My admiration grows while my grades quietly slip, something that would have once terrified me. Now, it barely registers. Deep down, somewhere I try to avoid, I resent this version of myself. I miss the girl I used to be. She was quieter. Less impressive. Less exhausting. Every morning feels like the opening night of a play. I paint on my thick mask of makeup, pull on a costume from Alice's carefully curated collection, and march out the door, leaving my old skin behind. Before, all I had to worry about were my grades. Now, it's everything else layered on top: the clothes, the fake friends, the social events, the endless performance.

By nightfall, all the noise blurs together into static. While I lie in bed, the façade finally dissolves. That's when I'm just me again. Vulnerable and scared. And beneath it all is a voice so strong it nearly wakes me up from sleep. A reminder.

The note is still in the drawer of my dresser. *"Shelby Jones, you're not who you think you are. Your entire life is a lie."*

CHAPTER 16

BANANA BREAD

It had been nearly six months since the incident with Moses.

My new routine demanded more attention, enabling me to stow that dreadful memory away. I slipped back into classes and familiar hallways. The days behaved themselves, and I was catching up on my schoolwork. My grades were finally back to where they needed to be.

At night, my thoughts still lingered, shamelessly deliberate. Unanswered questions constantly knocked at the door of my mind. Mostly about my mother. Who she was. Why were there no photos? Why Papa never spoke of her. Why have I never met any other relatives? I had no siblings with whom I could share this burden. And Papa. Well, Papa stopped making sense a long time ago, so this little world that was created out of thin air, the world with Alice, Jared, and River, became my crutch. One could call it accidental friendship.

One night, I lay in bed while the house formed its usual orchestra—the refrigerator buzzing, the radiator humming, and wind brushing against the window softly. The nagging thoughts drained my energy. The lids of my eyes eventually succumbed to the exhaustion, and my hands folded on their own, as if they knew exactly what to do, while I silently recited my nightly prayer. Sleep came quietly. Swiftly. I didn't need a book that night. Off to another land, I drifted, to a place close to home, with familiar faces and voices.

I was now standing in the university courtyard. I don't remember walking there. I don't question it either. The usual group was spread out across the picnic tables, eating lunch and talking over one another. Everything looked normal. River was in his form, boasting about the last football game, sensationalizing every play, acting each one out like a one-person show. A cluster of followers hung on his every word, devouring the attention he fed them.

"Thirty seconds left in the fourth quarter," he announced loudly. "I take off down the sideline. I'm thinking there's no way it's coming to me. The ball's spiraling down in slow motion, the crowd's losing their minds," he jumped to demonstrate, arms flailing. "I leap, four feet in the air! It almost slips through my hands, but I catch it. I tuck it under my arm like a stolen bottle of vodka from the corner store. Some guy dives for my legs…nah, not today, buddy. I spin out, leave him in the dust, and BOOM. End zone."

The crowd around him erupted in cheers. Jared sat nearby, more invested in his ham sandwich than in the story. He smiled between bites, clearly hoping River wouldn't drag him into the performance. Jared hated being put on the spot. "Well, yeah," Jared muttered through a mouthful of food. "Keep yuckin' it up, why don't you?" River ignored him, completely absorbed in his own aura.

Alice's laugh cut through everything. She had many laughs, but this one was cruel. The sharp and condescending one that was usually followed by a verbal attack. Her eyes followed a girl crossing the courtyard. Margaret Jacobson. Alice's face twisted with judgment and scorn. She leaned forward, enjoying the moment as a sneaky smile spread across her face.

"How does Margaret even leave her house looking like that?" she sneered, admiring her recently painted nails. "She's a sad mess from head to toe. The irony is she actually thinks she's something special."

Something in me rose. I felt offended *for* Margaret. Because not long ago, I was her target. I was Margaret. Now that I crossed to the other side, am I supposed to tolerate this behavior? Two girls beside her snickered. "Wait." One of the girls paused her snickering. Daringly, she looked directly into Alice's beady eyes and said the unthinkable. "Wasn't Margaret the girl Scott Rodgers chose over *you*? You had a thing for him, and she took him right out from under your nose." The two girls burst into laughter. For some reason, they felt extra bold and challenged the fierce lioness.

Alice turned slowly toward them. Their courageous spirits were instantly deflated. Her stare landed like a punch. They snap back to reality, and one of the girls immediately looks down, mumbles something about the ladies' room, and disappears. She didn't come back for the rest of the afternoon. This was Alice at her worst. No matter how much I'd changed, I couldn't stand her when she became like this. I never understood why she always needed a target, whether it was boredom, cruelty, or pure sport.

I pretended to be absorbed in River's dramatics, turning my face away from her completely. In that moment, I was ashamed to be associated with her. Switching my mind over to River, I look over in his direction, facing my back to Alice. River caught the sunlight just then, his olive skin glowing, his energy filling the courtyard. He could charm a rock if he wanted to. Sometimes I envied how easily life seemed to flow through him. Being with River was a daydream nearly every girl on campus had entertained at some point. And somehow, I was the one living the reality. A drunken smile appeared on my face. The thought barely had time to settle before a harsh coughing sound tore through the air.

Then choking. I turned. It was coming from Alice. Her face was bright red. Both hands clawed at her throat. Her eyes bulged, panicked and wild, pupils darting in all directions, in search of someone to save her.

A piece of banana bread was lodged somewhere deep inside her. It happened all too fast.

She'd been talking while eating. She never shut up long enough to swallow properly. Jared rushed behind her, arms wrapping around her waist as he tried the Heimlich maneuver. He drove his fist in again and again, trained hands moving automatically.

Nothing came out.

Her pupils rolled upward until only the whites showed.

Students crowded around, shouting. Some stood frozen, too afraid to make any sudden movements. A wet, squelching sound echoed from deep inside her throat, something shifting and sliding, trying to break free. Something that didn't belong there.

Alice's mouth opened into a silent scream. We barely had time to process what was happening. Beneath the thin skin of her neck, waves rippled, moving and writhing, like they were searching for an escape route. And then something slithered out. The first one came out, then the second. Small black tips emerged first, followed by about a dozen.

Slugs. Thick, slimy bodies poured from her mouth, her nose, her ears, leaving trails of mucus behind. Her body convulsed violently, veins flashing like blue lightning beneath her skin. "Help!" Jared screamed. "Someone, help her! Call an ambulance! Call someone!"

River rushed forward, grabbing her, trying to hold her shaking body still. A bluish hue crept across her face as her consciousness began to slip.

"Oh God, no," River shouted. "Alice, wake up! Her skin is freezing, and it's...it's rough, almost like leather!" The convulsions continued, and for one brief moment, her eyes snapped open.

River stumbled back, gasping. When he moved, I could see why he was anxious to get as far away as possible. Alice's eyes were open, but completely black. There were no pupils, no iris- just black. Blood erupted from them, trickling down to the base of her neck.

A wicked smile lifted one side of her mouth. The convulsions stopped. The choking stopped. Her breathing had become slow and heavy, with a hoarse undertone. River let go of his hold on her and began to slowly back away.

Then her arms shot forward and grabbed River's throat with impossible strength. Her fingers tightened, nails bending backward until they cracked, piercing his skin. River clawed at her wrists, choking, unable to scream, small slits of his skin ripped open by her ferocious grip.

Jared and I threw ourselves at her, screaming at her to let go, prying her frozen fingers. She was impossibly strong. An inhuman strength that could probably have lifted a truck with her bare hands. With one final, violent kick, she sent River flying into a stonewall. His back slammed hard against the building.

Her eyes flicked towards me. I stumbled back, too afraid to shift my gaze. Afraid to move too fast. My eyes were fixed on her. As much as I wanted to look away, I couldn't. Alice cackled, delighted by the terror she was causing. She covered her mouth with her leathery fingers, almost sheepishly. Students and staff scattered in every direction, screaming, fleeing.

When the ambulance finally arrived, paramedics strapped her into a stretcher. It took four men to hold her down. The entire time, her eyes never left me. No smile. No anger. Just staring. Right into my soul. Her eyes seemed to be accusing me of betrayal, or maybe it was my own guilt for not being able to help her.

Her gaze locked me in place. I didn't know where to look, so I stared back at her lifeless expression, a sharp contrast to the moments before. A part of me felt sorry for her. A part of me feared her. And a part of me never wanted to see her again.

As the ambulance doors slammed shut and the vehicle pulled away, the crowd watched in stunned silence, relieved she was gone. As it drove away, we got one final look at her as her face slammed against the rear window. Laughing, waving goodbye.

It was the last time we would ever see Alice Whitman.

CHAPTER 17

THE DEMONIC LITTLE CHERUB

The tea kettle whistles downstairs, jolting me awake. Thank God. It's not real.

Papa is up and about early. I can hear him puttering around the kitchen. I savor the familiar sounds.

My heart pounds as I call Alice immediately, gulping down a glass of water before she answers. My eyes scan the room as I wait for her to pick up the line, searching for my robe. The temperature in my room seemed to have dropped drastically.

"Alice! Is that you?"

"No, it's your hot pizza delivery guy," she groans. "It's 7 a.m. on a Saturday, Shelby. And I had a late night. What the hell do you want? You're ruining my beauty sleep. My beautician says I need at least 9 hours a night, and I'm barely getting 7. If I have bags under my eyes today, it's on you." Relief floods through my veins just hearing her voice, but I scramble for a reason to be calling her this early. I know her weakness. Shopping.

"Oh," I say casually, forcing calm into my voice. "I was just wondering if you wanted to go shopping today. I hear far-out sales are happening at the mall." Alice yawns loudly. Barely coherent, she responds, "You are such a strange girl, calling me this early about *that,*" she mutters. "But fine. Let's meet around noon by the fountain. I'm going back to bed." The line clicks and goes dead.

I rub my hands together for warmth, grab my robe, and quickly tie it around my waist. A cool breeze floats through the room. The window is open. I didn't open it. It's mid- April, and there would be no reason for me to with all the pollen in the air. I shut it, locking it for extra security. I stumbled into the bathroom and splashed my face with cold water, scrubbing hard, as if soap might wash away the nightmare. Scrub. Rinse. Scrub again. The lavender scent calms me slightly. I splash my face one more time and crack my eyes open, too afraid to fully close them. Soap burns my eyes, but I welcome it. At least I'd see something if it was coming for me. I grab a towel and pat my face dry. *Everything will be fine. Deep breaths, Shelby.*

As my vision focuses, I glance toward the mirror. Alice is staring back at me, head peering above the shower curtain. Not the Alice I know. Her face is twisted, black eyes, distorted features, the one from my dream. Her head tilts slightly, lips stretched into a smile.

My breathing stops momentarily. I force myself to turn around.

She's gone.

No. No, no, no.

This is *not* happening.

The dream with Moses was just a coincidence. That's all. There is no way. This is not going to become something real. I bolt into my room and collapse onto the bench at the foot of my bed with my hand on my chest. I can hear my heartbeat, racing. But curiosity drags me back in. I tiptoe into the bathroom and slowly pull the shower curtain aside.

Something moves in the corner of the tub. I step closer inside. "What the hell...?" A black slug. I have *never* seen slugs in the house before.

"I need air. I need to get out of here."

As I turn to leave, the door is masked by a cloud of fog. I stretch my arms out to navigate my way out of the bathroom, and my eyes catch a word written on the mirror. The fog surrounds the mirror, but the center is clear, illuminating the letters appearing on the glass.

Letters trace themselves through the steam. **L-I-E-S.**

Am I still dreaming? I touch my face. Then slap it. "Ow." This is real.

"L-I-E-S... where have I seen that before?" The buried memory hits hard. Moses' collar.

There's no going back to sleep after this. I skip making my bed and head downstairs to brew a cup of tea. The refrigerator hums. The heater groans, struggling against the cold. The ordinary sounds suddenly feel cryptic.

I sit on the edge of the sofa, television blaring to drown out the noises.

In the center cushion, there's a small dip, as if someone has just been sitting there. The cushion slowly rises back into place.

My hands shake as I check my watch. 11:30.

****

The sense of relief hits me as I get into my car and drive away from my house. The mall will give me some reassurance that what I witnessed this morning was strictly in my mind. Watching people do ordinary things will put me back at ease. I already feel better after seeing people walking towards the mall from the parking lot, excited to check out all the weekend sales, grab a bite to eat at the food court, or just window shop.

It's five minutes until noon when I reach the central fountain at the mall. The sound of water behind me fades as a faint ringing fills my ear, growing louder and louder, then abruptly stops.

A small child nearby coughs. Not a normal cough, but a violent one that would cause concern. The coughing turned to choking. His face flushes red, then pale blue. The parents panic as a crowd forms. His father tries to dislodge a peppermint candy from his throat. The ringing slams back into my ears, drowning out the world. Everything moves in slow motion. My body feels heavy, disconnected, as I sit frozen on the fountain's edge.

The father flips the child over his leg, pounding his back again and again, desperate. The mother clasps her hands over her mouth, whispering prayers, bargaining with God. Promising to do everything right this time around, as long as her boy can be saved. On the fifth strike, the candy shoots out and lands in the fountain beside me, making a plopping sound. A tiny splash of water jumps onto my face, and I can feel the sting. The water turns blood-red. Immediately, I jump away from the fountain with my hand on my chest. Am I the only one who can see the water turn red? Why is no one else reacting? The crowd is busy, cheering and applauding the parents, who have their arms wrapped around the boy. A sense of relief floats through the air. The water turns clear. The show is over. Everyone has resumed their normal activities of chatting, shopping, and eating. I can't shake the feeling of dread, even though the boy is fine. I should be celebrating, but it's not over. I know it's not over. Gut-wrenching anxiety fills my every pore. The child faces me while his parents hug him, now about ten feet away. His color returns. He catches my skeptical gaze. I try to look away. I can't. I'm locked into the moment, paralyzed, wanting to know more.

One corner of his mouth lifts. *Told you so. It's just a matter of time. Just wait*, his eyes communicate with me.

His chubby hand rises. I lift mine to wave back, but he doesn't wave. His cherub-like face turns grim, and his middle finger sticks straight up in the air. For a split second, his eyes go dark. Empty.

Alice's voice catches me in a trance. "What's with the crowd? Shelby! Shelby!" She snaps her fingers in front of my face.

"Hey, Alice..." I begin, but she barrels on.

"It took *forever* to put together an outfit today. I felt so bloated. Do I look bigger to you?" She turns sideways. "Ok, you don't have to answer that." Waving me off, she continues, "I can't believe you woke me up so early just to tell me you want to go shopping. You can be so weird sometimes, Shelby." I wasn't really paying attention to her. My mind was still on the boy. He was a sign. A sign of what lies ahead.

Continuing her rant, she walks forward, using hand gestures and dramatic expressions, barely realizing that I'm lagging.

"Anyway," she says brightly, grabbing my hand, "let's go have fun. This was *your* idea, remember?" She pulls me along.

I glance back at the boy. He's leaving, between his parents, hands clasped, bouncing lightly with each step. No one knows what I'm seeing. No one knows what I'm carrying.

"We'll check out the sales," Alice says, already moving, "but first we have to stop at Seaside Bake Shop. You've probably never heard of it. It just opened last week. I've been twice already."

She grins. "You know what the best thing on the menu is?"

I shake my head.

Her eyes light up.

"The banana bread. You *have* to try it, Shel. It's my new favorite."

CHAPTER 18

THE RADIO REQUEST

I was dreading the following Tuesday. The three-day mark, if there was such a rule.

I hoped it was all a mix-up. A coincidence. All in my head. But no matter how hard I tried to wave it off and focus on other things, the knots in my stomach tightened with each passing hour. Because deep down, I knew this was no coincidence. My ability to concentrate, to formulate the right words, to carry out a simple task had long gone. Mid-conversation, I'd often forget what I was saying. The looming thought of Alice invaded every brain cell. Last night, I left the stove on. I never do that. Luckily, I went downstairs for a glass of water and caught it before the house burned down. Today, I left the house without my wallet. I never do that either. I woke up this morning to the window open again. I still can't figure that one out, but it's another strange occurrence to add to the list.

What do people do when anxiety hits an all-time high? I don't drink. I don't smoke. After the episode at the party, I stopped completely. But I need *something* to take the edge off. Fresh air. I step into the backyard to pace, to clear my mind. I sit on the grass, grounding my thoughts and my body. It's still damp from the earlier rain. Moisture seeps through my pants as I fold forward, resting my head between my knees, hoping gravity might pull my frantic thoughts out.

Closing my eyes, I drift away into a daydream. One that I wanted to be in.

River and I are swimming together at the beach. Sunlight warms our backs as waves crash around us. He lifts me effortlessly and carries me toward the sand. His breath is warm, close, familiar. He leans in for a kiss—

Alice's face slams into the scene. The gruesome one. Smiling at me. "Damn it!" I yank myself back to reality, fists tearing at the grass beneath me. Moses' burial site rests about fifteen feet away, but something was wrong. It takes a moment to register. Something was missing. The cross was gone. I'd staked it deep into the earth. There hadn't been any strong winds. There's no reason it should have disappeared. A miserable laugh floods my ears. I clamp my hands over them and run inside, but the sound follows me, wedging its way through my skull.

Outside, the sky darkens into that uneasy hour between day and night. Threatening clouds loom low. From the window, I see a flock of birds swooping down toward Moses' grave and begin pecking violently at the soil. "Hey! Get going!" I charge at them, bolting through the side door and into the backyard again. They don't move. I'd never come across such stubborn and fearless birds before. The leader hops toward me and lets out a harsh squawk. The others follow, obediently. Up close, they look eerily familiar. The same kind of birds from my driveway. They begin to organize, some forming a straight horizontal line. Others align vertically, intersecting it.

I take a step back, squinting. They've managed to synchronize into a cross. A perfect holy cross. All at once, they lift their heads to the sky and shriek in unison. The leader launches upward, and the rest follow— ascending together, flawless in formation.

Every sign points in one direction. The inevitable.

****

After a hot shower, my softest pajamas cling to my skin. I light incense, trying to create an atmosphere that might coax me to sleep. I need it desperately. Lately, I feel like a zombie, half alive, half absent. I rub lavender-scented moisturizer between my hands until it warms, then smooth it over my face. The radio hums softly in the background. A lavender candle flickers beside my bed. For some reason, it's the one scent I'm always drawn to. The only one that calms my jumping nerves. One more song, then I'll turn the radio off. Music has a way of rescuing me from my own mind.

"Hot 101.5. Heartbeat Radio, your favorite station of today. Welcome back, all you night owls."

Rap. Tap. Tap.

"This is Debbie, here with you live, and I'll be taking requests all night long."

I had been listening to her segment, "Night Cap Radio," for two years now. Her voice is so familiar and friendly.

Rap. Tap. Tap. The sound hits the window. "Must be a bird," I mutter.

"The lines are open, and we have a special request," Debbie continues. "Let's see who the next lucky caller is. Good evening! Who's on the line?"

RAP. TAP. TAP. RAP. TAP. TAP. I yank the curtains back.

My eyes search for the thing causing the noise, disrupting my segment with Debbie. A face stares up at me from underneath the streetlight. For a moment, I couldn't recognize the person standing there. Expressionless. I grabbed the binoculars from my desk.

Alice.

She's wearing oversized overalls. No makeup. Hair wild and tangled. The cross from Moses' grave hangs heavy around her neck, dragging her shoulders down.

The radio host continues, "Hello there, who do we have on the other line with us tonight?"

"Yes." Her voice crackles through the radio. "Thank you for taking my call. This is Alice Whitman."

"We have Alice Whitman here with us tonight. Alice, dear, what song would you like to dedicate, and to whom?"

"'Dreams' by Fleetwood Mac," she says. "This is for my dear friend. She's listening right now. She's not near me, but I can see her." Alice looks straight at me. Her mouth twists into a wicked smile. Her hollow eyes gleam.

As the song plays, she sways gently to the rhythm, eyes never leaving mine. Dirt and dried blood mark her skin. Sweat trickles down my spine. I can't scream. I can barely breathe, momentarily paralyzed and terrified. My mind drew a blank, unsure of what to do, but my feet somehow ran me down the steps and out the front door, right by the streetlight where she stood just moments ago.

She's gone. Nowhere in sight. Had I blanked out long enough for her to leave, or was she never here to begin with? Just a figment of my imagination.

No. She left a trace. There's evidence. I'm not going insane. The streetlamp illuminates something on the asphalt, a crumpled piece of paper where she'd been standing. I pick it up. If I throw it away without opening it, will this end? I walked away slowly, ignoring the paper on the ground.

A whisper invites itself into my ear. "Open it."

My fingers twitch as I unravel the paper.

"I lost. Tomorrow, it's coming for me, Shelby. It's coming for me."

It's Alice's handwriting. Tomorrow is Tuesday.

Day three.

CHAPTER 19

HELPLESS

Fear kept me awake most of the night.

I might have slept two hours, if that. Mostly, I lay there listening to sounds that didn't belong, watching the darkness fade until the sun finally rose. The television, the radio, a book, nothing helped. My mind was pulled in one direction: Alice, like a drain sucking the water in when unplugged. There was nowhere for me to hide.

Maybe I can change the sequence this time. Disrupt it. Outsmart it. If I already know how it's supposed to happen, I can scramble the pattern. There has to be a way to interfere with its plan. It's early, and yet again, I call Alice out of desperation. I wanted to know where she was last night, dressed in overalls with no make-up. I'm too afraid to ask. She finally answers after three rings. "Alice? Are you awake?," I blurt out anxiously.

"Shelby, why are you calling me so early?" she snaps. It was slightly annoying the first time. Now she's irritated. "Is this some joke to you now? My alarm doesn't even go off for another six minutes!"

I was prepared for the verbal lashing, but I continued. "I was thinking we should ditch classes today," I say quickly. "We could spend the day at River's beach house. I know where they hide the key."

Silence.

"Hello? Hello, Alice? Are you there?" The line goes dead. "Damn it." My fingers fumble through the drawer for my keys. Moving on to Plan B.

I'll drive to Alice's house, pick her up myself, and take her *anywhere* but the university. I can stop this. I *have* to.

My mustard-yellow 1971 Ford Pinto, my loyal companion since the day I got my license, waits at the end of the driveway. I threw a bunch of snacks and a few cans of cola into the trunk. We can trick this thing. It has no hold over us.

Click.

Click. Click.

Click. Click. Click.

The engine struggles, draining itself with every failed attempt.

There's no way. I just had the car inspected last week. Everything had cleared, and it passed the inspection. The radio snaps on by itself.

"Good morning, beautiful people, and welcome back. This is Mac with 101.5 Heartbeat Radio. Today's hot topic is dream interpretation. What do your dreams *really* mean?"

Back and forth, back and forth, the windshield wipers jerk to life, creating a harmonic sound. The car's lights flicker, adding to the chaos. The dashboard glows and dims, breathing into the spring morning.

But the engine remains dead. Nothing makes sense. I slammed my fist into the steering wheel, setting the horn off. The car erupts into disordered convulsions—clicking, whining, sputtering, creating sounds I've never heard before. It was complete chaos. After a minute or so of this fit, the car moans loudly, belching thick, black smoke from the engine and clouding my vision. My patience is waning. Holding my breath, I fling open the door and run through the black smoke. I coughed my way to the neighbor's house three doors down.

Wesley.

I ring the doorbell, desperate. *Please be home.* I hear his footsteps approaching the door, slow and steady. Wesley answers the door in his robe. Eyes full of sleep, he squints to get a better look at me. "Uh, hi, Wesley. I'm really sorry to disturb you so early. My phone line is down and--"

"Sure, come on in, Shelby," he interrupts smoothly. "Would you like a cup of coffee? I was just about to put a pot on."

"No, that's alright, thank you," I say quickly. "May I use your phone, please?"

"Sure, right over here in the kitchen." He points to a corner of the counter used as a workstation with pens and paper, a phonebook, and a message book. I'm not sure if he notices my trembling hands or smells the smoky car fumes that penetrated my hair, but I didn't care. I just need to talk to Alice.

The kitchen is meticulously arranged. Spotless. It *smelled* clean. Lemony fresh.

While I call Alice's number, he stands there watching me press each number on the pad. Hands still in his pockets, studying me. Why is he doing that?

There's a necklace around his neck, silver. Quite simple, with the initials WJ engraved on the charm hanging front and center.

After three rings, the housekeeper finally answers. "I'm sorry, honey," Mrs. Robbins says. "Alice has already left for the university. She had a paper to turn in and didn't want to be late. Would you like me to give her a message?"

"No, thank you, Miss Robbins. I'll catch up with her there. It's too late anyway."

"Excuse me, dear? What is too late?" Mrs. Robbins asks.

I pause. Defeated. "Nothing, sorry." Putting the receiver down, I thanked Wesley and swiftly made my way towards the door.

The doorknob doesn't turn. I twist it left. Right. Jiggle it. Push it.

Nothing happens. My chest tightens. Why won't it open? Did he lock me in?

Behind me, Wesley watches calmly, with his arms folded across his chest, leaning against the wall, almost amused. Ted Bundy. He was all over the news, in the papers, and in the minds of women all over the country. The gruesome images flashed through my mind. What if Wesley is a psycho?

C'mon, Shelby, stop overreacting.

"Could you please open the door?" My voice trembles.

He saunters over, standing far too close; his morning breath lingers in the air next to me. He grips the knob, gives it a small lift and tug.

Click. The sound of freedom.

"It's these old houses," he says lightly. "They all have their tricks."

"Thanks," I say, already halfway down the front porch steps. He calls after me, "Hey Shelby." The tone is no longer amused. I freeze, just able to turn my head slightly toward him.

"Sometimes the truth has been there the whole time," he says. "Just beneath the stairs of your mind, waiting for you to find it." Wesley smiles faintly. Without waiting for a response, he turns around and disappears into the house.

I don't have time for riddles. Alice needs me. I rush back to my car and slide into the driver's seat, knowing it's pointless. Nothing has changed. I'm not sure why I bother trying to start it again. I turn the key. To my surprise, the engine roars to life.

For one foolish second, I think my prayer worked. But this thing, whatever it is, is stronger.

It wants me to be there, front and center, to witness the chaos about to be created.

CHAPTER 20

THE COURTYARD

The university bell rings for lunch hour, and students pour out of their classes from every direction. We drifted toward the courtyard as usual, but today we were being pulled by something else. And only I knew.

I tried one last time.

"Why don't we go to McDonald's today?" I suggest, forcing cheer into my voice. "Just for a change." If we leave campus, maybe it won't happen. Maybe I can break the pattern. But the Devil doesn't let you outsmart it. Everyone resists the idea. Excuses. Shrugs. Lunches have already been packed. They're drawn to the courtyard like it's magnetized.

The temperature drops. Not gradually, but violently. At least twenty degrees in a matter of seconds. The wind kicks up, sending leaves skidding across the lawn. The flowers lining the courtyard lose their color and begin to wilt, drained of life. The sky dulls to an ugly gray. Students glanced upward. Some muttered, unable to fathom the sudden change. A few hurry back toward the dining hall, assuming a storm is about to hit. But I knew.

River is in his element, talking. I hear him highlighting the last game. His grandiose gestures mimic the game's winning moves. His voice fades into static. Jared silently eats his ham sandwich. I watch Alice carefully. She opens her backpack and pulls out a small paper bag.

My mind races to another place, the mall. The logo stares at me.

No. No, no, no.

Seaside Bake Shop. She reaches inside and pulls out a thick slice of banana bread. My heart starts pounding so hard I swear the people around me can hear it; I can almost see it through my blouse. I can't just sit here and watch. I spring forward, arms outstretched, trying to knock it from her hand. Too slow.

She pivots away. "Have you lost your mind?" she snaps.

The words left my mouth so fast before my thoughts could process, "Alice, all that banana bread is making you fat!"

Two of her other girlfriends stand by her and gasp in horror, staring me down. Alice looks at me the same way people look at Papa, confused, annoyed, and slightly afraid. No one has ever spoken to her that way before.

"You can sit by yourself today." She angrily turns her back on me and joins the others, even more determined to eat her slice of banana bread. I drop back onto the bench and bury my face in my hands.

Please. Please. Please. Make it stop.

A few minutes passed. The choking begins, and the sound of sheer struggle and desperation cuts through the air. A faint ringing fills my ears, swallowing everything else.

I froze. Everyone around me was moving fast. Helping. Running towards Alice. Then, running away from Alice like a stampede of wild animals, causing the ground to rumble beneath the weight of their panicked footsteps.

The wind picked up. Leaves blew in circular eddies, swirling around the courtyard.

Time stood still for me.

Because I knew. I knew it would be the last time we would ever see Alice.

CHAPTER 21

RUMORS

Alice wasn't completely gone, but she wasn't present either. A cold room, painted in mint green, was now her refuge. Hung on the wall across from her bed was a painting of a secret garden with a small waterfall. At the end of the waterfall were animals gathered around a pile of rocks. She was now a patient in Room 312 of the Intensive Care Unit at Wilshire Pointe Memorial Hospital.

She didn't know where she was, nor was she able to see the painting or the green walls, because she was in a coma. The only sign of life was her chest, being lifted up and down by a ventilator.

Our first thought was simple: should Alice wake from the coma, it would be best if she changed her name and moved far away. A fresh start, because no one at the university will ever associate with her again. Not after what they witnessed. I'm ashamed to admit, I'd think twice before being alone with her in a room. And I'm her friend.

Life changed for the three of us. As River, Jared, and I passed by groups, the whispers would follow. Quiet enough for us know it was about us, and loud enough to catch certain words: *cult, Satan, demonic, curse.*

The town knew Alice was in our circle. The questions began.

What were they associated with? What exactly did they do in their spare time?

All eyes were on us. We weren't the only ones under scrutiny.

The town had no mercy for the Whitmans. The irony became evident. Everything they worked for, the grand image they created, the important associations they made, went up in flames the moment word spread about Alice. What took years to achieve took only 24 hours to undo. The Whitmans played a crucial role in rebuilding poor communities, sponsoring church activities, and providing scholarships to underprivileged students. Alice claimed they did it mostly to show how "godly" they were. The charity served as a tax break for them as well. Either way, Mr. and Mrs. Whitman were silently erased and dropped by the boards of advisors with no explanation. Club memberships were denied. Invitations stopped coming in the mail.

Weekend mornings, they'd wake up to see toilet paper hanging from trees that lined the front of their home. Eggs splattered across their iron gates.

Instead of receiving compassion, they became a target.

CHAPTER 22

THE CONFESSION

Panic sets in. A part of me feels like I am going crazy. Maybe I am. Maybe I carry the same gene as my father, and it just found me earlier in life. I have to tell someone. The burden is too much to bear. But authorities won't believe me. I have no proof. A dream? Signs? They may send me to an asylum, along with Papa.

Benson Robert Jones. My father's full name. He was a renowned lawyer in his day. One of the most respected in this town. He appeared on television and radio shows. Reporters lined up just to get a few minutes of his time.

He had a presence, always dressed to the nines in a three-piece pinstriped suit. Shoes perfectly shone. A confident grin was fixed in place. People would pause when he walked into a room, hoping to absorb even an ounce of his poise. They wanted to be near his energy.

Papa had a gift, an extraordinary one. He made everyone he met feel important. He spoke their names, looked them in the eye, and shook their hands, giving them his full attention. A light touch on their shoulder, as if transferring an electric current. In that moment, you were the most important person in the world. And it came from a genuine place because most of those people he encountered had no power. They couldn't offer him any special favors. His calm and collected composure, even in the most tumultuous situations, made him the most powerful person in the room.

Now he looks twice his age. The medications have added another forty pounds to his frame, causing extreme lethargy. He sits on the same side of the sofa, worn and tattered, with his imprint on the seat, mindlessly flipping through the channels, waiting for each day to pass. There are times when he stares at the wall without blinking, mumbling unintelligible words, snarling, snickering, sometimes even barking. A few days ago, I found him crouching behind the sofa, biting his nails vigorously, to the point of drawing blood at the corners of his fingers.

What do I do? How do I go about the rest of my life like this? It's all too much. Papa. The secrets. *The secrets.* I feel like a balloon being pumped with air. Too much air. One more breath, and I would explode.

So, I decided to tell River. The constant chatter in my mind was driving me insane. Like this force, it *wanted* me to share this secret. Maybe it was a selfish thing to do, but at this juncture, *I didn't even care.* Releasing this demon was all that mattered; it took over my mind, and eventually, I felt physically exhausted. The guilt was too heavy, even though I didn't do anything. Maybe that's the problem. I'm not doing anything. I'm just watching it unfold, knowingly.

"River," I called through the throngs of students scattering about the hallway. He signaled to wait one second, as he was finishing his conversation with another student. Wrapping it up, he winked at me and started in my direction.

"What's going on, my lady? Have you been losing sleep?" He uses a finger to trace the dark circles underneath my eyes. Ignoring his concern, I bluntly steer the conversation in a different direction. "Can you meet me by my car in ten minutes? I need to talk to you."

"Oh?" He grins, sliding over to me. "Just to talk or..." His hands wrap around my waist. "Knock it off," I snap. "I'm serious." Tears sting my eyes. He immediately straightens. Pushing a strand of hair behind my ears, he gently kisses my forehead.

River is there before I am, leaning against the door of my car with his backpack slung on one shoulder, giving me that look—the one that makes me instantly forget why I ever get angry with him. He's genuinely concerned.

"I don't even know if you'll believe me," I begin, voice shaking, "but that thing with Alice…"

His face flushes instantly, and patches of red appear along his face and neck. The sight of Alice and being so close to the action himself is something etched in his memory. He swallows hard and gives me a look that says, 'Do we have to talk about this?' I'm the only one who knows about his weekly therapy sessions.

"I had a dream about it," I continue quickly. "Three days before it happened. Every detail. From start to finish. And it wasn't the first time." His eyes narrow, listening intently. I can tell he's not following me. I take a deep breath and start over.

"Six months ago, I dreamt about my cat. And then I found him under my neighbor's car, exactly like in the dream. It's like something tested me with Moses first. And when it worked…Alice was the next victim."

It was all word vomit. It came out so fast. Too fast and too messy. I could almost see it splattering on his face. But I couldn't stop, just like I couldn't stop the dreams. I even rehearsed it repeatedly in front of the mirror so eloquently, with hand gestures and perfect expressions. What was happening now was an act of desperation disguised as panic. I stop talking after he winces, removing his hands from my waist. His gaze shifts to the students walking past us.

I waited, relieved yet anxious to hear his response, unable to breathe for a moment. An uncomfortable silence floats around us. I had no idea what he was thinking. I wanted so badly for him to believe me. He sighed, scratched the back of his neck, and shook his head. None of this was good. I knew these signals.

"Shelby," he says softly while leaning in closer so that students nearby can't hear, "I mean this with all sincerity. It might help to talk to someone.

It's a lot to process. We are all dealing with things. I could give you the number to my therapist."

I cut him off. "I shouldn't have told you." My bottom lip starts to quiver. But I control my emotions. "I knew you wouldn't understand."

And then I said it. "I need some space. Some time apart." His face sank. "Shelby, come on. Why are you acting—," I put a hand up in the air, signaling him to be quiet. I didn't want to hear anything else from him. Walking away with his hands in his pockets, he kicks a stone. I watched the dust settle as my anger began to escalate. I had so much to say, but the rage clouded my ability to speak. He left me behind to ponder my own emotional wreckage.

I'm not sure what made me think he would believe me. But the damage is done. I can't take back what I said, and now I have no one to turn to.

Pounding the windshield with my fist, warm tears emerge and trickle down my cheeks, dripping onto my lips. They taste awful, so bitter, almost like whiskey.

CHAPTER 23

SOCIAL OUTCASTS

It's now the middle of May, and Alice is still in a coma. No one visits her except for her parents and me. Jared stops by occasionally, but River can't bring himself to face her again. He also hasn't spoken to me since our last interaction. I don't blame him.

The doctors don't have any hope for a recovery, nor do they have an explanation for the terror that took over her body that day. A team of Harvard-educated physicians was assigned to her case. After a series of physical exams were administered, they alluded to several mental disorders, possible seizures, but could never narrow their diagnosis. Her parents won't allow any photos of her condition to be released to the public. They were too gruesome. At the hospital, the nurses keep a thin veil over her face.

Wilshire Pointe, known for its conservative views and ultra-religious community, was convinced the devil himself had visited the Whitmans. Too many versions of the stories had spread, each gaining more shock value as they were passed around. I overheard a man retelling the scene, confidently confirming that Alice levitated off the ground.

People stayed clear of our paths, from River, Jared, and me, as if we were infected with a contagious disease. Rumors spread that we were part of a satanic cult. That evil lurked around us. That being near us invited darkness. Store owners kept a close eye on us. Some pretended to work around the store while following our movements, dusting and sweeping near us so they could maybe catch us in the act. One shopkeeper threw holy water on us to see if it would burn our skin. To her dismay, nothing happened. We got stares and gasps as people sped up when passing by us. Exorcism flyers were tucked into our mailboxes and left on our car windshields. Missionaries shoved pamphlets under our doormats and ran as soon as they saw us.

Once, a man spat at the ground when I walked by.

Plastic skeletons, normally used for Halloween decorations, hung from our trees like warnings. Our mailboxes were smashed. A devil's face with horns was sprayed across Jared's van in red spray paint. People were relentless. Cruel. We had become the town's source of fear.

What they didn't realize was that we were scared, too.

CHAPTER 24

CRY ME A RIVER

My phone rings incessantly. I know it's River. After the sixth ring, I finally answer.

"Shelby! It's me. Please don't—"

I put the receiver down. Ruthless? A little bit, but he deserves it. He can suffer a little longer.

The phone rang again. I ignore it.

I imagine him—pacing, yelling, even punching a wall, cursing under his breath. He can sit with it. He can feel the weight of his words. The lack of his empathy. The questioning of my...my mental state. If he passed me in the market square or the library, I'd cover my face and change direction. Now that June is creeping in and classes are coming to an end, there's little chance of running into him at all, which is in my favor. My wounds are still raw. He poured salt into them, and the sting hasn't faded.

Outside, rain pounds the ground in thick, violent drops. The kind that soaks you in seconds. I step onto the porch to bring in the cushions from our small, covered area, just enough for two people to sit. Movement catches my eye. Someone is running toward me from down the street, arms flailing, stumbling through the rain. For a moment, I can't make out his face through the heavy rain. Then I hear him as he gets closer.

"Shelby!"

My stomach turns. It's River.

He looks like a ghost, pale and thin. His eyes show that he hasn't slept for days. His hair is plastered to his forehead, rain streaming down his face, but I can't tell where the rain ends, and the tears begin. I've never seen him cry before.

Good. Serves him right. I imagined him tossing in his bed, unable to sleep due to the guilt he felt, the way he dismissed my confession. The thought almost makes me smile.

He reaches the porch, breathless, wheezing, out of energy, and desperate to see me. Trying to catch his breath, he bends forward and grabs his knees. Fresh tears pour down his face as he apologizes, repeatedly, voice breaking and shaking.

This is not the River I know. Crying? Begging?

This is more than just me. This is deeper. Something is wrong, very wrong. The hairs on my arm lift. I step forward and pull him inside before he collapses, guiding him to the couch. I pat him dry with two towels and wrap a warm blanket around his shoulders. It's unsettling to see someone so full of bravado reduced to a bundle of nerves. His hands shake as he pulls out a box of cigarettes from his pocket.

Another first. I'd never seen him light up a cigarette before. At least, not in front of me. If it were a habit, I would have smelled the smoke on his breath or on his clothing. He lights it, inhales it too hard, and coughs violently.

"You were right," he blurts. "Everything you said, I believe it."

My chest tightens, and my hands make their way to my stomach, forming knots as he continues.

"There's something out there," his voice rising with each word. "Something is out there. It comes into our minds. It plays out stories in our dreams. And then it makes us watch them happen. What is it?" He repeats even louder, with a quivering voice, "What is it?" The cigarette in his hand trembles.

Papa peers out from his bedroom, confused, almost alarmed. I give him a steady nod. A reassuring wave. *Everything's fine.* He retreats into his room.

River pulls the blanket up to his shoulders and props his feet on the couch after removing his wet sneakers. Shock has taken over his mind and body. A part of me doesn't even want to know.

I sit on the ottoman in front of him and take his trembling hand, warming it between mine. He grips it like a lifeline.

He stares at the wall, eyes empty, and begins to tell me everything in a frail voice.

CHAPTER 25

WHAT HAPPENED TO JOHNNY?

"Johnny, wake up! It's time for school, shithead!" River takes a pair of dirty socks, worn at football practice, and shoves them in his brother's face.

"Ugh, gross, you scumbag!" Johnny spat out whatever fibers touched his lips. "You're a sick freak, you know that?!"

"Looks like you're awake *now*! C'mon, let's go." River yanks the covers down to the floor, along with Johnny, wrapped in them. He falls to the floor, landing with a thud.

"I'm taking you to school today. Mom and Dad have some big meeting in the city, and they told me to drive your sorry ass." River smirked. "I'm not waiting. I've got things to do and people to meet." Johnny rolled his eyes while massaging his backside, untangling himself from the blanket. He let out a moan. "I can't wait until school is out. I just wanna *sleep.*"

River stares down at him, gripping the back of his head with both hands. "Quit your whining. It's the last day. You can sleep all you want tomorrow. Now get your lazy ass up and get dressed." River laughed as he lifted him, giving Johnny's bottom a quick kick.

They both scarfed down Pop-Tarts and chased them with a cold glass of milk, wiping their milk mustaches with the backs of their hands, then using their jeans as napkins. Slamming the door shut, they jumped into River's Jeep Cherokee. River popped in a new mixtape and turned up the volume, windows down. One of their all-time favorites, "Somebody to Love" by Queen, begins.

River dramatically sang while Johnny backed him up as the chorus. That's how it usually went at home, too; River was always up front and center, the one telling jokes and narrating stories, and Johnny was in the audience, beaming with pride. Windows down, music up, they both move their heads to the beat, aware that the life they lived was pretty damn good.

This was River's last memory of his brother.

****

River closed his book after the last class at the university. Usually, Shelby waited for him outside, and they chatted about their evening plans, where and when to meet up, but she was angry with him. So angry, she had been ignoring his calls and avoiding him on campus for the last few weeks. River noticed that Shelby had been acting stranger than normal, even before the day she confessed her dreams to him. She started biting her nails again, combined with mumbling to herself. She kept a small notebook with her, occasionally scribbling dates with words next to them. He could never really get a good look at it. She kept it hidden. He saw one sentence that seemed to read, '*How do I control my dreams?*,' but was too embarrassed to ask her about it. It would make him seem like a nosy boyfriend.

The professor's voice became distant and unclear as River's eyes wandered to the door, looking for Shelby. He was accustomed to having her around for second opinions, guidance on certain subjects, someone to talk to about future careers, and, most importantly, for emotional support, especially after the episode with Alice. He seemed to be unstable without her.

There was no sign of her.

The professor finished his speech, emphasizing that students should continue to use their minds in the summer and engage in some form of intellectual stimulation.

Forget the books; the only stimulation he wanted was Shelby.

The lecture came to an end. Before the professor could even finish his last sentence, the students darted out of the classroom, like caged animals in a zoo. The gates were open, and they ran wild. Music blared in the cars, and people were discussing all sorts of plans and vacations for the summer. Excited chatter filled the spaces. River didn't waste any time socializing and drove straight to Wilshire Pointe High, his old school, to pick up Johnny. He planned an ice cream treat at Denny's to finish the year strong, for being responsible and getting good grades. It was a celebration, just the two of them. He was proud of his little brother but would never tell him to his face.

River pulled his jeep up to the pick-up line at the high school, remembering his younger self walking out of the double doors with a crowd of friends around him. He waited for Johnny to come out, books in hand, because his backpack was always stuffed with more books. He was usually surrounded by one or two of his buddies. Quiet kid. Not a fan of too much attention.

His two main buddies walked out, but Johnny wasn't with them. River jumped out of his Jeep, plowing over a group of nerds, purposely knocking their books to the ground. "Oops!" It was an old habit he couldn't shake. He was excited to take his brother out for a treat.

"Hey, guys, have you seen Johnny?" His keys whirl around his index finger.

One of them hesitated. "Yeah, it was weird. He was here for the first three classes, we had lunch, and then we didn't see him after lunch." River stops swinging his keys and looks at the other friend for more of an explanation. The other friend added, "I saw him get into a car with another guy...right after lunch. Didn't think anything of it. I figured he was just playing hooky, or maybe he had some place to be."

River's voice escalated. "Didn't think anything of it? Has he *ever* played hooky? What kind of friend are you? You don't know him at all. Johnny's not the type to ditch class. Idiot!" He paused to think and put his hands on his hips. His eyes gaze beyond the boys. "Do you remember what the car looked like? Did you get a license plate number?"

The friend answered, realizing the situation was getting serious. His voice quivered. "It was a cab, and I don't remember what the driver looked like, and no, I didn't think to get the license plate number either." He looked down. "I'm sorry."

"Oh well, that's just great." River hits him on the back of his head and storms off. The boys watch him speed out of the parking lot. He drove around in a frantic search, from street to street, looking for Johnny. *Shit, this is the one time Mom and Dad ask me to take responsibility, and I've lost Johnny.* His thoughts unravel, creating mental scenarios of his parents' reactions. The mixed feelings of fear for Johnny's safety and the wrath of his parents set in.

"Have you seen a young kid, blonde hair, blue eyes, about 15, wandering around? He would have been wearing an Wilshire Pointe High uniform?" he asks the gas station manager. The manager saw the sweat beading up on River's forehead and offered him a free bottle of water. "No, son, but I sure will keep a lookout. I'm sure he'll turn up." River made a stop at the market square, the deli, and Moody's record store, but no sign of Johnny. He slowed his car as he passed the park, but no one was there. He passed by Denny's on the way home, and an unsettling feeling gnawed at him.

The iron gates at the front of the driveway were already open. His parents had just parked and were getting out of their car. River hoped to have more time to prepare an explanation. He parked his Jeep next to their car and reluctantly removed his seatbelt.

"Hi, son. How was your last day at the university?" his mother asked.

"Alright, but I have to tell you something. There's really no other way to say this, but… um… I went to pick up Johnny from school. He didn't show up. I can't find him anywhere." Mrs. Smyth gasped with her hands covering her mouth. "What do you mean, you can't find him anywhere?"

Mr. Smyth told her to go inside immediately and make some calls to the parents of Johnny's friends, his soccer coach, and the school. She ran into the house without bothering to close the door behind her.

"Must be off with some friends and celebrating the end of the school year. He should've given us some notice. Can't be taking off like that, worrying your mother and me." Mr. Smyth shook his head and grabbed his briefcase from the car. He muttered something, but River couldn't quite catch it. He only heard the words 'irresponsible kids.'

But River knew something was off. This wasn't like Johnny at all.

Edward Smyth hung his hat on the rack and loosened his tie. "Any news on Johnny?" he asked his wife. She sat at the kitchen table with a notepad, crossing off the last name on the list. She had called everyone who might have known about Johnny's whereabouts. She let out a small cry, "Oh dear, I'm afraid not," followed by tears. Her hands shook as she straightened out her dress.

"Ok, that's it, I'm calling the police." Edward grabbed the receiver and took over.

The receptionist answered and transferred him over to one of the officers. River heard him on the other line. "Mr. Smyth, you know we can't do a search until your child is gone for 48 hours."

Edward Smyth angrily retorted, "What in the fucking hell?! So, we just sit around and wait for 48 hours? Do you know how much damage can be done during that time, and you want us to be patient? Well, fuck my patience! Do you know who I am? Get the sheriff on the phone. Actually, forget it. We're coming down to the station." He slammed the receiver and violently motioned everyone to get in the car, face red and back as stiff as a board.

River and his mother followed Edward Smyth as he marched to the receptionist's desk. One cop whispered something in another cop's ear, possibly alerting them of the storm about to hit.

"I need to speak to Sheriff Gibson, NOW!" Edward slammed both fists down on the desk. Sheriff Gibson strolled out of his office, balancing an overweight belly over his skinny legs, as he ate a slice of pizza straight from the box. "What's all this commotion?" The sound of his chewing was obnoxious and untimely. "I'll tell you what the commotion is about. You're gonna send a squad out to find my kid. I don't give a rat's ass about your 48-hour rule. Ya understand? I hope you know who you're dealing with, *Gibson*."

Gibson motioned them to follow him into his office. The distraught family sat across from Gibson. His fingers were interlocked, resting on his round belly as he leaned back in the chair. The buttons on his shirt struggled to keep the two sides from splitting apart. "Now, you're aware of our rule, Mr. Smyth. I understand how distressing this may be for you and your family. But you know, kids, they run off all the time. It's a rather rebellious age. We see this all the time. Really, it's nothing to worry about. Soon he'll realize there's no place like home and will be back before you know it." He licked marinara sauce from his thumb and rubbed his hands together.

"Johnny's just not the type. He's an extremely responsible child," Theresa interjects sternly. The officer dismissed Theresa and leaned forward, his eyes intensely glued to Edward. "Well, let's see what we can do for each other, shall we?" Edward raised his eyebrows, mentally questioning what Gibson was about to say. On a piece of paper, Gibson scribbled something and slid it to Edward. Angered, Edward's face became red. He shot up from his chair, fist clenched, ready to swing.

"Now, you know that will land you straight to jail, Mr. Smyth, and I'd hate to do that to you and your family, especially during this stressful time. Keep your calm, because it's the only way you can get us moving. You, especially, should understand what I'm about to ask for, right, Edward? Or do you need a friendly reminder?" He gave him a wink.

Edward took his seat, defeated. Theresa and River were lost, unable to follow the conversation, but knew there was some hidden secret between the two men. "Can I assume we have a deal?" Mr. Smyth stared at him for a long moment, then nodded. Later that evening, Mr. Smyth handed River a zipped pouch. "Son, you don't need to say anything. Just hand Gibson this pouch, and no matter how tempted you are, DO NOT open it." He didn't tell River what was inside the pouch. But River knew.

The Smyths had barely slept, worried sick about Johnny, hoping he would show up in the middle of the night. River was sure his brother was home with each noise he heard, but when he checked, no one was there.

It was around 9:00 a.m. when the doorbell rang. Mrs. Smyth was in her robe, holding a cup of coffee. She answered the door. Two cops stood there in silence; upon seeing Mrs. Smyth, they removed their hats, and their eyes solemnly met the stone steps. Losing grip of her coffee, Theresa Smyth fell to the floor. Mr. Smyth ran over to console her, tears in his eyes. River watched his family fall apart from the kitchen door.

Edward Smyth looked to the officers for answers as he held his wife upright.

The officers began their speech. "I am Officer Heinz, and this is Officer Brown, and we are here to talk with you about your son, Johnathan Smyth. We express our deepest condolences and are here to inform you that your son was pronounced dead this morning at the corner of 9th and E Street."

River and his parents couldn't grasp the words coming from their mouths. Just yesterday morning, everything was normal. A regular day in their lives. And today their world was turned upside down.

Officer Brown continues, "Would you please come down to the morgue to identify his body?"

His last sentence sent Mrs. Smyth into hysteria. She threw a ceramic vase from the foyer onto the floor as she screamed for Johnny. She didn't accept it. None of them accepted it.

Mr. Smyth held her tightly while River silently motioned to his father that he'd go down to the morgue to identify Johnny. He didn't believe the body lying in the morgue was Johnny's. He wanted to see for himself. River looked over to the empty passenger's side of his Jeep. Johnny was sitting there just yesterday.

"Somebody to Love" by Queen played on the radio. The reality slowly sank in; he would never see his brother again. The strong façade he kept up for his parents melted away, and he cried. He cried so hard he was unable to breathe.

An autopsy had shown a drug overdose.

River knew there was more to the story. Johnny would never get mixed up with drugs. There was just no way. He told River everything.

The next few days at the Smyth household were somber and unbearably quiet. Endless questions swarmed their minds. Who did he get the drugs from? Why Johnny? How did he get involved in this mess? His friends were questioned but had no idea about Johnny's double life.

Once the drugs were found in Johnny's blood test, the cops chalked it up to 'rich boy gets involved with the wrong crowd.' They concluded the investigation and closed the case. The Smyths wanted no news coverage and made sure the media stayed out of their private life, not wanting their son to be remembered as the boy who died because of a drug overdose. He was so much more.

There was nothing the Smyths could do except to mourn their child and accept their new fate.

****

I held his trembling hands as he finished the story, feeling an avalanche of sympathy for him and his family. "River, this is terrible," I whispered. "I'm so sorry. I'm so sorry I wasn't there."

He shook his head hard, eyes wet. "Shelby, I'm sorry for not believing you." I squeezed his hand tightly. I wanted to know one thing. "I need to ask you something, River. Did it happen three days after you dreamt it?"

He looked at me, terrified, "How did you know?"

CHAPTER 26

THE BOOGIEMAN

A chill ran through my spine.

He sobbed again, wiping his face with the back of his hand.

"And the funeral is tomorrow. I can't go. I can't go, Shelby. I don't want to see Johnny like that!" I wrapped my arms around him and held him tight. Now I knew.

"Boogieman!" Papa suddenly yelled from the hallway, half- peering around his doorframe. He giggled and disappeared back into his room like a child caught eavesdropping. "Boogieman!" he shouted again. Then again, three more times, each one quieter, like he was chanting it to himself.

"I'm sorry," I said gently, embarrassed. "That's just Papa. He isn't in the right frame of mind. He's been that way a long time."

River was unfazed by Papa's behavior. He was staring at nothing. I leaned closer. "River, please listen to me." I pulled his chin over in my direction to ensure he was listening. "Listen carefully. This thing, whatever it is, I think it spreads." He blinked slowly, trying to understand. "It spreads when we talk about it," I continued. "I told you about my dream, the one I had about Alice, and the one about Moses."

My throat tightened. "Now look what happened. You're pulled into it, too. Infected, or whatever you want to call it." His eyes widened, but he didn't interrupt. I didn't know the rules of this game just yet, but I also didn't want to take any chances. "Don't tell a soul about your dream.

Apparently, it feeds on vulnerability. It wants us to share the dreams, because that's how it grows. Like a virus, causing destruction and chaos." I swallowed. "This thing hates our community. Hates this town. It wants to destroy us." I stared at him as the sense of dread loomed over me. "The only question is...why?"

CHAPTER 27

INFERNO AT ST. THERESA

I tucked my hands between my knees while my head collapsed onto the pillow. The warm air danced into the room from the window across and softly caressed my face as I drifted into another world. A world where I was uninvited. A world I never wanted to be in. Something inside me sensed the imminent doom, but I was too tired, too worn-out, to care.

****

The church bells of St. Theresa were already ringing cheerfully.

It was a clear Sunday, not a cloud in sight. The rays of the sun bounced playfully off the stained-glass windows, causing me to squint, taunting me. I stood outside near the entrance, confused about how I'd arrived. I don't remember walking. My car was nowhere in sight.

I was just...there.

Mrs. Baker's sharp voice pierced through the air like daggers, aiming straight for my ears. She was the town's gossip queen, and the local newspaper could hardly keep up with her fabricated stories. There were hints of truth, but she had a way of adding a twist here and a twist there to gain an audience. Round and robust, she gathered a small cluster of women near the doors and launched into the weekly gossip, with not a second to waste. Mrs. Baker dominated the conversation, while the others clutched their handbags, gasping and covering their mouths at the right moments. She had a real knack for telling stories, especially since she took the liberty of spicing them up.

Who was having an affair? Whose child had been caught stealing from the market? Who had been excluded from the latest luncheon? Empty talk. None of it their business. Yet it filled the women with pleasure, dulling their own discontent. It was really their main reason for going to church. I never liked Mrs. Baker, and Mrs. Baker never liked me. It was unspoken, something we just knew.

The crowd quietly began funneling into the main hall. People filed past River in the aisle like he was part of the pews. He didn't belong here any more than I did. He barely ever went to church, and I would attend maybe twice a year. We made eye contact, mentally questioning each other about our presence there.

Children squealed near the front, giddy, barely containing themselves. They couldn't wait to bolt toward the new playground after service. Eventually, everyone was ushered into the pews and settled in. The day looked perfect. The sky was bright blue. The air smelled faintly of lavender. Father Clemmons stepped up and began his sermon.

River and I sat in the back pews, stiff and uneasy, pretending we were normal parishioners instead of two lost souls who happened to wander into church. We weren't religious. We didn't belong. Nothing came naturally to us, and we had to look to others for cues. It was too late to leave. The doors were closed. We were now trapped and had to sit through the next hour, pretending we knew what to do.

Six tall candles glowed behind the pulpit. One by one, they went out, as if there were an invisible breath blowing out birthday candles. I tilted my head towards River. "Did you see that?"

"Yeah," he whispered. "Maybe a draft?" There was no draft. No open window. No shift in the air.

Clemmons continued speaking, unaware that the candles behind him had gone out. From his view, everything was normal, but the congregation had changed. Every parishioner stared past him, unblinking, eyes fixed on the altar. Smiles stretched across their faces, too wide, almost disproportionate.

A chant began, low and tender. "Lies, lies, everything's a lie." The sound grew. "Lies, lies, we're all gonna die."

Cold air brushed my neck. I jerked my head around, but there was nothing behind me.

They were all staring in one direction, smiling. Their eyes were fixed on the cross. As the crowd tilted their necks clockwise, the cross followed the same movement. It slid slowly at first, then faster, until it flipped completely upside down.

Clemmons, undisturbed, still preached. He couldn't see what we saw.

River grabbed my hand. His palm was damp. "We gotta get out of here, Shel. Something weird is—" He was interrupted by uncontrollable laughter from the congregation. Not normal laughter, but the sound one makes when they are on the verge of insanity. Animals in the wild. They jumped up on the pews with both feet, dressed in their best clothes but behaving inappropriately, hissing, sticking their tongues out, and screaming with delight, eyes bulging from their sockets.

We couldn't hear ourselves anymore.

Then the heckling began. Clemmons became the target. Bibles flew through the air, hardcovers launched like weapons, aimed at the pulpit. "Foolish man! Disgusting pig! Get off that podium! You don't belong there! We know what you did!"

Clemmons froze, breaking out of his spell, and finally saw what we saw: complete chaos. Without wasting another moment, he bolted, vanishing through a side door like a thief in the night.

I grabbed River's arm and pointed at the children. "We need to get the kids out of here!"

It was too late. All twelve children stood at once, forming a single file line, unbothered by the chaos. They began to march towards the exit, eyes black, in a trance. The grand wooden doors creaked open ever so slowly, welcoming them to the outside. The day shifted to dusk in a matter of minutes. When the last child was outside, the doors slammed shut, creating a loud thud that echoed through the main hall, jolting the parishioners out of the spell. Boom. The latch slid loudly across the door, locking us inside, sealing us into our demise. The parents screamed after they realized their children were gone, scrambling to the door, banging on it, pulling on the handles. "Let us out! Let us out! Help!" Cries of desperation that no one on the outside would ever hear.

We were trapped.

From a window, I could see the children. They weren't joyful, nor did they run and scatter to the playground. They walked in a disciplined, single-file line. A moment later—swinging, sliding, laughing, and playing as if nothing had happened.

River yanked my hand. "Side exit! Let's go!" We ran, tripping over a woman who had fainted. The side exit was jammed.

Intense heat pressed in from every direction. Screams turned silent. Smoke followed the heat, barging into the room. At first, it was a thin black ribbon sneaking along the ceiling. Then it thickened, gushing towards us. Within seconds, flames burst through the ancient stained glass, cracking it with violent rage.

Dense smoke rolled down the steps outside, curling hot lava, like the church was trying to cough out deathly poison.

The parishioners ran in all directions, attempting to escape. Through the window, I could see the silhouettes of two nuns dropping to their knees in the courtyard, rosaries clenched in shaking hands. Smoke filled my lungs, and breathing became difficult. My body was slowing down. River slammed his shoulder into a window until it shattered. We climbed through the jagged glass, cutting ourselves on the way out. A shard of glass sliced through my right arm, cutting it deep, but the shock numbed my pain.

We stumbled into the open air, gasping and coughing. We wanted to let the others know about the window, but the thick smoke wouldn't allow us to see our way back.

Behind us, inside the church, the crucifix buckled, warping, twisting, and bending in impossible ways, until it crashed to the ground, debris scattering across the altar. Part of the ceiling collapsed onto the organ, producing a morbid sound, before the roof came down in a thunderous roar. People were trapped inside. Bodies roasted in the heat. Two of the women gossiping earlier were now covered in black, one screaming, one silent, and then the wooden beams came down on them with extreme force. We couldn't help them. It was too late. The building was collapsing.

Firefighters arrived at the scene within seven minutes. They shoved past River and me, hauled hoses, shouted orders, and dragged coughing parishioners away from the doors. For two full hours, they fought the fire until it finally surrendered to smoke and rubble. One by one, bodies were carried onto stretchers. Some gone; some holding on by a thread. When the worst of it was over, the firefighters began to move away, exhausted, furious. One of them shouted, "Kids! Over there by the playground!" I turned. Across the lot, the playground was still full of laughter. The children were there, playing as if nothing happened, totally oblivious to the church fire behind them.

I ran toward them, but something stopped me. It wouldn't allow me to move closer. A pressure barrier surrounded the playground. It shimmered faintly in the air. I could see the children perfectly, hear their shoes scrape the slide, and hear the giggles. But I couldn't cross. I waved. They couldn't see me. Moments later, the barrier shattered and turned to dust, falling to the ground. A firefighter jogged over and began to question the children. "Are you alright? Do you know what happened at the church? How did you kids end up here?"

I tried to answer. "Hello, sir! I'm right here!" I wave my hands. "They were inside. And then they left. The doors shut, locking us in…" No one looked at me. I was talking to the air. I grabbed the firefighter's arm. My hand passed through him. Cold rushed up my spine. Am I dead? I tried again. It went through again. A little boy stammered. "No, sir. Before the service started, we were called to the playground. Our parents said we'd be a distraction because we were too excited. We just wanted to play on the new equipment. We couldn't sit still at the service. They didn't even get mad, barely noticed we were gone. They were just staring straight at the altar—smiling. They were really happy for some reason."

"And who told you to come out here? Who *called* you?" the firefighter asked.

A little girl with pigtails and a frilled dress yelled, "That man…in the woods over there." She pointed toward the wooded area known as *The Witch's Womb.* No one ever went there. It was rumored to be a cursed land. The firefighter raised his eyebrows, unable to find the right words. The firefighters exchanged looks—relieved that the children were spared.

I staggered backward, dizzy, feeling like my body would float away. I felt light, almost half my weight. I turned toward what was left of the church.

River was on the ground, staring at the rubble with dead eyes. His hands were shaking. "River," I whispered. My voice sounded thin, far away. "Do you hear that?" He blinked slowly, coming out of a fog. "Hear what?"

"Listen closely," I whispered, moving my ear in the direction of the sound. Inside the ruined church, the organ was playing beautifully. A hymn they played every Sunday. "Here I am, Lord."

"No," he said. "There's no way in hell. How is that even possible?"

We moved into the wreckage, stepping over debris, ash, and broken glass. The building was empty, but the music continued to play. A white cloud of dust hovered near the organ, as if someone invisible had been sitting there, creating melodious tunes, celebrating the destruction. The strong force pulled the dust upward, yanking it through the broken stained-glass window. We watched it disappear before our eyes.

The music stopped. Then the scratching sound began. We followed the sound to the side of the organ. Intense scratching, words being etched in a rage.

L. Scratching. I. More scratching. E. More scratching. Then, S.

The scratching became even more violent and frenetic. *BURN IN HELL. ALL OF YOU.* This wasn't a freak accident. It wasn't random. This was intentional. Outside, the playground was empty. Yet the swings moved, back and forth, chains clinking joyfully. Tiny footsteps appeared on the slide in a faint dust trail, then disappeared. Reporters arrived before the smoke was fully cleared. Cameras, microphones, headlines, and reporters were in position, ready to dissect the situation. This was the beginning of a very dark reputation for Wilshire Pointe. They filmed the rubble, the standing wall, the playground, the altar—and the upside-down cross, but they didn't see what we saw. They didn't hear what we heard. River and I didn't tell anyone. We couldn't. No one would believe us. And if they did, they would fear us, like they feared Alice. The town demanded answers but received none. There was no foul play, no faulty wiring, nothing that could explain the tragedy. The media dug deep. They heard about Alice. They smelled a story that could make headlines.

"Wilshire Pointe: The Devil Has Awoken."

"Evil Reaches New Heights in Wilshire Pointe."

The papers were printed.

****

The sun rose on a beautiful Thursday morning.

The smell of soot woke me, and I rubbed my eyes. My body ached in unusual ways. My hands were black. On my right arm, a long cut. It took me a moment to understand. Soot covered most of my body and trailed onto the sheets. Grabbing the receiver, I dialed River. "It's all over me," I said, voice shaking.

On the other end, he swallowed hard. "Me too."

We didn't understand what was happening. All we knew was that our dreams were synchronized. We were in this game together. A game that started in our minds and became the town's reality in a matter of three days. That was all the time we had.

Sunday came, and the church bells rang their last tune.

CHAPTER 28

HURRICANE OWEN

Normalcy was never regained at Wilshire Pointe. The reconstruction of our historic church began, although it would never be the same. Lives were unfairly snatched on those very grounds, and there was still no explanation.

Although I already knew it was going to happen, I had no control over it. I couldn't stop it. Neither could River. People already labeled us as cult members, and if they knew we had a premonition through our dreams, it would just further confirm their theory.

Wilshire Pointe was quiet. Too quiet. Like the town was afraid to make noise; afraid to conjure up another disaster. The people didn't realize—it wasn't up to them.

The church ruins cooled. The bells stayed silent. Reporters packed up their vans and left. People rebuilt what they could and avoided what they couldn't explain.

And still, nothing felt healed. A Band-Aid was applied to a wound, but it would soon tear open.

This time, River was next to me. That feeling of dread came over me. The one that warned me to stay awake yet created a dull sensation in my body. My eyelids became too heavy to fight. My limbs went numb. River had already surrendered as I heard his breathing turn into light snores. My hand clutched River's arm tightly, but the hum of the fan finally took me into another land. I released my grip and something took me to another place.

****

The cold, wet feeling on my legs sent shivers across my body, waking me from a deep sleep. I stared into the murky water. I was knee-deep in it. Sewage floated around my legs. I tried not to look, but the atrocious smell invaded my sense, causing me to gag. Vomiting into the water would only make it worse. I called out for help, but it was of no use. Most of the town was hiding in their homes, afraid to come out after the hurricane had passed, afraid to face the floods that haunted the town for the last two days. People wading by just wanted to get to their destination, disgusted by the filth touching their skin, looking ahead and avoiding eye contact.

Papa needed his medication. All the stores were shut down. He only had enough to last another week, and I didn't know when this curse would end.

My wet jeans grew heavier with every step. By the time I finally got home, it took me another half hour to peel them off my cold legs. I wrung them out and threw them into the washing machine out of habit, even though the power was out.

River refused to leave my side. He didn't like the idea of me being alone with Papa.

When I returned to the living room, River was sitting on the floor across from the television with his knees pulled to his chest. Water dripped steadily from the ceiling into a bowl between us, creating a rhythmic sound that was almost hypnotic.

"It's been doing that all night," he said, then glanced toward Papa. Papa sat on the couch, smiling at the blank television screen as if it were showing his favorite program. Totally oblivious.

He kept repeating one phrase. "There's a boogieman, but you can't see him. He lives right here." Those words sent waves of discomfort through my entire body. I never understood, nor did I want to.

Phone lines were down. Families couldn't check on one another. I stood at the window and caught faces staring back from other houses—hopeless, hollow, waiting for help, asking the same questions without saying a word.

When will this end? What did we do to deserve this?

Their blank expressions felt like surrender.

Stagnant water bred mosquitoes. Then sickness. The town whispered about the end, about punishment, about God. Government agencies arrived, but not soon enough. That's when the rain finally stopped, and we were able to regain some control over the mess.

The clear sky offered a bit of relief. It was no longer a threat. The sun rose after days of gloom and destruction. But for many, the sky didn't matter. The sun didn't matter. Because for them, life had changed forever. They were preparing funerals.

Wilshire Pointe looked disheveled, stripped down. People wandered the streets with dirty faces and matted hair, moving like zombies, staring through one another as if their bodies kept walking, but their minds were elsewhere. Somewhere far. Windows were boarded up on businesses and office buildings. "Closed" signs hung on most of the doors.

During the blackout, the backup generator failed to work at the west wing of Wilshire Pointe Memorial Hospital. The patients who depended on life support machines didn't make it through. One of those patients was Alice.

We knew it was a matter of time. Her parents still held on to a thread of hope. They finally let go and fell into a deep state of depression. Their only daughter vanished in front of the entire town, and in the most violent way possible. They could do nothing but watch her disappear. No amount of money could bring her back. They had no one to turn to.

The townspeople looked away. It seemed easier for them to pretend the Whitmans didn't exist. They reminded the town of evil.

The flooding subsided. Stores slowly reopened. The town was heavily bruised, but the people came together and rebuilt with help from neighboring communities. Everyone *knew* what happened, or at least, they thought they did. They believed the devil was here, and he was unleashing havoc on the community. The latest theory in town was that Alice was the start of it all. The disasters began after her episode at the university courtyard. She was the epicenter.

I still didn't know how I felt. A part of me was glad she was gone. For so long, she wasn't *with* us, yet she wasn't completely gone. And when we heard the news that she had finally passed over, it gave me an eerie sense of relief.

At the university, things had changed. The courtyard was abandoned after the incident with Alice; landscapers were too afraid to maintain the area. Weeds and grass swallowed the stone paths. Nature had reclaimed its territory. Students swore they heard muffled laughter when they passed the location where it all happened. They would walk quickly by the site, only if they absolutely had to, sometimes running by to avoid contact with any evil forces. Rising high school seniors thought twice before applying, usually accepting offers from other universities. Wilshire Pointe University became the backup choice. They sent their applications elsewhere. Anywhere but here. It was tainted.

A Hollywood producer was set to film a horror movie in the courtyard. During the night hours, all the film equipment had been destroyed. Any film captured was somehow erased. The production crew packed up and left the very next day, confirming the town's theory. The courtyard was cursed. Forever.

****

There was one last formality to complete. One we were dreading but couldn't avoid. Alice's funeral was small and short. There wasn't a crowd.

A few reporters attempted to arrive with cameras, but the priest sent them away. The only attendees at Alice's funeral were her parents, River, Jared, the priest, and me. River didn't want to go. He wasn't fully recovered. None of us were. But he showed up. His therapist suggested it would bring closure for him.

River's parents refused to attend. They didn't want to be associated with the Whitmans anymore. Being ostracized by the community wasn't an option for them; they had a reputation to uphold.

Mr. and Mrs. Whitman stood there, dressed in all black; Mrs. Whitman wore a slender black dress and an elegant shawl. A netted veil stemmed from her hat, hiding her bloodshot eyes. They looked swollen, puffy with grief and guilt-ridden tears.

And still, she wore diamonds. Pearls. I couldn't help but notice.

Mr. Whitman looked like he'd lost weight. The death of his daughter had aged him in a way money couldn't fix. I'd heard rumors they planned to move to California, to start over where no one knew their name. There was no reason to stay in a town that had blatantly disowned them. The constant harassment would drive them out. That was the town's goal. It was a small community full of people who feigned support; people who would turn on each other in a heartbeat.

The priest conducted a brief ceremony. He was supposed to reserve judgment while performing funeral rites, but he couldn't hide his discomfort. He fidgeted, coughed, lost focus, and forgot words. When it was over, he offered a quick, awkward condolence and left as fast as his body would allow. If he could have run, he would have. It was more like a speed-walk, the kind that showed you were desperate to get away. Away from the casket.

The three of us, River, Jared, and I, stood in silence. River was having a difficult time being so close to the casket. His mouth twitched from time to time, and he blinked more frequently than normal. I took his hand between mine.

We were relieved that the coffin was closed. I had seen her face. Up close, during the wake. I wish I hadn't. It didn't matter what makeup they used or what jewelry they placed on her. She looked horrific, a face that would haunt my memory for as long as I lived. The beautiful, once charismatic Alice was long gone. What remained looked like something unreal and distorted, shown only on the screen for shock value. Her skin had turned leathery, tinged with a faint green undertone. Her lips were parched, almost black. Scrapes and cuts lined her cheeks and forehead. Her expression tightened with anger. She hadn't been resting. She'd been tormented, and she wasn't ready to go. Something had taken her against her will.

We turned to leave the cemetery grounds, sad, drained, and relieved to put a close to this chapter. Her parents were already halfway up the hill, walking hand in hand, heads down.

Clouds gathered above us. The sky darkened as the sun slipped behind them. Something moved beneath the ground. A ripple under my sandals, like tiny waves under my feet. Slow and intentional. I froze.

Slugs. They emerged from the earth in every direction—slimy bodies sliding forward with purpose, as if they'd been called. As if they knew exactly where to go.

They did.

I nudged River and Jared with my elbow. The slugs crawled up the casket, and in formation, like synchronized swimmers, they spelled a single word across the top. *L-I-E-S.*

A painful groan rose from deep within the casket.

Then muffled laughter, thin and sharp, almost taunting, followed. Without hesitation, we ran. But the air around our legs thickened, heavy, as if running under water. Something was trying to keep us there. It wanted us to stay and watch. It didn't want to be alone. She didn't want to be alone. I yelled, "Alice, let us go! We were the only ones who were loyal to you." Just then, the grip loosened, and we fell to the ground.

Across the street, my eyes caught a tall, lanky woman walking her Labrador. The dog stopped almost immediately, refusing to move forward. It stood rigid, like an ice sculpture, its nose aimed towards Alice's grave and growled in a low tone.

"Come on, Rex," the woman said, tugging the leash. The dog snarled, then lunged. Its teeth clamped down on her wrist. She screamed, yanking back as blood ran down her hand. A passerby hurried over, cautious, trying not to startle the dog.

"He's never been vicious," the woman cried, pressing her free hand to the wound. "He's never hurt anyone. I don't know what's gotten into him!" For a split second, Rex's eyes went black, then normal again, like nothing happened.

We made our way up the hill, not looking back. Not even once.

The next day, River and I took a detour by the Whitman residence on the way to the market. It was boarded up. All the cars were gone. The housekeeper, Mrs. Robbins, was closing the gate when she saw us approaching. "I'm sorry, but I cannot let you in," she said without making eye contact. She started sweeping the remains of trash from the driveway that people had dumped over the gate.

"It's okay," I said quickly. "We don't mean to disturb you. Where did Mr. and Mrs. Whitman go?"

She kept sweeping. "They left this morning. Purchased a place out in California." Her voice was flat. "Probably for the best. This town would've made their lives a living hell."

I didn't argue. We both knew it was true.

"Are you staying to look after the property?" River gently asked. She stopped sweeping and stared at us for a moment. Then she looked back at the house. "Oh, heavens no. I don't want to stay here for one more minute. Can't wait to get my things and leave." She shook her head. "Those noises at night, they could wake the dead." As she said it, a silhouette brushed past the front window. It stopped, drifted to the next window, then disappeared. The chair on the front porch began to rock, slow and steady.

We wished her well and left, feeling jittery and uneasy. That evening, River and I tried to distract ourselves. A crossword puzzle calmed my nerves. River played solitaire at the coffee table, flipping cards, concentrating. Papa sat at the kitchen table, finishing dinner.

BREAKING NEWS flashed across the television screen.

"Evil has reached a new level here at Wilshire Pointe. Another mysterious death has occurred, just hours after sundown. The body of Cynthia Robbins, a housekeeper at the Whitman residence, was found on the grounds of their property. The cause of her death is unknown. However, she was found with an expression of intense terror. In her right hand was a cross."

The camera zoomed in on the cross. I recognized it immediately.

It was the same cross I had staked into the ground at Moses's burial site. The one that went missing. The same cross that hung around Alice's neck the night I saw her under the streetlamp.

****

My arm reached over for River. He wasn't beside me anymore. His voice came from the hallway. "The faucet in the bathroom was leaking. I couldn't sleep. And there's water dripping from the ceiling over there in that corner." He eyes moved to the far corner of the room. A bucket sat directly under, slowly filling up, collecting water from the rains that had appeared overnight.

He stood there in his robe, looking down, curling one side of his belt tight around his fingers and letting it unravel again.

"Did the smell of sewage wake you up, too?" I asked.

He stopped twisting the belt. "Yeah," he said quietly. "It's coming from outside."

The clouds thicken and begin to rumble. The rain continued to fall, and the winds picked up. We turned on the television to see the weather report. Warnings flashed across the screen: HURRICANE OWEN was heading in our direction.

There was nothing we could do. We knew what was coming.

The sun disappeared, and with it, so did Alice.

CHAPTER 29

HOARDER'S PARADISE

They couldn't sleep. It wasn't important anymore. They studied the dream sequences. They made charts. They took turns dissecting symbolic events. Timing. Patterns.

"Shelby, this wasn't random," River said on the other end of the line. "There's a gap between the dreams. And right after the dream, it hits. Three days. Every. Damn. Time." Shelby paused. Guilt prickled beneath her skin. She knew the calling was hers. She's the one who wanted to be shown. She *prayed* for it.

"I can't think anymore," she whispered, and set the receiver down. Taking a moment for herself, she closed her eyes.

A whisper slid into her ear.

You're so close. It's right here. Don't give up so soon.

Her limbs went numb, surrendering to the fear.

No, I can't let it get to me. This is what it wants. Get up, Shelby. Do something. First, I need to be me again. Nothing can be uncovered by this fake version of me.

Marching over to her closet, she yanked out most of her wardrobe, Alice's donations. The scent of Alice's perfume clung to the fabric. Sickly sweet and unwanted. It was time. She shoved the clothes into a large box and labeled it SALVATION ARMY. She never liked this new version of herself. Winning River over was the only silver lining, but it wasn't worth losing herself. Shelby was so embarrassed for allowing someone to crawl into her mind and toy with her identity. She thought she was strong, unshakeable, and level-headed. At least, that's how her Papa had taught her to be. She was angry at herself. It was a betrayal of Papa. He would never know, but she knew.

Either River would need to accept her old self, *her true* self, or they would be over. She couldn't wear someone else's skin anymore.

Shelby pulled on her overalls, wrapped her hair in a bandana, and got to work. Relief washed over her. She felt free. No more uncomfortable shoes and tight dresses. She took a deep breath, liberated from the burden of walking in someone else's shoes, literally. Tired, frustrated, and out of ideas, Shelby began to search for answers. She didn't know what she was looking for, but in her mind, she had to start somewhere.

Her room, her closets, the guest room, she found nothing. Towels and sheets filled up the linen closet. Nothing there. Her father's room was quite bare, with necessities, a bed, nightstand, and armoire.

Then the basement. "Hoarder's Paradise," as she jokingly called it. Trinkets from travels, old records, and hundreds of books filled each corner. Paintings Papa once created when time was kind to him were covered with old sheets. One in particular always caught her breath, a woman with angelic wings, wrapped in gray clouds, waving goodbye to a little girl standing beneath a rainbow. It was a sad painting. Maybe he painted it after her birth. Shelby would never know. She'd only recently found it, hidden beneath a dusty sheet.

A wooden bookshelf lined the back wall, crammed with encyclopedias. Every night, her father used to read to her from those volumes until her small eyelids grew too heavy with information. She ran her fingers across the spines. Monarch butterflies. Ancient Egypt. It was still there. Untouched for years but loaded with memories.

After rummaging through endless piles and finding nothing of significance, she dragged her tired body toward the stairs. Her head hung low, shoulders sulking. The steps creaked beneath her weight. Halfway up, she froze. Her heart began to pound as the words flashed through her mind.

Right beneath the stairs of your mind.

The thought slid in, uninvited, as her shoulders stiffened.

"Wesley." The answer to the riddle. *"Sometimes the truth has been there the whole time. Just beneath the stairs of your mind—waiting for you to find it."*

That's it. The small storage room beneath the stairway, the forbidden room.

Her Papa used to say it so casually, just to keep her out: "The boogieman sleeps there." As ridiculous as it sounded, the words stayed with her. There was always a latch. Always a lock. Eventually, the door faded from her awareness, either it became invisible, or she trained herself not to see it. But not today. Today, she was going in. *Maybe Papa said that because he was hiding something in there. A secret.*

Her hands trembled as she dialed. River answered on the second ring.

"Hey, River? Could you come over if you're not too busy? I need your help."

Within an hour, he let himself in through the kitchen door. She was standing by the kettle, making tea while waiting for him to arrive, too afraid to venture into the storage room alone. Her appearance didn't seem to faze him at all. He kissed her forehead. Relief softened her chest. As strong as she tried to be, there was a part of her that needed River close. "Now, why did you call me here?" he questions, popping a Milk Dud into his mouth.

Shelby grabbed his hand and led him to the stairway, telling him about this forbidden room on the way there.

The rusty latch hung loose, untouched for years. River reached for it and hesitated. "You sure you wanna do this?"

Shelby nodded, feeling the knots twist and turn in her stomach. The door creaked open and stale air rushed out, cold, damp, and unfamiliar.

Whatever her father kept inside had been waiting for her.

CHAPTER 30

INSIDE THE STORAGE ROOM

I slid the latch to one side, and the door creaked open, slowly.
Darkness inhabited the room, along with a musty stench. I hesitated
for a moment, feeling like a disobedient child for exploring the forbidden
walls. It was a sneaky move on my part. Should I be going through these
things? Even though Papa wasn't in his right mind, and hasn't been for a
while now, he still deserved privacy. I tugged back and forth between my
emotions and my integrity.

No, this is important. It's necessary. Something nudged me forward
with the plan, an invisible pressure, a mental shove. My body moved before
my mind could continue battling with itself. Before I knew it, I stood in
a room I had never dared to enter. The flashlight beam illuminated a
dangling cord. It controlled the small bulb hanging from the slanted
ceiling. I held my breath and tugged at the cord, afraid to awaken the
items in the room. The bulb flickered, indecisive, unwilling to wake up
after all these years. Cobwebs sagged from the angular ceiling, but there
were no spiders in sight. The sudden light must have sent them scattering.

From the corner, a slug slowly emerged. A memory of Alice. I
shuddered at the thought. Nausea crawled up my throat. *Focus, Shelby.
She's gone.*

The walls of the tiny storage area were scuffed and stained, as if
something heavy had been dragged across them. Several boxes sat stacked
beneath a thick film of dust, labeled in Papa's careful handwriting. *Law*

School Books, Pots, Blankets. Yellow and brown crocheted throws with herringbone patterns spilled from one box. Two old suitcases were neatly stacked in the corner, unused for years. And beneath a stack of books, half-hidden, sat a Puma shoebox. It looked insignificant. We almost missed it.

As I pulled on the Puma box, the books on top of it toppled over and fell on my head. River first laughed and then asked if I was okay. I was more startled than hurt. Then the bulb flickered violently and died after a few seconds.

Darkness. Something was playing with us now, leading us to clues and then creating obstacles along the way. A cruel laugh could be heard, too distant to be located, too real to ignore.

"Are you sure you're okay? River's voice cut through the dark. "Those books could've given you a concussion."

"I'm fine," I spoke too soon. My head was thumping. "Go, get a flashlight, please. Garage cabinet, top drawer. Hurry." I wasn't in any hurry to see what was in that box. I didn't want to be there alone for too long. Back within seconds, he had a flashlight in hand, and together we carefully brought out the Puma box.

The lid slid off with no problem.

Inside—relics. A time capsule?

Movie ticket stubs. A set of keys. A small flask. And a necklace with a pendant. The pendant glimmered between my fingers—an oval emerald, cool and heavy. It was magnificent, almost magical.

There was also a photograph. Papa stood there, smiling with eyes full of hope; his arm was wrapped around a petite woman. They were both dressed up. Papa in a suit, tie, and hat; she was wearing a beautiful dress with long gloves up to her elbows. Around her neck was the same necklace I was holding in my hand. The woman's face was blurred in the photo, like water had spilled but just enough to cover her face.

June 3, 1959. About a year before I was born. The words on the back read "the love of my life," in cursive, blue ink. My mother. I had never seen her face. After she died, Papa erased any trace of her. No photos, no stories. I grew up studying my reflection, trying to guess what parts of her lived in me.

I slipped the necklace into my pocket and later hid it in my nightstand drawer. Papa would never know. And even if he did, he wasn't well enough to remember.

"Nothing," I said, as I could feel my heart slowly sink. "We found nothing of importance." River smiled, trying to stay hopeful. He then said something stupid. "Sometimes answers show up when you stop looking." I hated cliches. We both knew better. His eyes sheepishly gazed at the wall while he scratched the back of his neck, not knowing how to console me. We were still scraping the surface. No map. No rules. No protection, and the threat still lingered. We didn't know when the next nightmare would visit us.

We put everything back in silence. A tall shadow darkened the room. It was Papa, and he stood by the doorway, wide-eyed. His breathing turned heavy. Uneven. With a quivering bottom lip, the words narrowly escaped his mouth. "What have you done?"

CHAPTER 31

THE 'F' WORD

Firework stalls were intentionally lined up along the most visited corners of Wilshire Pointe. Shop owners and officials proudly raised American flags around the town. Red, white, and blue bunting draped the storefronts along the main street. The town was gearing up for Independence Day celebrations.

With July came the heat. And my birthday. I wanted a day off from it all. I deserved it. I needed it. River and I called Jared and made plans to head to the shore, a mental and physical escape from reality. It was the one F-word we were craving. *Fun.*

Hanging on Jared's arm was a tall, slim girl with a bohemian ease about her. She wore a long, flowing maxi dress over her bathing suit; her loose, wavy hair just brushed the tips of her shoulders, topped with a crown of flowers. Her name was Caroline.

Jared had a type he was drawn to. The hippie types. The girls who barely wore makeup and smelled like incense and freedom. Caroline was a yoga instructor who had spent a year in India learning Hatha Yoga, determined to share her knowledge with Wilshire Pointe. The older and more religious folks here were skeptical and associated her practices with voodoo, afraid of anything different that threatened their comfort zone. They never took the time to understand it. The younger generation adored her. She already had enough students to open her own studio— *Namaste Yoga.* As cliché as it sounded, it caught on. "Namaste" shirts. "Namaste" keychains. "Namaste" bumper stickers on cars. Everyone knew the word. I came to know what it meant. "The divine light in me honors the divine light in you." Immediately, the word was hanging from my keys and plastered on the back of my car. I couldn't think of anything more beautiful than those words.

I thought she was brave for doing what she loved, especially in a town that frowned upon anything slightly different. We all knew this was just a summer fling. Jared bolted when things got too serious. Being answerable to his mother was more than enough commitment for him. His mother's paranoia wanted answers to where he was going, what time he would be home, who he was with, and it drove him insane. He made it clear that he had no intention of answering any of those questions from whoever he was dating.

Caroline and I set up our beach chairs and umbrellas while the boys went to grab sodas and burgers. An "Om" ring hugged her right ring finger. On her left wrist was a lotus tattoo. I asked her about it.

"In Hinduism," she said softly, "the lotus flower symbolizes purity and spiritual enlightenment because it emerges untarnished from the murky waters it grows in." I was mesmerized. She sounded older than she was. Wiser. Touched by a world far beyond Wilshire Pointe. Her voice had a rhythm, slow, grounded, almost hypnotic. She almost turned *me* on.

There was so much more to life than what we saw at Wilshire Pointe. I wanted to ask her about the ring but stopped—that could be another conversation. Or maybe I would go to the library and research it myself so that I wouldn't appear an unlearned fool.

This is exactly what we needed. We talked. We laughed. Caroline shared stories from her exotic travels. I returned the favor by telling embarrassing stories about Jared. He groaned and tried to change the subject every time. We had grown close over our short span of friendship. "Copacabana" blared on someone's stereo. Two of the couples in that group got up and started to dance. People wanted their lives back after the back-to-back tragedies—some semblance of normalcy.

Then it got quiet.

"What happened to Alice Whitman? The *real* story. I heard all sorts of versions, but you guys were her buddies." Caroline stared at the sand while drawing circles in it. Her ring reflected the sun's rays. She didn't look up when she asked, knowing that question would cause discomfort. River's face flushed with anxiety, and he excused himself, surfboard in hand. He muttered something about the water being perfect and took off. I knew that look. He still saw and heard her. And he still went to therapy.

She looked at Jared, who then shifted beside me.

"C'mon, babe," Jared said quickly, forcing a smile, "let's go in the water." He removed his orange "Namaste" t-shirt, showing off his six-pack, and motioned her to follow. Caroline didn't push the conversation about Alice. She followed him into the ocean.

And just like that, a wave blew over Alice's story and washed it into oblivion.

We baked in the sun for another hour. Then Jared did something we never expected. He invited us to his home.

CHAPTER 32

BIRTHDAY CAKE

I had only been to Jared's house one time, to borrow a record. He had left it on the front porch before leaving for his shift at Moody's.

Today was different. His mother had the day off. Jared said she'd always taken this day off, every year since he could remember.

Today, she was cooking his favorite meal: meatloaf and loaded baked potatoes. Jared swore that when she cooked, she made enough to feed the entire street. As a courtesy, he still called her from the pay phone to warn her he'd be bringing guests in the evening.

There was a time when River would never have been caught dead on this side of town. The working-class side. The last few months had humbled River. He became easier to talk to. More grounded. I liked this version of him better. We parked along the street. A bed of flowers neatly planted lined the front steps of their ranch-style home, made of red brick, with a porch just big enough to fit two small chairs. Two newspapers sat at the bottom of the steps, overlooked and forgotten. River picked them up, prepared to hand them to Mrs. Mitchell when he met her inside. He quickly combed his fingers through his hair, then put his hand on the small of my back as Jared turned the doorknob. Moments like these made our relationship feel more official.

The door opened, and we were greeted by a fusion of smells—meatloaf, cigarette smoke, and lavender potpourri. A decorative crystal bowl sat on the console near the door, filled with after-dinner mints. Dishes and utensils clinked against the wood surface as his mother prepared for our arrival. Their foyer walls were covered in a William Morris green-and-yellow floral print. I couldn't help but envy Jared at that moment. I would do anything to be surrounded by the comforts of these smells and sounds.

"Jared, is that you?" his mother called. "No, Mom, it's a burglar," he replied. "I'm here to rob you of everything you've got," he teased.

"Well, you'll be disappointed," she shot back. "Not much here to offer." There was humor in her voice, but also truth. Mrs. Mitchell bustled around the kitchen in her yellow apron embroidered with delicate flowers. "You kids must be starving. Sitting at the beach all day will work up an appetite." Her gaze held mine for a second. The ladle in her hand slipped from her fingers and clattered to the floor. Startled, she picked it up quickly. I grabbed a towel and helped wipe the small mess.

"Oh, don't worry, it's alright," she said softly. "I can be a bit clumsy sometimes." Her hands shook.

We all sat at the dining table. "We never sit here," she said, looking at Jared. "It's nice. We should do this more often, honey." He smiled and nodded.

My growling stomach echoed during the quiet moments. "Sounds like *someone* is hungry," River murmured. I kicked his leg under the table. I must have inhaled my meal in under eight minutes. Caroline ate delicately, putting me to shame. "Mrs. Mitchell, where did you learn to cook like this?" she asked, wiping her mouth at the corners with a napkin. "Everything is so delicious."

A pinkish hue flushed his mother's cheeks and trickled down to her neck. "Working at the diner now for over ten years. I ought to know a thing or two about cooking." She winked and continued her meal. "I have to say, it's nice having you kids over." She looked up at us, talking between bites, and then directed her words to Jared. "The house seemed empty without you or Mathew around today. So, tell me, who's ready for dessert?"

Jared and his mother excused themselves and disappeared into the kitchen. The rest of us kept talking, laughing, relaxed in a way we hadn't been in a long time. The light feeling of regularity almost felt daunting.

Jared and his mother returned holding a cake lit with candles. The singing began. "Happy birthday to you. Happy birthday, dear Shelby…" Heat rushed to my chest, climbing up my neck and into my ears and face. It had been so long since anyone had celebrated my birthday. Papa used to make such a big deal about it. And then came my sixteenth. I blew out the candles. A small prayer escaped from my lips.

"Dear mother, please forgive me for this day. May you be at peace, and may you always shine your guiding light onto me. Amen." A prayer I recited every year on this day. Caught up in the emotions, I didn't realize I had said it out loud. I was jolted from my brief trance when Caroline squeezed my hand. The room fell quiet. Mrs. Mitchell's eyes filled with tears. She turned away quickly, dabbing them with a napkin. "Oh, I forgot plates." She excused herself and went to get them.

They were sitting right next to the cake; all five dessert plates.

To lighten the mood, River played Zeppelin on the record player, and we all enjoyed a slice of chocolate cake. This was a birthday I would hold close.

In that moment, I didn't realize how special it was. Until it was too late.

CHAPTER 33

THE PHOTO ON THE WALL

We probably ate more than we should have, and the long day in the sun left us feeling heavy. Drowsiness had set in. Caroline and I helped Mrs. Mitchell with the dishes while the boys disappeared into the den to flip through records and enjoy a casual smoke. After clearing the dishes, I sank into the sofa and curled beneath a blanket with Caroline, resting my head on her shoulder. "What a perfect evening."

"Mmmm." She closed her eyes and smiled in agreement. My gaze drifted around the room. Fragmented images appeared behind the smoke. Wood-paneled walls wrapped the space in warmth. A deep, gold shag rug was spread across the floor, thick and plush beneath our feet. In the corner, a record player sat atop a low cabinet with an assortment of albums. Carole King, Bob Marley, Janice Joplin, and other great artists. The coffee table was jumbled with an ashtray and glass candy dishes. The lower shelf housed *Reader's Digest* and *Vogue* magazines, stacked in a neat pile. I could have lost hours in that room.

Along the wall hung a line of framed family photographs, perfectly spaced. We laughed as we saw Jared in diapers, one with him holding his baby brother, his parents' wedding photo, camping trips, and candid shots. His father held a quiet smile. Mrs. Mitchell's body was slightly faced away from him. They barely touched one another. Jared had a strong resemblance to his father.

"Where's your brother tonight?" I asked. "Sleepover," Jared called from the other side of the room. I smiled and kept scanning. A professional studio photo, the four of them posed in front of a Christmas tree, was centered on the wall. Jared was dressed in a tiny suit with a red bow tie. His brother, grinning, was held by Mrs. Mitchell. His father stood stiffly by her side, again, barely touching her. Then there was a smaller one next to it. Mr. Mitchell wasn't in it, just Jared, his brother, and his mother.

My head spun, mind blanking momentarily. I couldn't feel my feet, all the sure signs of a panic attack. I tried to control it with deep breaths, not wanting to ruin the evening.

It was hanging around Mrs. Mitchell's neck—the necklace with the emerald pendant.

I couldn't breathe. I needed air. I felt dizzy. No. No, no. Not here. Not now. This is *my* day. I need to get out of here. Why was she wearing that necklace? Can I not just have one day? One day of sanity?

"I'll be out on the front porch," I announce quickly.

Outside, the air was still, but my heart was running circles. River followed me and closed the front door behind him. My trembling hands sparked his cigarette. A minute or so passed by until he finally spoke. "I saw it too, Shelby. The necklace." The front porch light flickered, and the trees began to dance in the wind, mocking us.

C H A P T E R   3 4

FRAGMENTS

I barely felt the weight of River's arm around my shoulder. My mind was trapped inside that photograph, still searching for clues. Unanswered questions floated around my mind. "We should head back in," he says quietly. "They'll start wondering where we went."

I didn't acknowledge him. I didn't hear him. "Jared had to have been five in that photo, around the time around when his father disappeared," I whispered. "It was a scandal. The whole town knew about it. I just...I know we're missing something. I can *feel* it."

A gust of wind curled against the back of my neck and sneaked up to my ear. Like someone was trying to say something. But no words came out.

That night, my sleep was fragmented. Pieces of my life, mixed images, unresolved feelings; half-formed shapes were trying to move into place to form a picture. The shapes were in different shades of green. The alarm went off. In my mind, it couldn't be 7:00 a.m. yet. It felt as though I had just fallen asleep minutes ago. I hit the snooze button twice. My arm swung blindly off the bed, searching for my robe. My eyelids could barely move up, heavy with restless nights. Exhaustion hit in a way sleep couldn't fix. My motivation in school and in life was waning. These were all bad signs. I knew they were.

I came to a road that suddenly stopped. Not even a dead end. It just stopped. There was no other place to go. No signs. Nothing. I opened the nightstand drawer to check. The necklace was still there. It was my only evidence of…I'm not quite sure what.

I called River while brushing my teeth, foaming at the corners of my mouth, words tumbling too fast, something I would never have been secure doing before. But now, I stopped caring. We had reached a new level of comfort.

"The photo from the storage room, where the face was blurred out, what if that woman was Jane Mitchell?" I say quietly, even though Papa was downstairs and probably couldn't hear anything. "What if that means she could be my…"

"Shelby," he cut me off. "Right now, all we have are bits and pieces, assumptions, no solid facts. We need more information before we can draw any conclusion." There's a pause. I knew that pause. He wanted to say something, but hesitated. "What if we told Jared? He might know something we don't, something key."

That didn't even cross my mind. I was too afraid to tell anyone anything. "And say what? We can't even tell him about our dreams."

"Just show him the photo that you found in the box. See what he says. Don't say anything. Let him come out with any information he has."

I didn't like this plan at all, but I knew he was right. It was our only hope.

Jared answered the phone after three rings.

"Hey, Jared, it's Shelby. Sorry to disturb you. Uh, I know you're working, but this is important. I have something I need to tell you. Meet me at the playground by the church at 9 p.m. tonight." I put the receiver down. I didn't give him a chance to talk, or to agree, or to disagree.

He had to be there. No discussion.

****

The playground was empty. During the day, the playground by the church was full of children's innocent laughter, swinging and sliding, giggling and singing songs. After hours, a dark, eerie silence lingered in the air, as if someone was watching. This wasn't a place to be once the sun went down. The slightest of winds caused the swings or merry-go-round to creak into motion.

Jared sat on the cold metal bench and waited. The streetlamp highlighted the right side of his face. He played with his watch band. I could see the irritation on his face as we approached. He stood up immediately upon seeing us. Hands in his pockets, he tried to act casually.

"Why here?" he muttered. "This place is creepy as hell, especially at night. You guys playing some kinda joke on me? Such an Alice thing to do." Jared realized he went too far as River stiffened. Alice's distorted face and cackle came to my mind. I shuddered at the thought.

"Oh, c'mon, man, let's not go there," River said under his breath.

"Yeah, you're right…sorry, but why are we here?" he asked again.

I reached into my bag and pulled out the photo. His eyes scanned it once. Then twice. "I don't get it." Confusion stretched across his face. "Why are you showing this to me?"

I paused. "Look closely—the necklace."

His mind concentrated on her neck. He quietly whispered to himself, "I've seen that before. And that dress too. It was the one she always wore to church." His eyes abruptly snapped back into the moment. Anger replaced his confusion in a matter of seconds. "But what is she doing in that photo with your father? With their arms wrapped around each other? With trembling lips, he slammed his fists against the metal slide, slightly denting one side.

"My mother would never!" he snapped. "You hear me? Never."

"Jared—" I attempted to interrupt his escalating rage, but he was inconsolable.

"There could be a thousand necklaces like that!" His denial is slowly replaced by unwanted awareness. He dragged a hand over his face and turned away, shoulders shaking. Covering his face, he succumbed to tears. I put my hand around his shoulder, but he jerked away.

"This is all just a big assumption right now. We don't know enough. That's why we came to you, so we can figure out what happened. It's a lot for me to take in, too." Puddles formed at the corners of my eyes.

"I was happy not knowing any of this. Why did you guys have to play detective? Sometimes it's best to leave things as they are. Just get out of here!" Jared yells between the sobs, wiping his face on his shirt sleeve. We left him alone at the playground. I wanted to stay back, to ask more questions, and console him, but he wasn't the only one devastated. Something was taken from me, too. I don't know exactly what just yet.

"If you wanna come over, you know where to find us. We'll be at Shelby's," River calls out to him. I could still hear his cries as we walked away.

"Should we go back?" I asked River.

"Let him be. He probably wants to be alone right now." River put his arm around me and glanced back at Jared.

Behind us, the swings moved. Slowly. On their own.

CHAPTER 35

WHISKEY-LACED MEMORIES

Jared remembered the lashings, the drunken evenings, and his mother's screams into the night, screams that were often muffled by a pillow, but loud enough for him to hear through the thin walls. By morning, she would be in the kitchen, humming. Her artificial cheer would confuse young Jared, as she twirled around the kitchen, creating a lavish breakfast for the family, as if nothing had happened the night before. But the evidence was clear. New bruises had bloomed along her arms and neck.

When Jared asked about them, his father would step in to answer, "Oh, son, you know how clumsy your mother is. Always tripping over something." And his mother would follow right on cue, as if they had rehearsed. "Yes, darling, I tripped over a chair in the bedroom. Silly me." She smiled and continued to whisk the pancake batter, humming a tune.

Lies. Jared knew. He saw his father in action through a cracked door once, in a rage. His father's cheeks were red as he straddled Jane, who received blow after blow, usually below the face, so she would be able to hide the bruises under clothing or scarves. Eventually, his father would be too tired to strike, roll over, and fall asleep, while he could hear his mother's whimpering cries until she drifted off.

She woke up in the same clothes. It was too risky for her to move around after the beating, for fear of awakening the beast. Jane stayed still and silent to avoid another round of beating and breathed quietly until morning came to the rescue.

Jared sang to his little brother, who was asleep in his crib, afraid that his mother's cries might awaken him. He tried to follow the rules carefully, because one wrong move, and his father would enter the room with a belt, ready to unleash his anger. At a young age, Jared learned how to disappear.

The dreadful episodes always occurred after his father drank that brown, smelly drink. He once tasted it and gagged. As a young boy, Jared thought it was an evil potion. Once you drink it, you become the devil. Later, he came to understand it was just whiskey, whiskey his father had stolen from the distillery where he worked.

It had all come to an end the day his father disappeared. *Good riddance,* he thought. *Now we can live in peace.* He hated to see his mother in such a vulnerable state. And even as a child, he knew his mother was pretending to be happy. Guilt and shame would flood his emotions as he remembered the sense of relief that overcame him that day, the day when he found out his father left. He wept tears of joy, mostly for his mother. Jane thought he was mourning his father, but she had no idea how happy he was. Now he had her all to himself, and she wouldn't get hurt anymore. At the tender age of five, he experienced emotions that one may never experience in a lifetime.

Jared wiped his tears and shook out his body, loosening up his muscles to relax. He swung open the gate to the playground and began to make his way home, stuffing his hands in the pockets of his olive-green corduroy bell-bottoms.

A familiar voice cut through the silence. His father's. Even as a child, that voice had always meant danger. It was a siren, a warning of what was to come.

"Just ask your mother about her little secret, would ya, son? You're old enough to know."

Chills ran down his spine; his throat was dry, and he couldn't swallow. Jared gathered himself and ran home, hoping to leave the dreadful voice at the park. He could barely feel his feet touching the ground.

The streetlamps turned on and off in a synchronized dance. The winds pick up. The clouds rumbled, gathering to form an angry face in the sky. Two illuminated hollows formed eyes, staring down at him. The clouds shifted to form the word L-I-E-S. Jared blinked a few times in disbelief. He looked up again, and the sky returned to its original state.

Arriving home, he collapsed on his bed, still wearing his shoes. As Jared lay asleep, he could hear his father's haunting voice; it was so real and so close, almost as if his lips were up against Jared's ear. Warm breath mixed with the scent of whisky from his old man's mouth brushed against the side of Jared's face while the familiar voice softly sang a lullaby, one that was always sung to him as a young boy.

The singing started sweet, but as it continued, the voice turned dark and slow.

"Rock-a-bye, baby, on the treetop.

When the wind blows, the cradle will rock.

When the bough breaks, the cradle will fall…"

His voice slowed. Twisted.

"And down will come baby, cradle and all."

Then laughter errupted. An evil laugh that lingered.

Jared sat up abruptly and clicked on the lamp by his bedside. The open window let in a breeze, causing a ripple in the draperies. He didn't recall opening the window. It refused to shut, no matter how hard he tried to push it down. He used all his strength. It didn't budge.

"What's all the racket?" Mathew, half asleep, staggered over from his bed. He pushed down on the lower sash of the window, and it slid down effortlessly. He shot a nasty look at his older brother for causing a ruckus at 3 a.m. and slipped back into bed.

The window stayed shut, but the voices screamed louder.

CHAPTER 36

MOODY'S

Morning came, and Jared felt like he had been beaten, tossed, spun around, chewed up, and spit out by something enormous and evil.

"You look like shit," Mathew commented, mildly concerned. Jane stopped whisking the pancake batter and looked toward Mathew with deep frown lines, "Language. Watch it," she scolded. "That's no way to speak to your older brother. Apologize right now." He glared at Jared and offered a half-hearted, mumbled apology. "Thanks to him, I barely got any sleep last night."

Jane Mitchell studied her eldest son more closely. "You should call in sick today. Take it easy. Your brother is right. You don't look too good, honey." Coming from her, that statement unsettled him. Jane was not an advocate of skipping work or school; never one to cut anyone slack, not even to her own kids. Jared looked at her oddly as questions swarmed around his head. He didn't know who she was anymore.

Grabbing his bag, he shouted at his brother, "Hurry up, Matt. Time to go." His younger brother squinted at him with a confused expression, "Time to go where?"

Jared answered while throwing a banana and a pack of nuts in his bag, "I'm dropping you off at summer camp." Mathew's face changed from a sulking appearance to one that beamed with excitement in a matter of seconds. No matter what happened between them, he thought his older brother was the coolest man alive. He loved riding around with Jared in

130

his van. The olive-green Volkswagen van, the loud music, usually Queen or the Rolling Stones, the effortless swagger, were all points to boast about in front of his friends. Jared wished he could swap places with him. Ignorant, untouched, and safe. Not a care in the world.

After dropping his brother off, he went straight to work. Five more minutes and his shift would begin. That would be five minutes he could snooze in his van. Those five minutes turned into nearly thirty as exhaustion pulled him under.

A sharp honk from a car pulling in next to his van jerked him awake. Ravi Chauhan. "Wake up, Jared! You're already late," Ravi scolded him as his elbow hung over a half-open window. "This is the second time you've shown up late to your shift. Mr. Moody won't hesitate to give you the boot. Three strikes, you're out. Remember his rule?" Ravi, his co-worker, was always looking out for him. Waving Ravi off, Jared knew he was right. He peeled himself out of the van, dragging his feet into the store, reminding himself of his responsibilities.

"What's going on with you, man?" Ravi asked. "Everything okay? Girl problems?" Jared almost laughed, wishing it were just girl problems. "No, nothing like that," he muttered. "Just been a rough few days."

Jared missed a part of his shift and now had to work through his lunch break. Inside, the bells jingled as the door slammed behind him. He avoided customers, avoided eye contact, and left customer service to Ravi. He could use the practice.

Ravi Chauhan was a smart, punctual, almost robotic medical student with a slight British accent, who secretly wanted to be a rock star. A calculus professor's son rebelling in the safest way possible: by working at a record store, where he could be close to the thing he loved most— music. Being in a rock band was a distant dream. His father threatened to disown him if he didn't pursue medicine and told him he would never stand a chance in the entertainment industry. Ravi mimicked his father's Indian accent, waving one finger in the air, moving his head from side to side while his soft, brown curls bounced around. "And what is going to become of you? You will slave for the rest of your life, begging for money." He sighed dramatically. "And I didn't make sacrifices to see my only son become a starving artist, and eventually, you'll end up killing yourself. That's what happens to a majority of these *artists.* Now get your head out of the clouds and come back to reality. You're a brown man living in America. The only way you'll get an ounce of respect is by becoming a doctor." Despite the morbid and demoralizing lecture, Ravi still believed he could be the next Freddie Mercury, whose roots were also grounded in South Asia, his absolute idol.

Jared shook his head and laughed at the thought of Ravi on stage, half naked and running wild with a guitar. Ravi was a dreamer, and Jared admired him for it. Envied him, even. Jared couldn't fathom putting oneself through *medical school,* one of the most demanding fields, for the sake of someone else. But that wasn't his battle to fight. Jared had his own issues to deal with.

Moody's has been around since the '40s; it was a landmark at Wilshire Pointe. Mr. Moody's father took over the store from his father, who took it over from his father. It was originally a hardware store where one could buy all sorts of nuts and bolts and somehow evolved into a record store during the transition.

Jared spotted the Knickerbockers album *Lies* out of place and slid it back into its slot. The phone rang for about five rings before Jared could jog over to answer it. Mr. Moody was too frugal to buy another phone, so they were always scrambling to answer it from different ends of the store.

"Good afternoon, this is Moody's, fixing moods through music. How can I help you?" He dreaded saying that lame slogan. No one was on the other end. Annoyed for having to run across the store to answer a blank call, Jared slammed the receiver down. "Easy, buddy." A look of concern flashed across Ravi's face as his thick, dark eyebrows lifted his hairline. "I've never seen you like this before."

Jared avoided eye contact, slightly embarrassed by his behavior, "Sorry,

I'm just tired." He stood behind the counter, pretending to stay busy, and neatly arranged the pens in a cup.

The Knickerbocker album *Lies* was out again. He turned to Ravi. "Hey, Ravi, did you take this album out to show a customer?"

"Nope. Wasn't me. I was over there, helping the last customer." He pointed. Jared shrugged his shoulders, scratched his head, and put it back.

Why does this album keep popping out of place, and who the hell listens to this?

Ravi called out from across the store, "Hey, could you cover for me tonight? I've got a hot date." He grinned. "I need to leave an hour early." Jared teased him, "You? Poor girl. Give me her number so I can tell her not to waste her time." Ignoring the sarcasm, Ravi puffed up like a peacock. "My father arranged it. Her name is Sarika. She's quite *foxy*." He growled.

Jared spit out his soda. "Arranged? You mean, your dad—"

"Yes, arranged. It's very common in India. My father met her parents at the temple. And they set it up."

"And dude, how do you even know she's sexy? You've never even met Saari-kah, or whatever her name is." Jared looked at him, puzzled.

"I know, I know. This whole idea is so foreign to you. It's an Indian thing. You wouldn't get it. I saw her photo, man. She's really hot. He wants me to get married, ASAP. I don't understand why he's pushing it, but hey, if she's that hot, how bad can it be?"

"Sure, no problem, Ravi. I got you covered. I'm sure she's excited to marry a doctor by day and rockstar by night." Jared pretends to strum a guitar wildly to the Led Zeppelin song playing over the speakers. Ravi gave him a playful shove, unamused by the mockery.

Closing time came too slowly. Minutes felt like hours with each second on the clock dragging to the next. Jared's head began to throb, and exhaustion set in. He gulped down a glass of cold water, hoping it would eliminate his drowsiness. The last half an hour couldn't end soon enough. Home was a short eight-minute drive away but felt distant.

Jared was left with his unsettling thoughts, along with thousands of records. He began the nightly ritual of closing. First, he wiped down the counters, then calculated and recorded all the sales for the day. He carefully put the money into a zip pouch and then locked it in a safe in the back office. The quietness of the store was music to his ears. No customers. No Ravi. No pressure for conversation.

As he closed the safe door, the stereo blared, almost knocking him down to the floor. *Lies* by the Knickerbockers. He never put that record in the player, and he made sure everything was turned off. Hands clammy, heart pounding, he bolted toward the record player. The music stopped right when his hand reached over to shut it off.

What the—

There was no record on the platter.

Was he hallucinating—hearing things? No, he wasn't crazy. He heard it loud and clear. Something was toying with his mind. He remembered the night at the playground and quickly shut down the memory.

Jared double-checked the safe to make sure it was locked, then got out as quickly as possible. He exited through the back door. His hands trembled while he tried to fit the key into the keylock. A buzzing sound came from the small light above the back door, and it began to blink slowly. The slow blinking turned into fast, inconsistent flickering accompanied by sparks, and then eventually shut off.

A violent force struck Jared from behind, knocking his body the pavement. Pain radiated up and down his spine. There was no one there. No one he could see. He lay on the floor holding his back, twisting in agony like a fish snatched from water. "What do you want from me?," he screamed into the empty parking lot, his body in a fetal position, scared, vulnerable and exhausted. It was at that moment, immense pressure crushed his chest, pinning him down. Jared's right leg was then lifted into the air and his body was dragged across the parking lot toward the dumpster. Blood soaked through the denim as his jeans shredded against the pavement. There was no one to save him.

His leg fell to the ground, limp and numb. Whatever grasped it had let go. It was too quiet. The evil was far too great to surrender so suddenly. It had more in store.

The engine of Jared's van roared to life. The accelerator was pounded repeatedly, mimicking the sound of a chainsaw. He patted his pocket in a frenzy to check for his keys. They were in his pocket.

"No. No, no."

The headlights turned on. The driver's seat was empty. The van jerked into reverse. The gear shifted, then moved forward, causing the van to charge straight toward him like an angry beast in the night. The van stopped just inches away from his face. Jared shielded his eyes with his hand. His mother's face flashed before him, as sweat dripped from his temples.

He flung open the van door and stumbled into the driver's seat. The smell of cheap whiskey floated through the air. A reminder of his childhood. A reminder of the fear. A reminder of the relief when it was over. Nausea unsettled his stomach. He opened the door and leaned forward, hurling whatever was left in his body. It hurt to move, and it hurt to think.

A shrill whisper slithered into his ear, "LIES. LIES. All Lies," was followed by dark laughter. "Leave me alone!" Jared yelled. He slammed his perspiring palms onto the steering wheel. Gathering an ounce of courage, he put the keys into the ignition and drove off, watching the streetlamp flicker in the rear-view mirror.

He drove into the night, desperate to get home, with no music or radio to accompany him. Determination took over. It was that night; he decided to confront his mother. As soon as he arrived home, he was going to ask her everything.

Jared rehearsed his speech repeatedly—how he would approach her, the careful words he would use, his tone, his hand gestures. He promised himself he wouldn't get angry. He'd stay calm. No accusations. No judgements.

He drove slowly and took deep breaths. A skill he learned from Caroline. It didn't work. He needed something stronger, possibly a reefer to take the edge off. He rolled the windows down and lit one up.

Tonight, he would ask her. And no matter what the answer, nothing would ever be the same.

CHAPTER 37

JANE

She tossed her keys into the large ceramic bowl that sat on top of the small table in the foyer and sighed, relieved to be home. Her loyal friend, a Marlboro, accompanied her. She tucked it behind her ear while searching for matches. Fridays were the busiest at the diner, and her feet had undergone the burden of a nine-hour shift, waiting on a bunch of thankless customers who barely looked her in the eye while ordering. The intoxicated ones had the gall to give her a little smack on the backside after she took their order. "That's just part of the business, hun," the manager said with a wink. "You're doing a great job, sweetheart." Jane hated Frank. He'd been the manager there for the last five years and made sure that a percentage of her tips went into his pockets.

"Brady!" she called out to her black Labrador. No paws padded toward her. No wagging tail.

Crouched under the dining table, he refused to come out. He was pressed so far back his black fur melted into the shadow.

"Oh, Brady, my sweet little puppy." Jane dropped to her knees and reached for him. "What are you doing down there? Aren't you a silly little dog?" She gave him a rub and a kiss on the head. He whimpered as she coaxed him to come out. He wouldn't budge. "Okay, Brady, you come out when you're good and ready. I don't know what's gotten into you, but I am too tired for these games today. Come out from there now. C'mon, boy, come get your treat." She dangled it near his face. After a few seconds, she surrendered and threw it in his bowl. "Okay, it's in your bowl." He still wouldn't move.

The stiffness in her bones and aches in her joints had her sitting on the floor for a few more minutes. She used the kitchen chair to prop herself up. After turning the tea kettle on, Jane stretched her legs out on the sofa. Eyes closed, she leaned back and rested her head on the armrest. For a few blessed seconds, her mind went blank. The heat of the cigarette pressed against her red lips and woke her from a short snooze. She jerked upright, heart thudding. The cigarette burned too close. "That could have been a bad scene," she muttered to herself as she stubbed it out. Angry at her carelessness, she got up to pour hot water and dropped in a Lipton teabag. The mindless chatter of the television kept her at ease. *Three's Company*, one of her favorites. Muffled laughter from the audience raised her spirits.

The kitchen lights began to flicker. *Damn loose bulb,* she thought, and continued onward toward the bedroom. She set a soft robe out on the bed, ready to be worn after a bath, her nightly ritual she looked forward to after a long day of work.

Steam filled the bathroom as water collected in the tub. She dipped one foot in to test the temperature. It was steamy, just as she preferred. Jane lathered lavender-scented soap over her shoulders, her arms, and her neck. The greasy smell of the diner washed away, along with the filthy stares of desperate men, some who were already married and others who passed through the town. They often left their telephone number on the bill, hoping to get a call from Jane. They never did.

The lights over the vanity began to flicker. Once. Twice. Then they died. Darkness flooded the room.

Jane froze with shampoo in her hair, suds dripping down her forehead, contemplating what to do next. She fumbled for the faucet and rinsed fast, blinking out the sting of the soap. "Goddamn it, I just wanted to take a relaxing bath and—" Her ears caught something, but it sounded like it was coming from a faraway place.

A faint tune flew through the radiator, barely recognizable. Jane stood still. The water ran over her bare body. The tune grew louder and nearer, circling through the bathroom.

No. Not that. Her skin prickled. "True Love Goes On and On" by the Chordettes.

"How—" Her voice cracked. "I trashed that record. I trashed it years ago."

The music swelled. Pressure built up in her ears, pushing her skull, sinking into her teeth, and vibrating behind her eyes. "Turn it off!" Jane screamed, cupping her hands over her ears. It only got louder. She felt herself shaking. Memories that were buried, boxed, and suffocated, ripped open all at once. The song pulled at her inner core, tearing through it.

A morose trepidation infiltrated her body and mind, and she fumbled her way out of the shower, grabbed a towel with trembling fingers, and tied it around her. She moved robotically into the bedroom. The lights turned back on. *Oh, thank heavens.* She took a deep breath. The music stopped. Brady could be heard whimpering from the kitchen. Jane stood in the doorway, chest heaving. She stared at her blistered feet.

Maybe I'm hallucinating. What was in that cigarette? Maybe I had one of Jared's cigarettes.

The lavender robe draped over her damp body. She bent forward and flipped her wet hair, patting the ends dry.

That's when she saw it. The antique doors stood wide open. A white lace fabric grabbed her attention. To her left, positioned against the wall, was an oversized, wooden armoire—a wedding gift from her parents. From the doors hung a gown, *her* wedding gown; a gown her grandmother had sewn. But why was it hanging on the armoire door?

She mumbled in a shocked whisper, "I never put that there. I haven't taken it out of the garment bag in years." She was saving it for Jared's future wife.

Confusion set in. She couldn't answer any of the questions that consumed her mind at that moment. A loud knock shattered her spiraling thoughts.

Knock. Knock. Knock.

She pulled her robe tight around the front and cautiously proceeded toward the front door. Her hand twisted the knob and cracked it open. No one was there.

Letting out a sigh of relief, Jane moved her hand forward to close the door, but before she could touch the doorknob, it slammed shut. There was no wind outside that could have caused it to close on its own. She was too afraid to understand what had just happened. Feeling vulnerable in just a bathrobe and the possibility of an intruder in her home, she motioned toward the phone to call the police.

KNOCK. KNOCK. KNOCK.

There was no one at the front door. This time, the door flung wide open, as if something was determined to enter the house. The door hit the wall, creating a dent, then slammed shut. She stumbled backward.

Again, three knocks, followed by silence.

Jane's first instinct was to run inside her bedroom and lock the door, though she had no idea what she was running from. She stood behind the bedroom door, barely breathing, barely making any sound, and closed her eyes. A prayer her mother had taught her flashed through her mind. She scrambled to remember the words. She moved her lips and recited the prayer, silently, for fear that sound itself might call it closer.

"Heavenly Father, I come to you today seeking your protection. Please keep me safe from all harm, danger, and evil. Surround me with your loving presence and shield me from anything that may seek to hurt me. In Jesus' name I pray. Amen."

Bang! BANG! A gust of air blew through her spine, knocking her forward. Jane staggered two steps; the breath ripped from her lungs.

All the questions in her mind faded into a vacuum. Then came flashes of her life: childhood, adolescence, marriage, births, bruises, apologies, nights she never spoke about. Everything spun together like a hurricane of photographs.

On the radio, "Miss You" by the Rolling Stones played, rumbling through the entire house. Jane's head hung down. She stood in a defeated position for a few minutes, her shoulders slumped, with her long arms by her side. Brady's treat still sat in his bowl, untouched; he was under the table with his paws over his eyes, as if he knew what kind of night this would be.

With twitching arms and trembling lips, she looked up, eyes blackened and hollow. A faint smile crept onto her mouth. Her movements were now sudden and impulsive, almost feral. Darting into the kitchen, she returned with a butcher's knife. She charged for the wedding dress and drove the blade straight down the center. The warped version of Jane ran to the other side of the room to gain more momentum.

She laughed, a wild sort of laughter, before attacking the dress like a mad bull, tearing and stabbing at it until the blade cut into her hands. There was no pain. There was no sadness. Blood trickled down her arms and onto the shag rug. Enraged, she slid her bloody hands down the dress, as the satin absorbed the crimson stains of her past.

She rocked her hips to the beat of the music, blaring on the radio, content with herself. Now wearing the tattered and tainted wedding dress, her bloody fingers gently caressed her face in a trance. The blood from her hands left a cherry-stained smear on her cheeks and neck. As her body moved from side to side, she danced with herself until her romantic moment was interrupted by an invisible slap. It cracked across her face and stole her temporary bliss, leaving her with a hot, burning sensation.

Red imprints stamped her face. The sting was familiar. So was the shame that followed. Jane crumpled to the floor, knees tucked under her chest, and head bowed. She sobbed. She knew she'd done something bad. Something unforgivable. Now she had to repent. The sobs faded into uncontrollable laughter, thin at first, then spiraling. Lunacy. Tears, dark and thick, leaked from her eyes and ran down her face. Blood followed from her nose. Gaining enough strength to stand, she admired herself in the mirror near the armoire, though a hideous appearance stared back at her.

Jane pulled the veil over her head, pretending to be a shy bride, pretending to be pure. She twirled and gently walked barefoot through the back door.

She paced her steps, slowly and steadily, in a daze, a new bride taking her first steps down the aisle. There was no audience. There was no crowd. She was all alone.

Into the darkness, she disappeared. Someone had waited a long time. She was being called home.

CHAPTER 38

WORDS LEFT UNSAID

As Jared hurriedly pulled into his driveway, he gave himself a pep talk, like the ones right before a football game. Except there was no team cheering together. He was alone, and this wasn't a game. He steadied his breath and prepared for the moment he'd been dreading.

The mother he knew had always been calm. Unshakeable. It took something catastrophic to rattle Jane.

This is just another curveball. Another disruption life throws at you. Everything can be figured out, dealt with.

The house was too quiet.

Where was Brady?

He'd never entered the house without Brady running up and circling his legs, then lying on his back for a playful rub. Tonight was different. The television, radio, a record spinning softly—his mother always had something on in the background for comfort, especially if the boys weren't home. For her, noise created an illusion of safety.

"And why is it freezing in here?" he muttered, rubbing his hands together and blowing warm air into them.

The smell of cigarette smoke lingered in the air, crisp and recent. A half-burnt cigarette rested in the ashtray; her red lipstick stamped clearly at the tip. Jared exhaled, reluctant to play detective and physically exhausted from the mayhem at Moody's.

There's one thing he did know. His mother was there.

"Mama?" No answer. "Mama, where are you? This isn't funny." His voice shook. "If you don't answer, I'm calling the police."

Silence.

He knocked on Mrs. Talbot's door. The neighbor. When she opened it, her eyes immediately travelled to his ripped, blood-stained jeans. "I'm sorry to bother you," he says quickly. "Did my mother stop by after work?"

"No, love." Her voice was gentle, clipped by her British accent. "Are you alright, son? What happened to—"

"Yes, ma'am, everything's okay. Thank you. Goodnight."

He turned away and raced down the front porch before she could ask any more questions. Calling out from the doorway, she added, "I did see the lights flickering about an hour ago. They seemed to fix themselves. Old wiring, maybe."

A tingling sense of doom teased Jared's every nerve. Inside, Brady was still under the dining table, whimpering.

"Aw, Brady. What are you doing under—" The dog barely moved. His brown eyes were locked on the wide-open back door. Jared ran to the doorway and scanned the yard looking for any trace of his mother. Nothing. No movement. No sound. He shut the door and locked it. He then lifted Brady's trembling body, as the lightbulbs in the kitchen began a blinking pattern. Panic crawled up Jared's spine, tightening his throat until he could barely breathe.

Along the wall, a spider emerged, slow and deliberate, until it arrived at a family photo and settled directly over his father's face. Jared stumbled backward and tripped over the coffee table; his eyes fixed on the spider.

He heads for his mother's bedroom. The wardrobe doors stood open. Nothing was missing. The bathroom smelled strongly of lavender soap, the kind she used every night. Water still dripped from the faucet. Her purse sat upright on her desk. Her wallet was still there, with a wad of cash. If a burglar had come through, they would have taken the money.

His eyes caught a shiny reflection that bounced off the mirror at the front of the armoire. A butcher's knife jutted from beneath the bed, its blade dark with dried blood. His thoughts fragmented with questions.

Did someone break in? Did she fight back? Did she run? Was she...taken?

His breathing turned shallow; the sight of blood weakened his knees, and dizziness took over. Shaking it off, he grabbed the phone and dialed Shelby, his first instinct. Almost automatic. Jared erupted, "She's gone!"

"Who?" Shelby, startled, asked. "My mom. She's gone. There's... there's a knife. With blood."

The line went dead. Within minutes, River and Shelby arrived. They never mentioned their dreams. They can't let it spread.

"We have to go to the police," Jared paced the room frantically. "I can't even make a fucking phone call." The lines are dead."

Shelby's face dropped as if she already knew that something dangerous was on its way. It was just a matter of time.

At the station, they signed in and waited in silence. Thirty minutes passed before a thin, stern-faced officer finally called them to the room in the back. "How can we help you?" Officer Leonard asked.

"My mother is missing." Jared rubbed his palms against his jeans, wiping away the sweat.

"She's never late. There was a knife under the bed. Blood on it. The back door was open."

His sentences were jumbled.

Officer Leonard raised an eyebrow while he jotted notes onto a yellow pad. His eyes then scanned Jared. "And can you explain why your jeans are torn? And blood-stained?"

Jared swallowed and shifted back and forth from one foot to another. "I, uh, fell, scraped my knees pretty bad."

"Well, son. Take care of that cut. Before you get yourself an infection. Let's go take a look and see what's going on at your home." He got up from the chair and lightly tapped Jared's shoulder. "Officer Miles will join us."

They pulled up to the house.

The officers approached River's Jeep. "You kids stay out here, while we take a look inside." They make their way towards the house, slowly, and with one hand on their holsters.

Back at the house, Brady had finished his treat. Jared heard the barks as the two men went in through the back door. The air had shed its earlier chill. The lights were in perfect working condition. Everything appeared to be...normal. Too normal.

Brady followed the officers into Jane's bedroom, tail wagging. Fifteen minutes had gone by, and Jared's patience was waning by the minute. They stayed quietly in the jeep and looked at the house for any sudden movements.

The officers emerged from the front door and walked down the steps to the driveway, unimpressed and slightly annoyed. Their demeanor was relaxed compared to when they had first arrived.

Officer Leonard cleared his throat, "Do you know it's a crime to file a false report?" Leonard said flatly. "There's no knife. No blood. Nothing."

"That's impossible!" Jared's eyes darted toward the house in disbelief. "It was right there under the bed, I swear."

"Save it for your next movie," Officer Miles snorted. "Or share whatever you're smoking."

The officers got back into their vehicle, shook their heads, and snickered. Miles murmured under his breath, "Unbelievable. The pranks these kids can play. Got nothin' better to do." The cruiser backed out of the driveway and disappeared down the road, into the night.

Jared turned to Shelby and River with desperation in his eyes, shaking—both fear and anger took over. "You saw it. Tell me you saw it."

They nodded. But the knife was gone. The blood was gone.

And now, so was his mother.

The front porch light blinked three times, teased, and turned off for the rest of the night.

CHAPTER 39

PIECES

He rambled through dates and timelines. Paced the room, looked for clues, and tried to force the chaos into some form of order. Where could his mom have gone? And why? At this time of night?

Shelby interrupted his spiraling thoughts. "Get a pad and pen. The police won't help us. They think we're lying. We have no choice but to do it ourselves."

"Right," River rummaged through the desk. "Let's take it step by step. Logic. The question—who was the woman standing with Shelby's father in that photo? Was it really Mrs. Mitchell?"

Jared felt a wave of encouragement run through his body. The uncertainty was morphing into a mission. He looked up at Shelby and started asking questions. "Shelby, your birth date?" She glanced over at River to ensure he wrote it down. "July 2, 1960."

He scribbled down the date.

Jared began with everything he knew. He still hadn't told them about his recent experiences at the playground or at Moody's but he knew his father was trying to tell him something. "My father came home from his deployment in December of 1958. He was here for about a year before being called back in January of 1960. Shelby was born six months later, that following July."

River exhaled, spinning the pen between his fingers. "Which means Shelby could easily be Nolan and Jane's child."

Jared stops pacing. "But if that were true, where does Benson Jones come into play? Why did he adopt Shelby?"

Silence occupies the room. Their brains were in full motion, working overtime as they tried to grasp any bit of information to piece together a logical story.

"And why was I told my mother died during childbirth?" The words quietly left Shelby's lips as she stared at the floor.

Jared leaned back into the recliner and spoke to the ceiling. "So *why* Benson Jones? If she were the child of Benson and Jane, that would mean they had an affair at some point in 1959. Then Mama had the baby while my dad was away on duty. He would never know."

His jaw tightened, and emotions ran through him, but he continued. "Maybe she was too scared of his temper—and I wouldn't blame her. Dad would have killed Mr. Jones."

River continued carefully as he saw something stir up in Jared. "She may have used a midwife to help navigate the birth—kept it quiet, and claimed the baby was stillborn. Well, at least that's what she would have told Nolan. When Benson found out, he insisted on raising his own daughter."

Jared sat up and straightened his back. "It was a perfect plan. My dad was away. He would never know."

"So, Nolan believed his child was dead, and Shelby was told her mother died during childbirth. This is a bestseller right here," River interrupted.

Something in Shelby snapped. "No! This is NOT *material* for a novel, River. This is my life. I was lied to!"

Her breath shuddered. "Do you know what it's like to grow up thinking you were the cause of your mother's death? That you were born wrong?" She covered her face with both hands. "I've carried that guilt my entire life. No wonder there were no photos. No stories. No memories.

Just pure silence." She could barely get words out between the sobs. "What a web of lies. All of it. Just to hide their dirty secret."

The tears dried up on her cheeks. Her eyes went distant. In a daze, her mouth formed the word, "Lies."

Moses's collar. The slugs.

It hit Jared just as hard. He never told them about Moody's. The song. *Lies* by The Knickerbockers. The playground.

For the first time, something shifted in him toward his mother. Not forgiveness, but something closer to understanding. The adultery, if it happened at all, was wrong. But he knew more. He remembered the screams into the night. He remembered the bruises. The fear. The abuse. The way Nolan terrorized their home. The irony was brutal. Nolan wore a uniform to protect strangers while he successfully destroyed his own family.

While River pulled Shelby into his arms, Jared drifted into his mother's bedroom.

What they had now was a complete fabrication based on pieces of a picture. There had to be something there. Just one more piece to solidify their story.

The hypnotizing paisley wallpaper put Jared into a trance. The room was untouched. Her clothes still hung neatly in the closet. Shoes lined up beneath. The keys were in the bowl on the front console. Where could she have gone?

Like a madman, Jared flipped everything over; pulled out the drawers, fumbled through receipts, papers, coupons, removed all the clothes from the closet, checked underneath the bed, and turned the mattress over.

Something caught his attention under the mattress, a large brown envelope with no writing on the front. He ripped it open. Letters. Dozens of them with neat, careful writing.

All of which had Benson's return address.

River and Shelby rushed in after hearing all the commotion as Jared's eyes glazed over at the pages. With a robotic voice, Jared informs them. "Guys, we may have something here." Jared read them aloud. One by one. They were love letters. Intimate. Detailed. Describing stolen afternoons, secret moments, and hopeful promises while Nolan was working at the distillery, or away on duty.

The last letter was different. It was a letter that answered the golden question: who was Shelby?

CHAPTER 40

THE LETTER

After silently reading it, Jared handed the letter over to Shelby. Shelby's hand trembled as she read it aloud.

My dearest Benson,

As a mother, it breaks my heart to be writing these words. I know we cannot live a normal life together, but please promise me you will raise our daughter, Shelby, with the most love and care and instill in her the highest morals. I wish I could be there, but circumstances would never allow us to unite in our sins. I guess this is my punishment: for me to never know my daughter, and for my daughter to never know her own mother. This is a curse a mother should never have to bear.

Yours for eternity,

Jane

Shelby's breath left her in soundless sobs. The search was over.

Jared spoke softly. "She was going to mail this, but then she probably got scared. Maybe scared my dad might get to it first. And forgot to throw it out. And it somehow got mixed up in this pile of letters."

They now had their evidence.

Before any of them could react, the letters ripped from their hands. Their eyes follow the letters upward as an unseen force pulls them. The pages whirled around the room in a violent spiral, shredding in midair. Paper explodes into fragments, raining down like snow.

Laughter erupted from the walls, low and taunting.

The brown envelope slowly floated upward toward the ceiling. It then flipped over, spewing out a photograph. It slid free and drifted to the floor, right between Jared and Shelby.

She kneeled over and picked it up. With numb fingers, she handed it over to Jared. It was upside down. She was too afraid to turn it over. Once he flipped it over, the truth was sealed. He looked at the photo, then at Shelby. Her eyes move to the photo. It was the same one from the Puma Box. But this time, the woman's face was crystal clear, no more secrets. There was no mistake.

The woman who stood next to Benson Jones was indeed Jane Mitchell. And around her neck hung the necklace with the emerald pendant.

CHAPTER 41

THE LAST RESORT

One piece of their story had been unraveled. But what about the dreams? The voices? The relentless nightmares that refused to release them?

They stared at one another, stunned. What were they supposed to do now?

Exhaustion and hunger eventually crept in. Their brains couldn't handle any more information at that point.

The boys ordered a pizza and collapsed in the family room as they mindlessly watched *Happy Days.*

Things were different for Shelby. The feeling of intense betrayal took over her. For nearly two decades, her mother had lived just minutes away, and she never knew. *What kind of mother does that? How do you live that close and never have the urge to visit your own child? Why did she keep herself away even after Nolan disappeared?*

The guilt she felt now morphed into anger, coiling in her stomach. All those years believing she caused her mother's death and carrying guilt that was never hers. Anger toward her mother blistered through her body. *And my complicit father, knowingly keeping me away—away from my own mother?* Rage rose into her heart, sharp and piercing.

She was barely twenty yet burdened with so much guilt and anger. The atrocious lies tore through her mind over and over again. What ached the most was her inability to confront her father about the lies. He was in no condition to even hold a sensible conversation. There was no one she could scream at. She pressed a pillow to her face and screamed into it. All the rage, the guilt, the sadness, the helplessness released into that pillow, wet with her tears; tears that were waiting to be shed for so long but didn't know why. Today, they knew, and there was no stopping.

Shelby later joined the boys in the living room, her eyes red and swollen. The boys didn't say anything as they handed her a plate of pizza. Nothing they could say or do would change the truth.

River gently massaged her shoulders as she ate in silence, attempting to absorb the truth. *Happy Days* continued in the background, but no one paid any attention. Pausing the massage, River came up with an idea that was too bold to be spoken aloud, but the words escaped his mouth, and he couldn't retract them. "We need to somehow travel through our dream."

Shelby froze, pizza halfway to her mouth.

Jared looked up at River with a puzzled expression. "I'm sorry, what the hell did you just say?" He squinted at him. "Are you high? What was in your slice? I'd like some."

Jared exhaled and glanced at Shelby. She shrugged, and her eyes spoke. *Don't look at me. I don't know what he's talking about.*

River didn't back down. *"Come on, Shelby, really? You know what has been happening."* Shelby's eyes tell him to stop speaking.

He still refused to take the hint. "Jared, something is going on with our dreams, but we can't explain everything. You gotta trust us." Shelby glared at him, warning him to stop talking.

River grabbed a piece of paper and wrote quickly. *We can't tell you. If we do, you'll be infected. Just trust us, please.*

Jared read it, looked up, and then he looked at Shelby. She shrugged again.

"Okay, what's going on? This isn't funny. Whatever you two are doing here. None of this is a joke." Jared threw the paper on the ground.

River's jaw tightened, and he rubbed his temples.

"I know this sounds insane. But here's the plan. We're going to call on your father's spirit. Something's been infiltrating our dreams, trying to give us a message, a warning. Maybe it's your father."

Jared's mouth fell open, unable to fathom what was said. He scratched the back of his neck with an expression of disbelief as he shook his head from side to side. "Uh...no, no, we are *not* doing that."

Jared wasn't buying it. He questions River, "Call on his spirit? How do you even know he's dead? All we know is that he left."

River continued, stubborn and not willing to take no for an answer.

"We don't know what happened. He's obviously trying to tell us something. All we know is that he disappeared in 1963. The town says time overseas broke him, that he packed up and vanished. But did he really? Maybe there is more to the story than anyone knows."

Jared stood there as he ate the last slice of pizza from the box and nervously chewed each bite. "You guys have officially lost your minds." Jared finished his pizza. "That's enough. I'm done. I'm too tired to think." He rubbed his face. "You two are obviously tired, or should I say, delusional. I'm going to bed. Oh, and how about we focus on finding my mom instead of some ritual to call on the dead—which is a complete assumption."

He turned down the hallway, hands buried in his pockets. But his chest was tight. He never mentioned Moody's. The parking lot. The van. The invisible force. The playground. He can't bring himself to tell anyone. He was afraid that no one would believe him, but after today, he knew—they're all being tormented.

The art of escapism was self-taught at an early age: drowning out the sounds of violence with music, hiding under his desk with his ears covered, making a pillow fort while talking to himself, and becoming invisible. It kept him alive as a kid.

He sat at the edge of his bed and bounced a knee up and down.

Shelby and River cleared out the living room, creating space. They were proceeding with the plan, with or without Jared. It was the only way. The last resort.

They lit several candles and pulled out a Ouija board—a game that became a household staple after the movie, *The Exorcist*. "Kids would entertain themselves during sleepovers, especially close to Halloween, and bring out the board.

It was under Mathew's bed. Jared showed it to River once. The board was crisp and smelled new. Never used. Jane didn't want it in the house, but Jared bought it for his brother, and they hid it under the bed.

Jared heard their whispers. *How long am I going to hide?*

The answer came to him fast. *Not for long. Not tonight.* The answer came all too quickly.

The curse of his father's behavior had kept him a loner most of his life, introverted and unable to trust people. He had to break the cycle, once and for all.

He knew he couldn't sleep while the two of them were out there. This was his puzzle to solve . His father went missing, and he was too young to do anything about it. Now that his mother was gone too, it was up to him to figure out where she went, or who had taken her.

Jared's curiosity could no longer be silenced. He got up and joined them in the living room.

"I'm in. I want to know everything."

Shelby patted the floor next to her, motioning her half-brother to sit down. She gave him an encouraging smile, but deep down, she was terrified of what might come through from the other side.

With rattled nerves, they lit candle after candle, twenty in all. The flame's shadows stretched and twisted along the walls, watching like an audience in the afterlife.

They took their seats on the floor around the coffee table. The planchette rested at the center, ready to be awakened.

Shelby's fingers trembled as she placed them on the planchette. She took three deep breaths to relax her mind and body. The candles flickered.

"Spirit of Nolan Mitchell," she closed her eyes, "we ask you to come through."

CHAPTER 42

THE SÉANCE

Surrounded by the glow of the candles, Shelby pushed forward. "Are we alone in this house?"

Nothing.

"I ask again, are we alone in this house? If you are here, please come forward. Show yourself. We want a peaceful meeting with no harm to anyone. We're just here for information, to understand the full story." With zero experience in talking to the afterlife, Shelby improvised as she went along. Her only guide was what she'd seen in movies or read in novels.

A whisky bottle at the bar slid off the counter and shattered to the ground, startling the three of them. The front door cracked open slightly, and a cold breeze allowed itself inside with a swift greeting.

"Oh, Lord... this is really happening," Jared said under his breath. River's mouth went dry, but Shelby pressed on. "What is your name?"

The planchette jerked violently. *N-O-L-A-N.*

The warm breath from Jared's mouth turned into a cloudy mist as the temperature kept dropping.

Shelby rubbed her hands together for warmth, beyond frightened, yet something inside her urged her to continue. The words kept flowing out of her mouth, like she was being hypnotized to conduct the interview.

"Where are you?"

The planchette scraped again: *B-E-H-I-N-D Y-O-U.*

A loud thump from the wall behind them echoed through the entire house. The wall's vibration caused a delicate figurine of Mother Mary to fall and crash to the floor.

They jerked their heads around and saw a solo photo of Nolan in his Navy uniform. It thumped back and forth, bumping against the wall. Spiders crawled from between the wooden planks and surrounded the frame in a ceremonial march. The frame formed a long crack down the center, and then smaller cracks veined throughout the glass, until it fell to the floor. Shards of glass exploded in all directions.

"What is it that you want?"

Silence. She waited about a minute and rephrased the question.

"Why are you not at peace? What do you need?"

With each letter, a candle was lit. The letters formed the word *R-E-V-E-N-G-E.*

The front door slammed shut. The windows rattled. River and Jared were in awe of her bravery, knowing they would have been too afraid to conduct the séance themselves.

Still, she carried forward, "What are you trying to tell us?"

No answer.

Shelby probed again. "Mr. Mitchell, please come forward and answer us. What are you trying to tell us? We need to know."

Still, more silence. The ticking of the grandfather clock, usually ignored, was particularly deafening at that moment. As the clock ticked, the melodious Westminster Chimes vibrated throughout the room as it struck midnight.

River, oddly quiet, sat across from Shelby, head hung as if he had dozed off. Jared lightly tapped him on the shoulder. The raw emotions of it all, the stress, the exhaustion, had them all drained mentally, eventually taking a toll on their bodies. But they all needed to be present for this to work.

"Hey, River, wake up. Don't sleep on us, man. We need you." Jared spoke in a loud whisper.

He tapped River's shoulder a bit harder and jumped back. "Holy shit! He's cold as ice!" River's slow exhalations created a cold, visible fog each time he breathed; the sound of his breath was similar to a ninety-year-old man who smoked a pack of cigarettes every day for an entire lifetime.

Shelby leaned over the coffee table to get a closer look.

River's face shot up from the slumber, eyes hollow. He puckered his lips together in sheer fury; his empty gaze pierced straight through Shelby.

In a lowered pitch with a raspy undertone, he barked coldly, "Stay away from me, you worthless girl! You're not mine! It should have been you, not ME!"

A loud noise grew closer toward her. She turned toward the sound. The TV unit slid across the room. It was headed towards her. Jared darted over to it and held it back with every ounce of his strength. It was too heavy, and the magnetic pull was stronger than he could handle; the unit knocked him over as it continued its way to Shelby, aiming to crush her. She jumped out of the way, just in time, as it crashed into the wall with such force that it created a massive hole and ended up in the room next door. Struck with momentary relief, she put a hand to her heaving chest and sat cautiously on the floor, unsure of her movements, careful not to startle the beast again.

Laughter ripped from River's throat. Not his. Something layered and vicious. Like one human and one demonic voice merging.

He abruptly stopped his laughter. Lifeless eyes were now looking in Shelby's direction. "You are a product of sin. You were born in sin. You are the definition of sin!" He charged towards her like an uncontrollable, rabid animal.

Shelby crawled backwards on all fours, desperate, as fast as she humanly could, far away to the other side of the room. He stopped in front of an enlarged, framed photo that hung on the wall, a photo of Jane and Nolan on their wedding day. River tilted his head and smiled as he admired the man in the picture. He yanked the frame in a rage and smashed it over his knee.

He swung his head from side to side in a trance-like state. "Look at what I have become. Nothing. I am nothing! After serving my country, I turned to dust, and no one remembers my name," the voice shrieked.

"You wanna know everything? The *real* story? You nosy, good-for-nothing, little assholes." Frothy saliva sat along the edges of his lips, and some drool dribbled down the sides to his neck. He leaned in closer. Shelby could smell Nolan's putrid breath laced with whisky. Both Jared and Shelby covered their mouths and noses, unable to handle the smell of a hundred decaying fish mixed with whiskey. Jared let out a gag but managed to control himself.

"Get yourselves into a deep sleep, and you will be shown the *truth*. You've been digging in all the wrong places. Now, it's time. You've finally knocked on the right door. All of you have been living one big lie, and you don't even know it!"

River's entire body shuddered and sweat dripped down his face and arms.

The planchette had gone wild, moving in all directions on the Ouija board. Huddled in the corner, Shelby cried for help; she wanted to help River, but knew Nolan invaded his body, and he despised Shelby. She kept her distance. She wasn't safe near him.

"River! River, come back! It's me, Jared! You're not Nolan. YOU ARE NOT MY FATHER!" he finally screamed out. He grabbed River's shoulders and slammed him on the floor, repeatedly, releasing all his trapped anger for his father. River's body created a loud thud each time it hit the floor. "I HATE YOU! You ruined my life, and you ruined my mother's life! You're an evil man, and I will never forgive you! None of us will! The day you disappeared was the best day of our lives!"

A black cloud of dust erupted from River's mouth.

It filled the entire room with the unbearable stench of rotten animal flesh, swirling around each one of them, and made a final exit through the large open window behind the sofa.

The floorboards beneath creaked and shook, creating waves that violently lifted them up and down. The windows couldn't decide whether to stay open or closed, and all the candle flames burned out. "Three Little Birds," Shelby's favorite song, played on the record player, but at an awfully slow speed, and backwards. Every light in the room turned on, then flickered, turned off, and turned on again, and flickered continuously.

All chaos came to a stop once the heavy wooden doors slammed shut. Nolan's army of spiders marched neatly back to where they came from. The picture frame featuring Nolan hung back on the wall in one piece. On the shelf was the whiskey bottle, with no evidence of its earlier fall.

A heavy silence covered the entire room like a wet blanket.

River remained on his back with his legs stretched out. Shelby still kept a safe distance and motioned Jared to check on him. "Hey, River, you there?" He touched River's arm. "His temperature is back to normal." River's eyelids fluttered open to the sight of Jared's face up close; he sat up quickly, putting his hand on his head as if in pain. He let out a groan.

"What the hell just happened? I feel like I got hit by a big rig. My head is pounding, and my back feels contorted. Did I get into a fight? Why is it so cold here? What's that smell? Ugh, gross. Did you fart, Jared? What the hell did you eat, man?"

They told him.

"Jesus fucking Christ. Are you shittin' me?" River went silent for a long minute, almost in disbelief. "I'm just glad I didn't hurt either of you.

That's wild. But why me? Why'd he pick me? You would think this kinda stuff only happens in the movies. Man, this is so eerie. I'm surprised you both still wanna be around me."

Jared shifted uncomfortably in his seat. "I kinda don't, dude."

River put an arm around Shelby. Still unsettled by the whole episode, she returned his half-hug with a mix of relief and fear, and he immediately sensed her discomfort. "C'mon, Shel, it's me. I promise." She forced a smile in his direction but was unable to make eye contact.

They put away the Ouija board in silence, hoping never to use it again.

River interrupted the awkward silence. "We need to get continuous sleep tonight. Nolan clearly wants to tell us something, and he communicates to us in our dreams."

"Sleep?" Jared asks. "After all that? And with you around? You're gonna try and kill us in our sleep." Jared got up and punched River in the arm.

"Jared, you got any sleeping pills lying around? We *need* to sleep. This is our chance; it may be our one shot to discover the truth. So do what you need to do to relax, take a hot shower, have a glass of warm milk, meditate, do those breathing exercises your yogi girlfriend taught you. Whatever the hell it is you do before sleeping, do that."

They prepared for sleep like soldiers preparing for a war, armed with sleeping masks, sleeping pills, scented incense sticks, heavy blankets, and comfortable clothing. All the windows and curtains were closed to block out any light. The phones were unplugged to prevent any interruptions. River and Shelby took the bed, and Jared slept on the sofa in the corner of the bedroom.

As soon as they lay their heads down, a force had taken over their minds and bodies, and they wandered into a deep slumber. This time, they were ready to confront their dreams. They were ready for the truth. It was time to know what really happened.

The fear subsided, and they welcomed Nolan into their dreams with open arms. Somewhere beyond sleep, something stirred. The curtain drew back. And the show began.

PART TWO: THE REVELATION

CHAPTER 43

THE BEGINNING OF DOOM

Sleep whisked them away into a different world, and a different time. A school bell rang into a hallway that smelled of books and leather jackets.

Shelby, River and Jared were no longer in the Mitchell house; they were transported across time. They were somewhere Nolan wanted them to be.

****

A 1952 Love Story

The bell rang into the long corridor of Seaport High as students were let out of class for the day. Different groups gathered in their usual clusters, waiting for their friends to walk home or ride the bus together. The jocks, wearing their uniforms with the Pirate mascot stitched on the front, stayed back for practice. Band members met to rehearse for the upcoming concert. The Hoods, with their slicked hair and leather jackets, stood by their motorcycles and decided on a location for the next rumble.

Between the scenes of Seaport High, stood a young girl, dressed in a conservative plaid skirt and buttoned blouse. Her wavy red hair was pulled back into bobby-pins, exposing cheekbones highlighted in a rouge shade, but never too much. She came from a conservative household with strict parents—a daughter of a schoolteacher and a police officer.

She twisted the corner of her cardigan, a nervous habit since childhood.

Her eyes searched the campus grounds until they spotted him jogging toward her. Tied loosely around his neck was a cashmere sweater that flapped in the wind with each stride. A smile immediately formed across her face as she lifted her petite hand to wave.

"Jane! Sorry, I got a little late. I had to help change a flat tire." He lifted his hands and cupped them together, showing her the black grease stains. He then lightly kissed her on the cheek. Helping others was built into his character, yet one would never have guessed it from his background. He came from luxury. His father and uncle owned and operated the steel plant, J & J Steel Co., which stood for their last name: Jones. Wealth followed him everywhere.

Benson Jones was a natural magnet. People gravitated toward him, eager to hear his stories. There was always a buzz around Benson, but that buzz died the moment he walked through the large French doors of his home.

Jane preferred to keep to herself. Attention made her uncomfortable. Fuss caused her to retreat.

They couldn't be from worlds more opposite; however, their grade-school connection made them inseparable. A classic story—from arched enemies to best friends to lovers. In kindergarten, he was the boy who threw mud on her during recess. The boy who ruined her favorite dress. That hatred eventually evolved into something special through the years. The anger softened, notes were passed, hands were held, and the whispers about their budding relationship began.

Now in high school, he was a year ahead of her, and everyone envied their love story.

They were in love, but they were also from different worlds. His parents despised Jane with every fiber of their being, and they would do whatever it took to separate them.

****

Fall approached, and with it came the Jones' annual brunch, held the last week of September, when the air was sharp, and the leaves burned gold, orange, and red beneath the afternoon sun.

The crème de la crème of Wilshire Pointe attended. Each guest was welcomed with a glass of champagne for the welcome toast and left with a personalized gift tote: a box of imported Swiss chocolates and a mesh bag of the finest dried fruits and nuts.

The gathering was intended for networking, social maneuvering, and, most importantly, for the Joneses to display their fortunes.

White tents towered over the gardens of their estate. The staff worked tirelessly to ensure that each detail was executed to perfection. Burgundy linens gracefully covered each table down to the floor, without a crease in site, topped with professionally arranged florals—a mix of hydrangeas, lilies, Queen Ann's lace, and garden roses.

Servers danced around in crisp bow ties and white gloves, addressing guests with the utmost poise, and serving them trays of food Jane heard for the first time: endive leaves stuffed with blue cheese and pecans, smoked salmon canapes, brie en croute, mini potato samosas.

Jane was used to her parents putting out an oversized bowl of chips and dip for guests, served by her mother.

The Jones family made a sport of humiliating her. They drew her into conversation, feigning interest in her life while testing her manners, her speech, and general knowledge of a world she was deliberately excluded from. Every wrong answer, every clumsy movement, and every mistake was noted. She became a source of their humor.

It was a cruel game they enjoyed playing. They found joy in highlighting her social faux pas, ridiculing everything about her, from the way she dressed to the way she spoke. Jane failed every hypothetical test that was thrown her way, making her an unfit match for their perfect Benson.

Their friends would erupt in laughter when she didn't know what to do with the many utensils placed at her dinner setting, and they purposely asked her questions about her travels abroad, which she never had the opportunity to experience. Benson's mother, Darlene, was the cruelest of all, casually displaying her Cartier watch and diamond earrings from Harry Winston; names that Jane wasn't familiar with.

"So, Jane, *honey*, what is it that your parents do?" Her smug expression said she already knew the answer but wanted to further embarrass Jane in front of her affluent friends. Jane clutched her elbows, palms damp. "Oh, my mother is a schoolteacher, and my father is a police officer. They love giving back to the community." The second sentence slipped out, unnecessary and vulnerable. Darlene raised her eyebrows in a superior manner and made eye contact with the other women at the table. A gloved hand covered her smirk.

Darlene's friend chimed in without making any eye contact, tending to her filet mignon. "And what do they enjoy for leisure activities?"

Jane paused and told them exactly what they wanted to hear, "A good movie at the drive-in, or we usually take a family camping trip once a year up at Kipper's Mount."

Laughter burst around the table.

Leaning into the neighboring woman, the friend snarled, "Why, that sounds like torture to me! Absolutely dreadful! Have they been to the social clubs, or on a dinner cruise, or traveled to Paris and tasted the fine cuisine there? Have they visited the ancient pyramids of Egypt?" She knew very well that Jane's family could never afford those kinds of trips.

"No, they have not. And they probably never will have those experiences," Jane replied in a defeated tone. Heat rose to her cheeks and engulfed her armpits. She was perplexed at how Benson could be a product of such a vile human. Jane excused herself to the ladies' room and heard the burst of laughter as she left the table. Meal untouched, she never returned.

That night, Darlene planned her next move. Destroying Jane became her ultimate purpose. She had to save her son from that no-good piece of trash. Benson's father was privy to everything, but since his wife was doing most of the dirty work, he sat back, puffed on his pipe, and pretended to be above all petty nonsense. Deep down, he enjoyed the show, hoping that Benson would come to his senses and find a girl who was on their level.

"That stubborn thing just won't take a hint. She's latched on to Benny like a damn leech!" she exclaimed to Robert, her husband. He was known as "Bobby" to his loved ones. She was seated at her vanity table, dressed in a white silk robe, applying cream to her face while complaining about Jane.

"It's a passing phase, honey. He'll soon realize that she's not Jones material. You're a tough one to follow." He gave her a playful wink and kissed her on the forehead. "Now don't waste too much time thinking about it. It's been a long day. Get some beauty sleep. We have a full agenda tomorrow."

Bobby Jones was a charming man and knew how to make others feel important to get what he wanted; beneath the charade, he was a narcissist, void of any emotion unless it affected him directly. Everything he did was for himself, including marrying his wife, who also came from an affluent family. Darlene was just another steppingstone; she was the mayor's daughter. Bobby saw an opportunity he couldn't miss. His steel plant would flourish if the mayor had the other plants shut down, and that's exactly what happened. Once they married, Darlene's father had the power to shut down any competition, anything that would affect his darling Darlene.

Each manipulative move Bobby made in his life was carefully executed to perfection.

However mean and condescending as they were, Jane kept her head high that entire day until Benson drove her home, and she finally burst into tears. A lump formed in his throat, and he pulled her to him. Anger and shame filled his heart. No apology could ever be enough to absolve his family of their miserable behavior. They had a lot of money, but no class; something that no amount of money could buy. He hated them for the way they treated Jane. The more his parents belittled and mistreated Jane, the more he was drawn to protecting and loving her.

The next morning, Benson galloped down the grand curved stairway, making quite an entrance. He had an important announcement that could no longer wait. His parents were seated at the long mahogany table while being served coffee; a full selection of breakfast items was spread across it, from hotcakes to baked beans and toast; his favorite was anadama bread, a molasses-sweetened bread. But he touched none of it; anger depleted his appetite.

"Good morning, Mother and Father. I'm not gonna beat around the bush. I love Jane. I'm gonna ask her to marry me. I'm old enough to make my own decisions, but out of respect, I wanted first to tell you before you hear it from anyone else."

Darlene slammed her empty cup of coffee onto the table and ran out of the room in tears. His father looked at him sternly. "Son, we will discuss this when you return from school. You're barely eighteen and have not a clue what life has to offer. Your mother and I will not allow you to make this mistake, understood?"

"Jane is not a mistake! I love her!" Benson pounded his fist on the wall and stormed out of the house. The front door slammed behind him, rattling the windows. He had no idea if Jane would even accept his proposal, but Benson was so adamant and ready to defy his parents, especially after the way they had been treating Jane.

He was only seventeen at the time, and she had just turned sixteen.

Benson was the third-youngest of four siblings. His older sister was married with four kids of her own and lived out in the country. She married the owner of a construction company and had staff watch over her children while she attended various Ladies' Club events. Everyone knew about her husband's extramarital affairs, but when she received the finest of silk dresses and jewels, all indiscretions were conveniently forgotten.

His elder brother was already handling the financial department of their steel company. They wanted Benson to follow the same path and move the company upward. According to them, Jane would drag him down, especially since she lacked the finesse to mingle with their social circle.

His younger brother, overlooked by his parents, seemed to be a lost soul. No one had time for him; he was different. His parents put him in a boarding school, and they would see him during the summers and some holidays. He was closest to Benson.

Benson was their last hope for the family business, therefore, Mr. and Mrs. Jones went into full-blown panic after hearing Benson's plans for marriage and immediately decided to move to Coral Springs, about four hours north. They owned another property there, and he could finish out his senior year at Coral Springs High. The unexpected turn took them by surprise. They had to act fast.

When Benson returned from school, Philip, the butler, had his belongings all packed and stacked neatly on the front porch, while his father brought the car around. Philip, now in his early sixties, cared for and watched over Benson, encouraging him to take his first step and teaching him to drive. Benson spent more time with Philip than he did with his own parents; he was almost like a second son to him. With tears in his eyes, he gave Benson one last hug and loaded all the bags and suitcases into the trunk of the car. Philip was instructed to stay back and manage the property.

Benson's mother, always dressed to the nines, sauntered daintily down the stairs and pinched his cheek, which he *hated*. "Now, you know we are doing this for your own good. You will thank us later. This is all for you, young man."

He moved his face away from her.

Darlene's expression turned grim. "And if you fail to comply, your father and I could easily have Jane's father demoted or even thrown out of the police force. You wouldn't want that for her, now, would you? They already seem to be struggling." She ran her fingers across the velvet sofa as she headed to the front door.

Benson felt himself turn red, and the anger rose into his chest. His mother was one of the most manipulative women in town, and often, he resented being in her bloodline. Feeling helpless and wanting to say goodbye to Jane, Benson was torn to pieces. Even at seventeen, he was unable to stand up to his parents; they had too much power.

They told him it would be just for a month or two, until he could get his thoughts together, but they lied.

His father hopped into the driver's seat and put on some tunes. As he drove into the horizon of a new town, Bobby Jones whistled triumphantly to the music, well aware that he and his wife destroyed the lives of two young and impressionable hearts.

CHAPTER 44

A SCENTED GOOD-BYE

Benson failed to appear at school for two full days. That's when she knew. Something was wrong. Benson never missed school, unless he was extremely sick. He found his home to be suffocating.

After the second day of his absence, she took the liberty of showing up at Benson's estate. Jane wasn't leaving until she had answers.

Phillip spotted her from the garden while he was reading the paper, peering through the windows in a frantic state, pacing the driveway, and talking to herself in a frenzy. Muttering to herself, her agitation escalated until she kicked the flowerbeds in the front lawn. She almost appeared unhinged. Desperate. A sharp pang of pity came over Philip. He had seen the young couple grow together since their elementary years. Their only time apart from one another was during family trips.

Phillip called her quietly to the side and pressed a letter into her hand with sympathetic eyes, covering his finger over her mouth. It calmed her momentarily. Benson had made him promise to give Jane the letter. He knew she would come looking. He knew her every move.

Jane had always been bold, spirited, and unafraid to confront anyone who disturbed her peace. She had sharp words for people she found obnoxious, except when it came to Benson's parents. Around them, her wit vanished, her defiance dissolving like a fierce dog silenced by the presence of a lion. The girl Benson's parents wanted for him was wealthy and malleable, a beautiful puppet to display or control. Not Jane.

Jane turned the letter over in her hands and lifted it to her nose. Benson had sprayed his cologne on it. Closing her eyes, she inhaled deeply, losing herself in the familiar scent; then she stopped, afraid the scent would fade if she breathed it in too many times. On the envelope, written in cursive, was "My Sweet Jane." Benson drew a heart next to her name. She ripped it open and read silently, moving her lips with each word while tears streamed down her pale cheeks.

My sweet Jane,

I had no intention of suddenly leaving town. Believe me, leaving you is the last thing I would ever want to do. I confessed my love for you to my parents and told them I wanted to ask for your hand in marriage. As you can imagine, they did not approve and grew angry with me.

It will just be for a month or two, and we will return. They think this time away will help me clear my head, but little do they know, absence makes the heart grow fonder.

I promise to write to you every day, my love.

Yours,

Benny

In a sudden surge of rage, Jane tore the letter into shreds. Almost immediately, regret followed. She collapsed into tears, furious with herself for destroying it. Hate filled her heart. Hate for his parents. Hate for Benson, for leaving, for obeying, for not fighting harder. Hate for the circumstances she could not escape. She even hated her own parents for being ordinary. She sank into the garden, folding her legs beneath her, sobbing until her body ached. Her hands crushed the envelope as she formed a tight fist. There was something hard inside. Forcing herself to breathe slowly, she wiped her nose and cheeks with her sleeve and turned the envelope upside down.

A necklace slipped into her palm. An emerald pendant caught in the light, luminous and flawless. It was the most beautiful thing she had ever seen. Without thinking, she clasped it around her neck. Her fingers closed around the pendant as fresh tears of loneliness fell. Deep in her gut, she knew the truth. Her life with Benson was over.

CHAPTER 45

THE NECKACE

He wrote dozens of letters to Jane, checking the mailbox every day in hopes of receiving a reply. As the days passed, his frustration grew. Benson began to believe Jane had moved on with her life. He never suspected the truth—that his parents had paid off the postmaster to intercept and destroy every letter he sent. They stayed one step ahead of him. Money had always been their greatest weapon, and they used it without shame.

Darlene stormed through the wooden halls, her heavy heels echoing sharply on the wooden floors as she prepared for a church event.

With immaculate hair and makeup, she draped herself in a white robe, and moved from room to room, barking orders and radiating impatience.

"Benson, honey! Have you seen my necklace?" she called. "The one with the emerald pendant?" She looked through her hand-painted jewelry armoire for a second time.

"No, Mama, I haven't." His voice wavered as he called out from his bedroom, though he held his ground.

"Well, I'll have to ask Helen if she has seen it anywhere," she said briskly. "And I can't ask your father because he wouldn't see it if it was two inches in front of his face!" She laughed at her own joke, finding joy in the little jabs she threw at her husband.

Helen had been their cook for fifteen years, brought over from the old house when Benson was still a little boy. She also did light housework, though they barely increased her pay for the additional duties. It was 'ironing day,' so Helen was in the guest bedroom with an electric iron in her hand, pressing the garments that were washed the day before. Darlene stood at the entrance with her arms folded across her bosom. "Helen, have you seen my emerald necklace?"

"No ma'am," Helen answered calmly. "I ain't seen your necklace since the last time you wore it at that holiday party. It was a mighty gorgeous necklace, Mrs. Jones. I'm sure it'll come up 'round here somewhere. I'd be happy to look for you, ma'am." She continued the back and forth motion with the iron, while the steam hit her face.

Darlene's expression hardened and she stomped her foot loudly against the floor and pointed toward the door. "Get out, Helen. Get your things. You have one hour to leave the property. Don't show your face here again. We have no room for thieves."

"Ma'am?" Her lips quivered in disbelief. With loyalty and pride, Helen had waited on the Jones family for most of her adult life and found her dismissal to be preposterous. "But I ain't ever took a thing from you, not even a dime. Where am I supposed to-" Helen began to form an argument.

"Out! Where you go is not my problem," Darlene yelled sternly.

And that was that. It was ruthless. And it was deliberate. It was classic Darlene.

Mrs. Higgins, the president of the Somerset Club, an elite, invitation-only society, waited in the parlor, sipping her Darjeeling tea. "This is quite a lovely home, isn't it, darling?" She asked her husband as her eyes scanned the Persian rug, velvet-upholstered cornices, and the sterling silver tea set. Raising his eyebrows, his bottom lip folded down as he nodded his head in agreement. He took a long slurp of his tea. She kicked his leg with her heel, motioning him to display proper etiquette. Tonight, they were scheduled to attend a charity event together with Mr. and Mrs. Jones.

Darlene used that moment, while they waited in the parlor, while the house was quiet, to her advantage. It was an opportunity to display her authority and to impress them. A seat on the club's board was within reach, especially after the charade with Helen. The couple sipped their tea and enjoyed the commotion from the parlor. "I think she would be a perfect addition," the wife said, as she dipped a biscuit in her tea.

Bobby Jones watched in stunned silence. He loved Helen's cooking, her intricate meals, her devotion, but fear kept him quiet. His thoughts drifted selfishly to what they would eat now that Helen was gone. Darlene could barely bake a dessert, let alone manage a kitchen. Most of her meals were inedible.

Benson stood frozen, disgust curling in his chest. He stared at his mother, shaking his head, unable to understand what he had just witnessed, though he knew he was the cause of it.

"Oh, don't look at me like that, Benny," Darlene snapped sharply while clasping a ruby- studded necklace around her neck. "These colored folk ought to be taught a lesson. Give them too much respect and trust, and they turn on you in a second. Don't be so naïve." She huffed around and then slipped into her evening gown. Darlene made sure her voice carried down the hall.

In that moment, Benson understood how deeply he hated his own mother. The shame of his silence stayed with him for years.

CHAPTER 46

A DULL FUTURE

After Benson moved away, Jane never heard from him again. She slipped into a quiet depression, and the jovial, spirited girl she once was, slowly abandoned her as well. Reluctantly, she dragged herself through senior year, the year that was supposed to be carefree and full of promise.

Day by day, Jane withdrew. She avoided friends because they reminded her of Benson. Simple routines like brushing her teeth and showering became unbearable chores. Her bedroom fell into disarray. Many nights she slept on the sofa, mumbling in her sleep, lost somewhere between dreams and grief. Deeply concerned about their daughter's mental health, Mr. and Mrs. Crawford began introducing other young men to Jane, unsure of what else to do. They carefully selected a handful of prospects.

One was handsome but lacked personality. Another had a charming personality but was physically unattractive. One man proposed to Jane on the first date, and another would not stop talking about his personal achievements, showing no interest in what Jane had to say. Each encounter left her feeling worse than the one before. It only reinforced what she already knew. Benson was perfect. There was no comparison.

Jane sat at her vanity table, mindlessly running the brush through her hair. Her mother peeked through the door, studying her once fun-spirited daughter; her delicate features, now dull, lacking the glow she once had. Her skin had become dry from neglect, and her nails, once carefully manicured, were now chipped and bare. Jane no longer saw the point of all the self-pampering.

She ran her fingers across the white lace nightgown folded neatly on her bed—the one Grandma Ruthie had made for her, a Victorian pattern with Jane's initials, J.C., embroidered on the sleeve. It had been a gift for her sixteenth birthday. Jane allowed herself a small, sad smile.

One more date, she told herself. If this date didn't work out, Jane vowed she would never marry anyone. She was happier alone than enduring another hollow evening with a man she didn't care for. Peeling herself off her bed, Jane slipped into a floral dress and threw on a cardigan. She almost reached over for the necklace with the green pendant, but stopped. It reminded her too much of Benson. This was not how it was supposed to be.

Downstairs, the doorbell rang. A nervous Nolan Mitchell stood on the porch, wiping the sweat that dripped from his temple with a handkerchief he kept in his pocket. His parents attended church with the Crawfords and had suggested he might be a good match for Jane. Jane's mother opened the screen door, "Why, you're looking mighty handsome, Nolan! Come on in. I'll call Jane down. She's upstairs getting ready."

"These are for you, ma'am." He handed her a bouquet of yellow daisies.

"Well, isn't that sweet. I'll put them in water right away. Come in and have a seat. Could I get you some tea?" She disappeared into the kitchen.

Nolan had recently returned from an overseas mission and had begun working at the whiskey distillery, hoping to rise through the ranks one day. He and Jane had spoken on the phone for two weeks. This was their first in-person date; a walk in the park, followed by burgers.

One date became many. A drive-in movie. A day at the shore. Horseback riding. Long drives. Walks beneath the stars. Hiking through the Blue Reservation. He merely served as a distraction for Jane, but never a replacement.

A year passed, and they were engaged. Jane told herself she was moving on. Yet deep inside, a gnawing ache remained. She longed to see Benson, even just once. His disappearance had been too abrupt, too final. He was etched into her core.

At times, when Nolan grew too close, she stiffened, waiting for the moment to pass. "What's the matter? Is something wrong?" he would always ask.

Everything is wrong, she wanted to reply. Instead, she politely dodged his question and moved on to another topic.

Nolan was kind, but he lacked Benson's effortless charisma. Benson's eyes had always lit up when he saw her; he would lift her off the ground, spin her, tease her, bringing her endless joy. Their bond had been playful, childlike, and rooted in years of shared history.

Benson had lived without responsibility, and the world had bent easily around him. Except for Jane, he rarely had to yearn for anything. Nolan, by contrast, had grown up too quickly. He lacked financial freedom and time for leisure. Nolan served as a Petty Officer in the U.S. Navy's Underwater Demolition Team—a frogman trained to enter waters no one else would. The things he witnessed stripped away his softness and buried his emotions beneath layers of discipline and silence.

The memory of his best friend, Billy, lingered over his sanity, almost challenging it. They had entered the water on a mission, two shadows slipping beneath the surface. Somewhere in the darkness, the current held a tight grip. Training and instinct took over, and Nolan drove himself upward, breaking through to safety. He looked all around, calling out for Billy, who never surfaced from the water beneath. Nolan never escaped that moment. It lodged itself deep inside him. He never spoke of it. It was the moment that shattered his spirit. The moment he learned what numbness and guilt truly meant.

His personality was a bit flat compared to Benson's. A dry sense of humor, a disciplined routine, and measured emotion were what Nolan had to offer. But Nolan was there. He didn't abandon her. He showed up to all the dates, and five minutes earlier than planned. Always punctual. The electrical spark was absent in their relationship; however, he provided stability and security. As a mature young woman, she was taught to settle for these qualities and move forward with her life.

At times, Jane felt as if a force inhabited her mind, pushing her toward him, urging her to forget Benson, but she never could.

She never did.

CHAPTER 47

THE GOWN

Grandma Ruth got to work, surrounding herself with an array of ribbons, lace, satin fabric, embellishments, and her beloved sewing machine. Her wedding gift to Jane was the creation of the most beautiful gown she had selected from a Dior pattern.

"Grannie," as Jane called her, transformed into a magician as her feet operated the large, cast-iron pedal that powered the machine while her hands carefully guided the fabric through the feed dogs. She ran her own small sewing business, an entrepreneurial woman ahead of her time. After losing her husband to tuberculosis at just twenty-six, she was forced to survive on her own. With three mouths to feed, she had no choice.

Sewing became her strength. She established a small business called *Ruthie's* and eventually hired four other sewists. It began in the parlor of her home, but word spread quickly. Customers could bring in a garment for alterations and receive it back the very same day. Ruthie's was the only shop in town who offered a true *rush* service.

Within a year of opening her business, Ruthie's expanded into a corner storefront that had once been a hardware store. Ruth was ecstatic about securing her very own dressmaker's shop, and was even able to upgrade to electric sewing machines. For her, this milestone signified resilience, strength, and the will to move forward. Since then, it has become the town's trusted source for alterations and custom-designed gowns.

Jane had always dreamed that her Grannie would create the perfect wedding dress for her. But she dreamed of walking down the aisle, in the gown, to a man she wanted to spend the rest of her life with. That man wasn't Nolan Mitchell.

While Jane's wedding was being planned, Benson was admitted to the University of Oxford in England, at the relentless urging of his parents. "We want you to have the best education," they told him. "Living abroad will give you a new perspective. Endless possibilities. The connections you'll make there will last a lifetime." In truth, they wanted him far away. Somewhere, Jane couldn't reach him, afraid she would somehow lure him back into her world.

Disheartened, Benson boarded the plane and wondered whether Jane had read any of his letters. As the aircraft climbed into the clear blue sky, he watched the roads, cars, and houses shrink beneath him, dissolving into miniature shapes. Somewhere below, lost in the maze he once called home, the love of his life was about to embark on a new journey—one that would exclude him forever.

CHAPTER 48

BLOOMING WITH GLOOM

The wedding was to be held that afternoon at St. Theresa Church. The house bustled with relatives from out of town and local friends from the church as they prepared for Jane and Nolan's ceremony; they all managed to help in some way. The flower arrangements were made by her cousin, who owned a small business as a florist; it was her gift to Jane. Their next-door neighbor offered to help with the decorations, and Nolan had a few friends in a band who agreed to provide the entertainment.

Jane's mother insisted the men arrive early to ensure everything was in place. The ladies made sure the small community room attached to the church had been set for the luncheon that would follow the ceremony.

When her mother and Grannie entered Jane's bedroom, they let out a soft cry of admiration. Jane stood in front of the full-length mirror, staring at her reflection. A timid woman stared back at her, rosy-cheeked, poised, and trembling beneath layers of satin and lace. Hesitation flooded her heart. She wanted to cry. She wanted so desperately to tell her mother everything; the fear, the grief, the truth she had buried so carefully. What she wanted to tell her the most was the truth—that she didn't love Nolan. She never loved Nolan. And she will never grow to love him. For her, it was always Benson.

She straightened her shoulders and forced a smile. They had worked too hard for this day. She couldn't bear to disappoint her mother or Grannie, not after everything they had done to hold her together in the months following Benson's disappearance. They had been her support when she nearly fell apart. She reminded herself that *he's the one who left. Focus on who's here. Who's real.* She repeated it silently but couldn't accept his sudden disappearance. She couldn't accept that Benson had forgotten her. That he had moved on so easily. And yet, that was exactly what she was about to do. Move on.

"We've been waiting for this day," Grannie said softly, with her frail hand on Jane's shoulder. "You are the most beautiful bride ever to grace Wilshire Pointe." She smiled warmly and straightened the gown's pleats. Jane's mother could feel her daughter's reservations. Call it 'mother's intuition,' but she knew her daughter held a secret space in her heart for another man. All she could do was pray that with time, Nolan would eventually fill that space.

Three generations of women stood before the mirror, hands intertwined, each shaped by loss, endurance, and sacrifice.

One of them was about to step into a future she never could have imagined.

CHAPTER 49

THE BLESSING

The car pulled up to the church, and Jane stepped out as her mother lifted the train of her dress from the ground and guided her through the back entrance.

It was almost time. She had doubts, she had cold feet, and she knew it was the wrong choice, but it was too late now. Everyone was waiting. There was no turning back. Her mother paused and cupped Jane's face with one hand, "Father Clemmons wanted to see you in his office before the ceremony for a special blessing." She pointed down the corridor. "He's in the last room to the left. I'll be waiting in the bridal suite with Grannie."

Jane knocked gently on the door. "Come in," a voice said. "You may close the door behind you." He turned around and faced the bride-to-be. "Oh, Jane, what a beautiful bride you are. I wanted to bless you before the ceremony, my dear. Please, come closer." His eyes examined her veil and slowly made their way down to her delicate shoes.

She moved toward him, her steps slow and calculated. He raised the cross and recited a nuptial prayer, his voice smooth and practiced. When he finished, he stepped closer. Too close. She felt his breath. Then his hand touched her head. As it moved downward, it brushed against her breast and lingered; lingered in an indecent manner. His breathing grew heavier. Time froze, and she felt suffocated under his bulky shadow.

Jane stepped back abruptly, nearly losing her balance. Without looking his way, she left the room trembling, fear and anger shooting through her, unsure of what had just happened, but she knew it was wrong, and wondered how many brides before her had endured the same "blessing," or even worse.

The organ began to play. Jane walked down the aisle, counting her steps, eyes fixed ahead. Her arm was tucked inside her father's. She felt his pride. She also felt his sadness. He was no longer her protector. Her gaze lifted to Nolan, who watched her with open admiration, but not too much. His expressions were controlled. There was no doubt she was the most beautiful bride ever to stand inside St. Theresa Church.

Opposite him stood Father Clemmons. He licked his lips as she continued up the aisle. Shame and disgust flooded her. She never told anyone. No one would have believed her over Father Clemmons. He was a force in Wilshire Pointe, untouchable. She buried the memory deep, hoping it would fade. It never did.

Jane was almost at the altar, but for some reason, she turned around. Deep down, she hoped for Benson to barge in and stop the wedding. Confess his love, as shown in Hollywood movies. Her father nudged her arm, bringing her back to reality. Benson wasn't coming to save her.

After the ceremony, the newly married couple and their guests moved into the community room for a luncheon prepared by Jane's mother and her friends. It was simple: finger sandwiches, baked ham, green bean casserole, and deviled eggs.

Jane and Nolan's first dance was unmemorable. They didn't have a special song. The band just played something slow. Nolan closed his eyes and imagined a beautiful life with Jane. Jane closed her eyes and saw Benson's familiar grin and felt his hands lift her and spin her around. She heard his laughter in her ears. Her best moments were now a distant memory.

Three tiers tall and trimmed with pale pink frosted roses, her wedding cake sat on a round table draped in pink lace and satin. At the top of the cake, there should have been two figures: the bride and the groom, but the groom was missing.

It had fallen onto the bottom tier, buried beneath a thick mound of icing.

CHAPTER 50

OXFORD

The historic City of Oxford welcomed Benson with bustling streets and busy students. His parents had called upon their most elite connections to ensure he was well looked after. A gentleman in a suit and white gloves stood in front of a Rolls-Royce, holding a sign with Benson's name on it. He closed the door as Benson entered the car and whisked him away to the university.

His accommodation was far from ordinary. He was booked into a penthouse suite shared with another student, someone who happened to be from Indian royalty. His roommate's name was Raj, which meant "to *rule*." A porter brought up Benson's final piece of luggage, and Benson made sure to leave a generous tip. His new roommate appeared busy unpacking and hadn't heard him enter the expansive suite, which sat on the second floor of a low-rise building.

A balcony wrapped around the front windows and extended down both sides, allowing each bedroom access to the outdoor space. It overlooked the High Street Deli across the way, open until midnight and ideal for hungry students studying late into the night. The common room was indeed a topic of conversation. Gold-framed original artwork and photographs of Oxford's history lined the walls above an ornate stone credenza, used mostly for liquor and fine wine. Two large, green-velvet sofas faced one another across a glass table. It was rumored that Shakespeare's original desk was once placed in this suite, but was later moved to the university library. A kitchenette, powder room, and the sweeping balcony completed the space. On opposite ends sat two bedrooms, each with their own full bathrooms.

The bedroom door finally opened and out stepped a small-framed man with thick glasses that magnified quick, darting brown eyes. His movements were filled with nervous joy. Nothing about him suggested royal blood. "Hello," he said briskly. "Nice to meet you, Mr. Jones. I am Raj Chauhan, from Jaipur, India. Please forgive me. I failed to hear you arrive." "Nice to meet you, Raj," Benson said. "Please, call me Benson." They shook hands. Raj's palm was round and clammy, and Benson held back, afraid his grip might crush fingers that felt strangely fragile.

Several rings adorned Raj's hands, each set with a different stone. Later, Raj explained that the stones were meant to stay close to his skin, to protect him from illness and evil. A family priest had foreseen danger and guided his parents to purchase them. The priest conveniently owned his own jewelry shop. Benson suspected it was a scam, but he nodded politely as Raj rambled on about each stone's supposed power.

Despite their different backgrounds, a genuine friendship formed between the two men. For the rest of their time at Oxford, Raj and Benson remained roommates. Raj taught him how to cook Indian dishes— biryani, chicken tikka, and rogan josh. The flavors were unlike anything Benson had ever tasted, and he couldn't wait to bring them back to Wilshire Pointe, a town that had nothing remotely similar. In exchange, Benson introduced Raj to Western fashion, escorting him to the finest tailors and helping him select modern suits and casual wear.

To distract himself from Jane, Benson threw himself into his books and joined several social clubs. His efforts paid off, and he rose to the top of his class, receiving several awards of excellence.

By his second year, bitterness had begun to replace hope. Jane hadn't written back. He checked the mail obsessively, convincing himself she had moved on. One evening, he decided to ask a young woman to dinner. He noticed her often in the library, beautiful and quiet, but friends always surrounded her. She was never alone. He spotted her reading by the courtyard fountain, unguarded.

It was now or never.

"Good evening," he said, forcing his voice steady. "My name is Benson. I've seen you around. May I sit next to you?"

"Of course," she said, scooting aside.

She was even more stunning up close. Porcelain skin. Soft pink lips. High cheekbones. Green eyes framed by long lashes. Dirty-blonde waves brushed her shoulders, and she smelled faintly of magnolias. A black pleated skirt stopped short below her knees, paired with a polka-dot blouse. Benson hadn't studied a woman like this in years. He had almost forgotten how to flatter a woman.

Part of him wanted revenge. Proof to Jane, proof to himself. Proof that he could move on.

She slid a bookmark into her book and met his eyes. "My name is Jane," she said, her British accent thick. His heart sank into silent defeat. He could never win. *Jane.* He gave a cool smile on the outside. Mentally, he was spiraling. Irrational, frenetic. Sweat pooled at his temples.

Why that name? Was this some cruel coincidence? A punishment? Was his Jane haunting him, refusing to let go? Memories flooded in: the laughter, the secret trips, the way they knew each other without words. Their last kiss. He tried so hard to forget, but the universe would make sure he never did.

"Are you alright?" she asked as she gently touched his shoulder. "You've gone a bit pale."

Without answering, he stood abruptly and apologized, muttering an excuse before walking away. She remained by the fountain, watching him go, confused.

Two more years passed. Benson promised himself he would return to Wilshire Pointe the moment he earned his degree. Raj planned to follow. Harvard was nearby, and he hoped to teach calculus there. With Benson's connections, an introduction to the mathematics department could be arranged.

The day Benson graduated, he boarded a flight home. He was done waiting. This time, no one, not even his parents, would stop him.

CHAPTER 51

A TRIP TO BAY & BASKET

Jared Noah Mitchell was born on December 26, 1958. Jane hummed softly as she fastened Jared into his stroller, tucking the blanket snugly around his small frame. Outside, the morning air was fresh, the kind that promised relief, if only for a little while.

She needed air. Room to breathe. A place to go, away from *him.* Jane reached for her scarf and coat. "Nolan, do you need anything?" she called from the foyer.

Bay & Basket, the local market, was her temporary getaway. An escape from the confinement of her home. An hour of freedom. Freedom from Nolan.

From the living room, the television droned on. Nolan didn't look away as he reclined on the chair, eyes glued to the television. "Pretzels and Coca-Cola." The order was short and sweet. What came next wasn't. "And cereal. We're out of cereal. Can't you keep track of this stuff? It's the one thing you're supposed to do, and you can't even do it right." His voice became louder and meaner. "Jesus. Do I have to do everything around here?" Jane didn't respond. She didn't even need anything from the market. Being inside that house with Nolan felt like slow suffocation. His temper had deteriorated by the day, and the flowery words he once whispered to her now turned into sharp daggers.

When he was called away to duty, the house became quiet again. Livable. She could watch the programs she liked without being told they were a "waste of time." She could listen to music without being mocked for her taste. She could be herself. Each time Nolan returned, something in him seemed darker, more mysterious. The humiliation, the fear, the anger, the emasculation, whatever he endured during his missions, he brought it back with him. They translated into stinging comments directed at Jane. And when that happened, her thoughts drifted back to Benson. She hated herself for it. But when Nolan was gone, she let the daydreams in. She *welcomed* them. Seeing Benson again was unlikely, and she knew that, but imagining him was safe, and sometimes it was the only thing that softened the days.

Nolan had secured a management position at the distillery, but the Navy still owned him. He could be called away at any moment. Jane quietly counted down the days. She had settled into a bland routine: caring for Jared, occasional trips to the library, knitting by the window, and meeting with another mother in the neighborhood from time to time, with whom she had nothing in common. Recipes and babies dominated the conversations. In another world, this would have been all fine. But in her world, all she wanted was Benson. The longing never went away. She knew, with dull certainty, that she would die with that feeling intact.

At Bay & Basket, Jane hooked a small basket over her arm and pushed Jared down the aisles. She made a point of dressing up before leaving the house. It always made her feel better. And she enjoyed the stares from other men. It gave her a feeling of appreciation and admiration, something she could only experience outside her home.

"Milk. Cereal. Pretzels. Cola." Jane made a silly song from the grocery list to entertain Jared, who was staring up at her from the stroller. Each item was dropped into the basket. She slipped in a candy bar and planned to hide it in her purse at checkout. If Nolan saw it, there would be comments. Lectures.

Mind your calories. You don't want to end up fat and sloppy like Susan. No man wants that around.

Susan lived two houses down, a woman who had gained weight after her second child. Some said it was a medical condition. Nolan called in laziness. He believed a woman's worth lived entirely in her waistline and her ability to keep the house spotless. Jane's parents noticed the changes in his behavior. At first, they tried to ignore it. Then they visited less, making excuses of why they couldn't meet. Eventually, they stopped coming altogether. It hurt them too much to watch their daughter disappear. Jane made an effort to visit them instead. If nothing else, her parents would know their grandson. Marrying the wrong person, she learned, didn't just ruin one life. It bruised everyone nearby.

As she reached the cereal aisle, a melody slipped into her mind without warning.

True love goes on and on.

She hadn't heard that song in years—on purpose. Benson used to play it in his Ford Thunderbird, parked somewhere quiet, while they watched the sun melt into the horizon. She thought she had buried that song along with everything else. Guilt flooded her chest. She was a married woman now. These thoughts came in waves—long stretches of restraint, followed by sudden, overwhelming longing.

Why now? Why this song?

It didn't matter. She stopped overthinking and surrendered to her raw emotions. She hummed the melody freely, suppressing the restraint. Boldness took over, almost like a sense of freedom. Nolan wasn't around.

A man's voice, somewhere down the aisle, hummed the next line of the song. Jane stopped walking. Her pulse thundered in her ears. *I'm imagining it,* she told herself. She pushed the stroller faster, turning the corner. Footsteps followed.

She hummed the tune again, barely audible. The man finished the verse.

Her heart slammed violently against her ribs. Jane slowed, then cautiously peered between two stacks of cereal boxes. A man bent down to the opposite side of the shelf and met her gaze. Jane's chest burned. Heat rushed up her neck, her face red and warm.

No.

It couldn't be.

CHAPTER 52

A BITTER REUNION

Jane ran out of the market absentmindedly, with a basket hung on her arm, and pushed the stroller with all her might. She wasn't sure where she was going. All she knew was that she had to get out.

"Hey, lady, you need to pay for those items!" the shopkeeper shouted, but Jane didn't stop. Her feet wouldn't allow her to. Jared's eyes darted wildly, absorbing his mother's panic. He let out soft cries. Jane slipped a binky into his mouth and watched his trembling lips latch on, the rhythmic motion calming him. Direction vanished. Thought dissolved. Her mind turned into a sea of molasses, and she was drowning in it.

Footsteps followed her. "Jane?"

Her limbs went numb as the anxiety hit hard. With a blurred lens, she slowly turned toward the direction of the man's voice. Her eyes landed first on his polished shoes, then pinstriped wool trousers, then a vest of the same fabric with a crisp white shirt beneath. She followed the line upward until she reached his face.

Benson.

He was more handsome than she remembered. The boyish grin she once loved was still there, softened now by maturity. A maturity that was steady and calming. A masculinity that could undo her all over again, a thousand lifetimes over. All the rage, all the grief, and all the regret she had kept caged broke loose. Tears erupted. Mascara spilled onto her cheeks. She pressed a handkerchief to her mouth, sobbing quietly.

It was too late.

Benson took half a step forward, instinctively wanting to hold her, but then he saw the ring on her finger and the baby in the stroller. He stopped. The town thrived on scenes like this. Benson wouldn't give them something to talk about. He wouldn't ruin her reputation the way others already had. He had caused her enough pain.

She wiped her face with another handkerchief pulled from her bosom, straightened her dress, and lifted her chin. "Why are you here now?" she demanded, her voice sharp and controlled. Jane's posture was direct and strict, almost like a schoolteacher scolding a student for being late for class. But this was worse. Benson's mistake of being late cost her a lifetime of sorrow.

Benson's dimples appeared faintly as he tried to smile, recognizing her range of emotions, remembering how they used to fight. "Jane, I wrote to you every single day while I was gone. You never answered."

She shook her head in disagreement. No words came out.

"I applied to Oxford. I thought distance would help." He exhaled bitterly. "It didn't. So, I came back. I arrived yesterday. My first day at law school starts tomorrow." His hands slipped into his pockets. He mostly looked at the ground. She wasn't his to look at anymore. "I came back to find you," he said quietly. "But not like this." His eyes filled as he nudged a stone with his shoe. Dust lifted between them.

Jane wished she could retrace her steps—her *mistakes*. Everyone knew Nolan was a rebound, a temporary distraction. Jane knew it too, but kept going along with it, because it was the easy way out. Her marriage was a lie.

"What did you expect me to do, Benny?" Her voice splintered. "I hated you. I *hate* you for leaving." Tears flowed again. She didn't bother to wipe them away. "My life isn't what I imagined. You ruined me. You ruined my life." She shook her head. "And I never got your letters. Not one."

His face fell.

"So what do we do now?" she asked quietly. "I can't go back to Nolan. Not after seeing you."

Benson swallowed and avoided eye contact. "You will go home to your husband," he said gently, though it pained him to say those words. "And I will stay away. We'll live our separate lives." He paused. "Maybe this is where our story ends. Too much has happened. I should have come back sooner. But it doesn't matter now, because we were over long before today. I was a fool to think otherwise."

They both knew who had orchestrated this ending. Mr. and Mrs. Jones had succeeded. They got exactly what they wanted.

CHAPTER 53

LOST HOPE

Benson dragged his feet back home with a heavy emptiness in his heart. This wasn't the way he had imagined meeting Jane after all these years. This wasn't the plan. He pictured it so differently in his mind.

A farm. Horses. Jane running into his arms, kissing his face. Children spilling out of the house behind her, maybe five or six. His picture-perfect scenario went up in flames the minute he saw her with the baby. Numbness took over his body, followed by uncontrollable anger. Because no one had cared to inform him about her wedding. Because Jane didn't wait for him. Because his parents usurped the letters. Because his life was never controlled by him. Because his parents were evil and selfish. And because *he* was born to *them*.

A defeated acceptance followed his anger. Jane now belonged to someone else. A closed chapter. A severed tie. Now she was just a memory.

Helpless and hopeless, his feet somehow carried him back to his childhood home, where fought with his parents and where he had secretly brought Jane when the house was quiet. The same house where he now lived. Alone.

His parents moved into their Nantucket villa. He barely saw them. Maybe on Christmas and Easter, and even then, he dreaded those holidays.

Benson finally arrived at the front porch and turned the knob slowly, almost automatically. He mindlessly sat down in the parlor on a velvet sofa, his mind blank. He needed a moment to himself, a moment to digest the news about Jane.

Raj and his new wife were expected for dinner that evening, and he should have been excited about seeing his best friend. He couldn't shake his encounter with Jane. His visit to the market had been for champagne and cheese, nothing more, and he returned with regret and heartache instead. His solemn appearance was evident to Helen. She knew his every expression, his gait, his tone, and what it meant, more than his own mother.

When Benson rehired Helen, she was hesitant, afraid to return to that house again. She agreed to come back as long as she never had to see his mother's face again. Benson didn't dare tell Helen the truth about the necklace. Instead, he absolved himself by hiring her and paying her double of what his parents had paid her.

"Benny, honey, what's the matter?" Helen asked gently. "Aren't you excited to meet your dear friend? I heard he's bringing his wife with him. It's goin' to be such a nice reunion for the two of you, and you'll be meeting *her* for the first time." Benson looked at her with sad, longing eyes, and his lips began to quiver.

"You saw her, didn't you? Oh, my child. I just knew it. You were bound to find out." She cradled his head in her arms. Though a grown man, he needed it. "Everyone here knows she doesn't love that man. Even on her wedding day, folks said her eyes wandered off into the distance, waitin' for you. I heard she walked up the aisle and looked back for several moments. That was the first time a bride had ever stopped to look *backwards*." She paused and shook her head, clicking her tongue.

"It's a bad omen, you know that?" She moved in closer to Benson and whispered, "To look backwards on your wedding day, away from the altar like that. No bride ain't ever supposed to do that. Oh Lord, no. She called the Devil to her. It invokes evil. She did it. She summoned up evil. And now her husband beats her, I hear."

Her last words broke him. *How could he beat her?* Anger surged through him. It was too much information. He broke, sobbing into Helen's shoulder like a child. When the tears slowed, he wiped his face and forced a smile. Benson couldn't take it. He didn't want to know any more. He was helpless; there was nothing he could do. Jane wasn't his to worry about anymore.

"I'm alright," he said, reassuring himself. He tapped her shoulder and stood up.

The doorbell rang. Raj stood there, beaming, his arm wrapped around his wife, a bouquet in the other hand.

Helen answered the door and had them sit in the parlor while Benson brought in a chilled bottle of Dom Pérignon to celebrate the reunion. Tonight was supposed to be joyful. Benson could hear Helen introducing herself and kept them company while he prepared the champagne and cheese platter. Usually, she would take care of that but today was special. He wanted to serve them, personally.

As he walked into the parlor, two warm smiles greeted him as they stood up. Standing before him in his home were Raj and Jane.

CHAPTER 54

A SURPRISE GUEST

Benson's memory flashed back to when he first met Jane by the fountain at Oxford. It was an awkward moment for the two, to say the least, but they both pretended to be meeting for the first time, strangers who had already met.

He extended his hand out toward her, "Hello, Jane. It's lovely to meet you," and motioned for them to have a seat on the velvet sofa. "Raj has told me wonderful things about you."

"Oh, yes, well, he's always got something to say, doesn't he?" she replied in her soft British accent, nudging Raj with her elbow. They sat close, a giddy new couple, filled with excitement for what the future held.

Benson never imagined running into her again after their brief encounter at Oxford, but now she was sitting in his parlor, sipping a glass of champagne, and married to his best friend. There was an eerie truth to the entire situation; he would never be able to rid himself of Jane's memory.

The two had married quietly at the courthouse. Raj's parents had forbidden the match from the start—royalty was meant to marry royalty, period. Jane was the opposite of what they had planned for him. The wedding was practical for them, and unforgivable for his family, who cut ties with him completely. He built a life with Jane, content to live without their approval. Benson respected him for making such a brutal choice but wondered if Raj ever had an ounce of regret. Their friendship solidified. It became stronger and closer than ever. The detachment from their families created a yearning for love, an unconditional love, a family they chose for themselves.

They became inseparable and celebrated birthdays and holidays together. There were long evenings of sitting by the fire during the winter. During the warmer days, they spent time on the shore. Life, for a while, became livable again.

Chubs, Benson's younger brother, joined their orbit soon after. He brought laughter into the house, a reminder of who Benson used to be. Chubs visited often, staying with Benson on weekends. It was his escape from New York City and the expectations of the steel empire. Mr. and Mrs. Jones refused to speak to Chubs, hoping he would abandon Broadway and join the family business. The brothers bonded over a common enemy: their parents.

Benson felt lighter. Almost whole again. Helen watched him from the doorway as he laughed and drank with his new family, coming back to life after his miserable encounter with Jane and the baby at the store. It should have comforted Helen. Instead, her left eye twitched, and in her world, that meant only one thing.

It was too good to be true.

Jane eventually became pregnant. She and Raj welcomed a baby boy, Ravi, who brought even more warmth into the circle. With brown curls and green eyes, he was the perfect blend of the two.

They were happy. Unfortunately, Helen's instinct was right. It was indeed too good to be true.

CHAPTER 55

A STEAMY SITUATION

It was a beautiful spring afternoon, and the courthouse had let out early that day. Benson decided to walk the mile home, absorbing the historical sites along the way.

He was anxious, but in a good way. From the payphone outside, he called Jane. *His* Jane. Nolan was away on duty, and the two had been meeting secretly for the last four months after another accidental encounter. This time, it was at the gas station. She wrote down her address on a receipt. At the bottom, a small note: *'I'll leave the side door unlocked,'* and stuck the small piece of paper on the windshield of his car. Since that day, they never looked back. No questions and no regrets.

When together, the rest of the world became a distant blur. It was only fair in their eyes to make up for lost time. Both felt wronged on so many levels, using every means to justify their actions, actions that would one day come back to haunt them.

Benson stopped by a French boutique around the corner from his house, *Maison Bellamy*. He picked up a gift basket of lavender-scented soaps, Jane's favorite. Something Nolan could never afford to give her. He had it wrapped in a bow, ready to present to her.

Benson went up to his bedroom to change into a robe and prepare for a long bath. A wave of excitement ran through his spine, the same feeling he had in high school before a date with Jane. Across the bedroom floor, clothes were scattered, clothes he didn't recognize. He never left his bedroom untidy. The shower was already on, and steam seeped from under the narrow crack at the bottom of the door. Confused, he put his ear up to the door to confirm the sound—the water was running. Helen wasn't home at this time of day. She took a two-hour break every day to run personal errands.

Subtle moans came from the bathroom walls into the bedroom. There was definitely someone in there. But he couldn't begin to understand who would be in his bathroom. Had someone broken into his home, to take a shower? Benson grabbed the gun from his nightstand drawer and kicked the door open. A cloud of blinding steam surrounded him.

"Who's in here? Show yourself!" His voice thundered into the fog. "I have a gun, and I'm not afraid to use it! Who's in here?"

Barely able to see, he waved the steam away from his face. The fog began to clear once the door was opened, and he could finally see a few feet in front of him. Once his eyes gained focus, Benson was floored, unable to process the scene before him. He froze. No words came out. He just stared at them with a bewildered expression. The gun slipped from his hand and hit the tile with a loud, hollow crack. What he witnessed in the bathroom was something no lifetime could have prepared him for.

CHAPTER 56

CHUBS

Standing there, wet and naked, was Chubs. He was slightly slouched over, hugging both elbows. Next to him was Raj. Both men stared at the floor, unable to look up at Benson, who stood there, mentally paralyzed. His brain was trying to piece together what his eyes couldn't unsee. Benson had no words, so he just ran, gasping for air. He ran down the hallway, down the stairs, and out the front door. He had no destination in mind.

He ran down the street, across the cemetery, and somehow landed on the steps of St. Theresa Church. The scent of the incense was familiar. He prayed. Prayed for his brother. He had heard of such relationships, but no one ever spoke of them openly. He never knew anyone who lived that way, let alone his very own brother and best friend, who was married and had a child. Two of the closest people in his life now seemed like strangers.

Benson didn't understand any of it, but he knew it was wrong, against the word of God. He caught himself in the moment. The faces of his parents flashed across his mind. The faces of the people of Wilshire Pointe joined, snickered, and condemned. Their frowns deepened. Their figures became larger and more oppressive. He heard their laughter. He felt their frowns. Their judgement. Was he becoming like them—judgmental, self-righteous? He lived most of his life trying *not* to be like them.

No, he wasn't one of *them*.

I need to go back. I need to go back and hug my brother and tell him it's okay. Everything will be alright. I'll fight for him. I'll support him. I'll take care of him. No one will ever raise a finger at him as long as I'm around.

Benson knew the town's cruelty too well. His parents were prime examples. The high society of Wilshire Pointe would make his brother's life a living hell if they found out. Maybe in New York City things were different, but not here. He became angry with himself for his reaction. It was insensitive. Unfair.

Benson gathered himself together after an hour or so and returned home. His demeanor was calmer and more settled. On his way, he rehearsed his apology and picked up Chubs's favorite dessert at the bakery. He wasn't quite sure about how to approach Raj. But at that point, his main concern was his little brother, who had always looked up to him for support and guidance. All he wanted to do was hug his brother. Tell him that he loved him. That he accepted his ways and would protect him.

The house was quiet. A bit *too* quiet. There was no trace of Raj.

"Chubs!" He called out; his voice reverberated through the quiet foyer. Benson ran up the stairs and barged into the bedroom. His brother was sitting on the bed, quivering, scared, and cold—still in shock. Still naked. Crying. His eyes were swollen and puffy.

In his right hand was the gun, aimed at his head. Benson took a step forward. "Chubs, wait! I love—"

His brother gave him a brief smile, then pulled the trigger.

It was too late. Chubs was gone. Benson stood there, frozen in time, with a box of freshly baked apple turnovers that Chubs would never eat.

CHAPTER 57

A FINAL FAREWELL

"Today, we mourn the loss of a wonderful man, who sadly passed away due to natural causes." The priest conducted a short ceremony. Only family and close friends attended.

Darlene and Bobby Jones accepted words of sympathy from their friends. He had his arm wrapped around her as she sniffled into an embroidered handkerchief. She was sure to wear her largest diamond ring over the netted black glove. Turning to Benson, Darlene met his cloudy eyes, "Oh, your poor brother. He couldn't take the pressures of life in the big city and his heart just gave way." She said it loud enough for others to hear. Suicide was a scandal and frowned upon by the church. The couple met with the priest beforehand to rehearse the cause of death. His parents, as always, were one step ahead.

Benson rolled his eyes and retorted, "You never made it easy for him either, Mother. You never accepted him. Ridiculed his passion in front of guests, took every opportunity to compare him to the children of your friends, who were successful businessmen." He scanned his mother's appearance with pure disdain. "You, Mother, are partly to blame for why we are here today." She let out a soft cry and looked at Benson in disbelief, waiting for her husband to defend her. His father opened his mouth to scold him. Benson put a hand up in the air to shield himself from the despicable words about to exit his father's lips, "Save it, Father. You know it's true. Your silence just gave way to her cruelty."

Benson turned around and left the ceremony, skipping the luncheon at the country club. He didn't want to be surrounded by all the people who had judged his brother for moving to New York and becoming a Broadway actor. They mocked him when he was alive and now mourned his death. *What phonies*, he thought.

From afar, he could see a man in a long black coat standing behind the bushes, watching. It was Raj. As soon as Raj caught Benson's gaze, he disappeared into the fog. Benson then heard a car drive away from the cemetery grounds.

Benson never saw Raj or his parents again after that day. Out of respect for his brother, he kept his secret. Didn't tell a soul. Not even Jane, Raj's Jane.

CHAPTER 58

THE CHURCH VS. NOLAN

I was going to begin my new role at the whiskey distillery the following week, as the manager, the highest position I'd ever attained. I was finally getting my life together with the small family I had created with Jane. For the first time, I felt like a man with direction, and my pride soared.

Until that dreadful day at church, a Sunday ritual that Jane had continued even when I was on duty. Something that gave her purpose.

It was a crisp December morning. Jane put on her favorite blue dress with a white scarf, and I wore my best suit and tie. Together, we ate breakfast in silence. Jane looked radiant that day as the morning rays reflected off her cheeks. But more recently, Jane felt a bit distant; when I spoke, her attention was elsewhere, far away. I often caught her daydreaming and drifting to another place, a place without me. I figured it must have been difficult for her, being pregnant with Jared while I was away. Something was off, but I never could figure out what.

The church was just three blocks from our house, so we bundled Jared up and secured him in the stroller. Off we went, one happy family. It was a special day; I was going to be recognized and given an award for my service to the country. I was beaming with pride for many reasons.

The historic Church of St. Theresa towered into the sky; a grand structure of red brick, with tall, stained-glass windows that glistened in the sunlight; ceiling fans spun slowly overhead, giving us just enough air in a room packed with fellow churchgoers. A silk material was neatly draped over the pulpit, and behind it, wooden panels lined the wall with a donated quilt hung across a rod that read "Peace and Love." Children squirmed uncomfortably in their Sunday shoes, hair slicked or tied with colorful ribbons that matched dresses.

Something was familiar, yet oddly strange. The town appeared to be split between the haves and the have-nots; all the elite and wealthy folk sat together, whispering to one another. The women held their parasols to their faces so they could quietly gossip with their neighbor. The lower-middle class sat in another section to the back left, obediently waiting for the priest to arrive for the sermon. Jane knew I noticed the changes but smiled and pretended all was normal.

She was always good at that, putting on a façade, masking the lies.

We took our seats towards the back left, where we belonged.

The few wealthy families in town conspired to create more wealth, while the rest of the town's resources were depleted. I found out later about the small, elite group of people whose wealth rose exponentially; they were involved in tax evasion and money laundering. I had no problem with people gaining wealth, but without a moral code, it was wrong, especially while the rest of us worked very hard to get by and keep the lights on.

The priest, Father Clemmons, had given a beautiful sermon about bravery that day, which was the theme in my honor. At the end of the sermon, he announced my name and presented me with a Medal of Bravery. Henry and Judith Whitman offered me a $500 check, and the congregation stood and clapped.

Could you imagine—a standing ovation for *me*. It was a swell day, and my heart was full of joy. I finally felt worthy of something good in my life. Jane and I were on a high, thinking of all the things we would do with the money. *Five hundred dollars*. Home renovations, new kitchen appliances. We acted like it would last us forever. Never before had we received so much money, and all at once. Jane even proposed leaving Jared with her parents so the two of us could go on a cruise. A cruise, simple people like us, going on a cruise. What a dream that would be.

I felt so much gratitude and love for the Wilshire Pointe community.

The next morning, I went back to the church to thank Father Clemmons personally; he was in his office with the Whitmans, and the door was slightly cracked. I could see the Whitmans sitting across from Father Clemmons, in a somewhat hushed conversation, but loud enough for me to hear. My jaw dropped at the words they spoke. The despicable words. They plotted and they schemed, their vindictive brains hard at work. Honest church members were told their donations would benefit sick children in hospitals, the elderly, firefighters, schoolteachers, and so on. By promising these noble contributions, people thought they were making a difference in the community. They had no idea their hard-earned donations would be used in money-laundering schemes, schemes that would enrich only a certain group.

They had bank accounts in places I had never even heard of. They preyed on the people of Wilshire Pointe, even those who lived paycheck to paycheck and made small donations for the sake of the community, hoping to add value in some small way. They snickered, and they grinned while totaling the amounts of funds received within the last six months, referring to the churchgoers as 'simple-minded idiots.'

I was in a state of disbelief. All the sermons he preached about loyalty, love, compassion, and kindness were a scam. Lies. Deceit. I couldn't believe what I was hearing.

As I removed my hand from my pocket, a coin fell out and clinked loudly against the tiled floor.

CHAPTER 59

EXCOMMUNICATED

Henry Whitman approached me calmly, with one hand in his pocket. As he scanned my cheap suit and polyester tie with disgust, he scoffed. "How long have you been standing here, Mitchell?" His demeanor was threatening. A cigarette hung halfway out of his mouth.

"Enough to see through your phony acts," I responded harshly, refusing to back down.

"You think you're high and mighty after receiving that petty award, huh? It was just a show." He blew the smoke from his cigarette on my face and motioned toward the door. "Now, get goin'."

Immediately, I turned away and headed toward the exit. Anger clouded my ability to form the right words. As I left, Henry called out, "Oh, and Mitchell. Remember, you heard nothing." He threw his cigarette on the ground and put it out with his leather Oxfords.

From that day forward, neither Jane nor I attended the church. We didn't want to, and we *couldn't*. We were excommunicated from the church. Father Clemmons was a clever man. He acted swiftly. The story was fabricated. According to Clemmons, I had snuck into the church and stolen valuable items from his office. The rumor had spread across town, and everyone believed him. He was a man of God. How couldn't they?

Edward Smyth, another vicious elitist, had cousins who headed the local newspaper. He paid them to write a shameful article about the theft, which falsely and *publicly* accused me of the crime. I had no way out.

One moment I was seen as a hero, and the next, a shameful criminal. It turned out that the Smyth family was also involved in money extortion using the church as a cover, so it was in their best interest to paint me in a bad light. That was the way to honor me and my service: put a medal around my neck and then snatch it off with lies, a befitting welcome for a Navy veteran.

But as you know, I was able to get my revenge through the dreams, by burning the church down to ashes. And the Whitmans, after the incident with Alice, are living a hellish life with no friends, status, or respect in the community. Why should I be the only one to suffer?

After that incident, we kept to ourselves, and I became a bitter man. With unlimited access to whiskey, I began to drink more, which led me to a downward spiral. I wasn't my best self, but who could be, given the situation? Jane often took the brunt of my frustration. We became more distant, and silence filled the home. The records started to collect dust. We never went on that cruise. The check for $500 was cancelled.

Night after night, I drifted off to sleep in front of the television. This lifestyle continued until I was called back to duty. It was almost February of 1960, and Jane was pregnant, due in July. I couldn't make it back for the delivery.

But there was no reason to celebrate, since I was told it was a stillbirth. *A baby girl.*

CHAPTER 60

CHRISTMAS OF 1960

It was Christmas in 1960 when I finally returned home from duty. To say I was disturbed, both mentally and physically, was an understatement. Everything I had witnessed on the missions, the violence and the feeling of despair, were deeply entrenched in my mind. I couldn't escape it. And the very community I fought for had turned its back on me.

Then came the death of my baby girl. Jane said she never wanted a burial for the baby, so she had the body cremated. The ashes remained in an urn above the fireplace. I personally never felt comfortable with that decision, but given the emotional turmoil it must have caused Jane, I allowed her to do as she pleased.

It was all too much. The drinking started again, slowly. It began with a single shot, then a double, then a triple, until my vision blurred and my speech was affected. Eventually, I stopped counting. Drinking led to depression, and the depression gave way to anger. I knew it was wrong. I knew when the rage was rising, when it was about to turn physical, but I couldn't stop it. It felt as though something feral had taken hold of me, hijacking my body, forcing me to do things I would never do in my right mind.

"Maybe you need help," Jane often suggested. I didn't believe anyone could *help* me. And who would help *me*, the outcast, the black sheep? I was a lost cause. More than that, I didn't trust anyone in Wilshire Pointe. All I wanted was to leave, to start fresh. Somewhere, no one knew us. The distillery became my refuge. It was the only place I still felt respected, the only place where I was *someone.* I managed to keep my position as manager, and it was the only thing I refused to lose.

At home, Jane was already gone. Not physically, but emotionally. She avoided my eyes, as if she couldn't bear to see the man I had become. And who could blame her?

Two years passed. Jane became pregnant again, and our son Mathew was born. Jared was five years old by then. I believed Mathew's arrival would save us, that it would be the turning point we needed. I cleaned up my act. I even started to exercise daily. I stopped downing whiskey. The anger dulled. I took better care of myself. For the first time in a long while, life felt *normal.* Everything was nearly perfect. New neighbors moved in. We became friends. We hosted cookouts, spent days by the pool, and watched movies at the drive-in.

This was the life I had imagined for myself on my wedding day.

I was finally climbing out of a dark place.

Or so I thought. Because it was then, on one cold winter night, when I discovered the letters.

CHAPTER 61

THE ULTIMATE BETRAYAL

Jane was out grocery shopping and had taken both boys with her when I found the packet of letters, hidden on the bottom shelf of our armoire.

There were letters, dozens of them. Letters from another man to *my wife.* I was looking for a tie that had slipped and fallen off the hanger. The distillery was having its annual holiday party for all the workers, and I wanted to get my suit ready and pressed before the party.

The edge of the brown envelope peered from beneath a stack of handkerchiefs. I sat there reading the words, one by one, fuming. These love letters dated back to when I was gone. The betrayal. It was more than I could bear. I finished my flask of whiskey as I read, and with each letter, my anger escalated. The words on the paper reeked of sin. Shame. While I was away, serving my country, my wife was spending time with another man. My hands trembled at the thought of someone else's hands on *my* wife. No. I couldn't accept it. I *wouldn't* accept it. Was there *anyone* whom I could trust?! I saw the name written at the end of each letter, signed in careful cursive—*Forever Yours, Benson Jones*

Quickly, I opened the large envelope to stuff the vile letters back into it. There was one more letter inside, folded and crumpled. I opened it up and read the words. It was a letter from Jane to Benson. She may have hesitated to send it and forgot to throw it away, and somehow it ended up back in this envelope. The words on the page confirmed that the baby girl who supposedly died, Shelby, was alive. And she wasn't mine. She belonged to Jane and Benson. I shot over to the fireplace in an uncontrollable rage and opened the lid of the urn. It was empty. There were no ashes. I slammed it on the ground, watching it shatter into hundreds of pieces.

Who was this Benson Jones? I found his whereabouts through the local directory. Apparently, he was a well-to-do, highly respected lawyer in town who came from an affluent family. Liars surrounded me.

Jane was one of them. My *sweet Jane.* She entangled me in her web and made a mockery of my existence. After everything we had been through, she was the final insult. The one that stung the most. How dare she?

Hot-headed and raging with fury, I got into my car and drove. As I drove towards his home, a thought occurred to me. This town wasn't built to support people like me. I needed to be one step ahead. I swerved the car and drove straight to the Sheriff's office. Before going in, I popped in a few breath mints and straightened myself out. They were surprised to see me there, but I put on a pitiful show. Even a fool would have felt sorry for my pathetic soul, an outcast, who was now a victim of adultery, and I had the letters to prove it. I made sure they knew everything about that dirty affair. I told them about my plan to confront Benson, because if anything happened to me, Benson would be the prime suspect. There would be no way out for him.

I then got back into my car, wiped my fake tears, and put on some music, laughing hysterically while I planned my next move. My car pulled up to a large, U-shaped driveway. Sitting out front was a gold Mercedes-Benz. The landscaping was professionally maintained, and the steps to the stained-glass front door were lined with potted plants. At the entry, there was a large floor mat with a gold J; the wind chimes hung on the front porch and chimed melodiously as I gathered the courage to ring the bell and confront the man who had been secretly meeting with Jane. *My wife.*

I rang the doorbell, and a few moments later, an older African American woman came to the door, dressed in a housekeeper's uniform. She cracked open the screen door. "Yes, sir, how can I help you? If you're sellin' somethin', we ain't interested." Her curious face stuck out two inches from the screen door, waiting for me to tell her why I was standing there on the porch, uninvited.

"Helen, who is it? I don't have time to meet with anyone today. I promised Shelby an afternoon at the library."

SHELBY.

"Sorry, sir, but you heard Mr. Jones. Could you leave your name with me, and I will be sure to give him the message?"

I pushed her out of my way and barged into the house. Today was going to be the day.

CHAPTER 62

THE MAN
IN THE PIN-STRIPED SUIT

A handsome man, dressed in a pinstriped suit, appeared in front of me. He smelled of wealth. His nails were perfectly manicured. His shoes sparkled as if they'd been shined. Rich, handsome, and poised. Everything I wasn't. "Excuse me, sir. You do *not* come into *my* house and push *my* housekeeper! Apologize to her immediately."

I took a step forward. "My name is Nolan. I'm Jane's husband."

His face turned pale as he began to step away and before I could say another word, he called out to his housekeeper with his eyes still fixed on me, "Helen, you can take the rest of the week off. I'll manage everything here."

I wanted to rip his head off, right then and there, but I had to stick with my plan. He removed his wallet and handed Helen a thick wad of bills. I had never seen anyone carry that much cash. Helen froze, one hand flying to her chest, questions filling her eyes. "But sir..."

He firmly interrupted her, "Helen, no discussion. I need you to leave immediately. You may return next week." At that moment, she knew he was serious. Helen gathered her things and walked toward the bus stop without looking back. I waited patiently—something I wasn't used to doing.

Once she was gone, I came back to our conversation. "I said that I'm Jane's *husband. You have been secretly seeing her, and I know it!*"

His face was ridden with guilt as he raised his eyebrows and looked at me coldly, "Jane who? I don't know who you are talking about." His audacity was unbelievable.

"Don't play dumb with me. You know very well who Jane is." I removed the letters from the envelope. "Who wrote these letters?" I snapped, waving them in his face. "You did. To my wife. While I was away, and I know exactly what you both have been up to."

I leaned in. "And she's going to *pay* for it. You better believe it. She will pay for it in the worst way possible."

Benson's eyes twitched, and his lips tightened. I could see his hand form a fist, positioning himself to strike. I continued to taunt him, "I would think twice before laying a finger on me, Benson Jones. The police know everything about this affair. I told them every last detail- they saw the letters. Now, if anything happens to me, they know who to come after."

His eyes widened in disbelief.

I continued to taunt him, "And I also told them you were planning to get rid of me. To get me out of the way so that you could live a happy life with Jane. But I won't ever allow that, not over my dead body. The cops know, Benson. I told them I was gonna confront you about it."

From the corner of my eye, I saw a little girl standing behind the grand piano, peering with red hair and blue eyes. She was a miniature version of Jane. My mind twisted, remembering the words on that letter. *That baby girl didn't die. She was kept a secret. A secret of sin. She was never mine. Jane was never mine.*

It all made sense. My anger rose uncontrollably. He couldn't touch me. I was safe. I could do anything. I lunged toward her. I meant to hurt her. To make her death a reality.

Benson reached over and shoved me to the wall. "Don't you even try to go near her or I'll—" I yelled back at him, "What? You'll what? I am going to kill her, that wretched little girl!"

Benson turned red in the face. I could see a thick vein appearing along his forehead, warning me. Something fierce took over his mind and body. He wasn't afraid of being framed. My plan was failing. Before I could think of my next move, he curled his fist and threw himself at me, slamming my body into the wall. His fist connected with my jaw, and I heard the snapping of multiple teeth. White light exploded behind my eyes, and a sharp ring pierced through my ears.

I caught another glimpse of the girl through my blurry vision. She was outside playing in the backyard. I wished her nothing but grief and a life of misfortune.

With ferocious eyes looking down at me, Benson pressed his fingers tightly around my throat. I could barely breathe. He drove my head into the corner of the television stand.

Once. Twice. The third time, everything went black.

CHAPTER 63

THE COVER-UP

I don't believe Benson intended to kill me. Once he saw the blood from my head pooling onto the floor, he snapped out of his fury and looked startled, almost confused as to what had just happened. He even tried to revive me at the scene. He scurried around the room like a squirrel, frantic and directionless. A big shot lawyer, brought down to his knees. For the first time in his life, he couldn't solve a problem. A problem that he created himself. I could see everything as my soul drifted upward like a silent gas cloud. Hovering. His ability to rationalize was hampered; I saw him pick up the phone, maybe to call the police, but then he looked out the window at Shelby and put the receiver down.

He wasn't a murderer, but his anger turned him into one. Taking a deep breath, he ran out to Shelby and picked her up with one arm. "Honey, I am going to take you over to the Goddards' home, where you can play for a bit." She clapped her hands with excitement. After dropping Shelby off to the Goddards, he was ready to deal with me. Benson dragged my lifeless body into the storage closet beneath the stairway and shut the door from the outside with a latch. He further secured it with a lock and key. It was a tiny storage closet with angular walls that smelled musty, like dirty, wet socks sealed in a box. He then drove to the nearest payphone. "Come on, pick up Jane. Pick up the phone."

"Hello, this is Jane." Benson blurted out to her, "He's gone forever." "What, what do you mean, gone forever? What did you do?" Jane asked impatiently.

Benson was silent.

"Oh my God, Benson Jones!" She let out a cry—not for me, but for Benson, and for what would become of Shelby. She didn't want Shelby to be in a foster home. Her mind was spinning over what would happen next. "We have to come up with something quick. We have to get rid of his body. There's no other—"

Benson cut her off mid-sentence. "Jane, come by tonight, and we'll figure this out. Leave the boys with your mother."

That night, Jane came in through the side door, wearing a long coat and a scarf around her head. Large sunglasses covered her puffy, red eyes. She didn't waste one minute, as if she had been thinking of a way out since the moment Benson had called her from the payphone. She removed her sunglasses and allowed her thoughts to unravel. "All you have to do is tell the cops that you acted out of self-defense. Tell them he threatened Shelby. And that would be the end of it. He never had the best reputation around here, and they would believe you over him. You're a respected lawyer!"

Jane's eyes twinkled with hope. Hope for a fresh start with Benson. She spoke quickly and continued. "Benny, this couldn't be more perfect. He's gone, no longer a problem. The cops will believe you. And we can finally be a fam—"

Benson put one hand up to stop her from the fantasy she was creating. "It's not that simple, Jane. There's something you don't know. Before he came over here, he went to the sheriff's office and told them everything. He showed them all the letters between us, whatever went on while he was away, and mentioned confronting me about it. Nolan even told them I had planned to get rid of him one way or another, so that you and I could be together. He framed me, Jane. He made sure that we could never be together."

Jane's face shrank. She prayed for a way out of her miserable marriage every day. A way to be with Benson. Now that chance was taken from her again. She let out a brief cry and then moved over to Benson's typewriter. "We must make it look like he disappeared. If you're convicted of murder, they'll take Shelby into foster care. I won't allow that." Her motherly instinct kicked in as she began pounding at the keys, typing a letter; it was a fake letter from me to her.

My dear wife Jane,

It saddens me to leave you this note, but it's the best way to move forward. All the years I served in the Navy have changed me in ways I can't undo. I will never quite be the same. I am unfit to be a good father and devoted husband to you, and I am sorry for any pain I've caused you. I am leaving town. Please do not look for me. It's better this way.

Nolan

For three days, I lay in that dark storage room. Benson warned his daughter not to go inside. "There's a boogieman hiding inside. If you go in, he's gonna get you!" It was cruel, but the only way to keep her out. On the third day, my body began to emit a stench; it was time for Benson and Jane to come up with something fast, because Shelby was complaining about the smell. She was a talkative child, and they feared she would tell the neighbors.

Jane brought the keys to the whiskey distillery with her and handed them to Benson. Their movements were robotic and intentional. Benson opened the storage room door and gasped, covering his face; the smell was so pungent, like rotting meat. Black slugs crawled over my neck and face. A truly atrocious scene. That was what was left of me. My clothes were stained with blood as it dried up behind my scalp.

Shelby was peacefully asleep in her bedroom when Benson planned to take my body to the distillery. Quietly, Jane lifted her daughter from the bed and took her home for the night. Jane sent her two boys off to her mother's house, and Shelby stayed with her. Shelby slept on my side of the bed.

Jane lit lavender-scented candles and sang a soft lullaby, sending her back to sleep in minutes. That was the only night she ever had with her daughter.

CHAPTER 64

THE NIGHT AT THE DISTILLERY

It was around two o'clock in the morning, and the town was silent. Benson backed a truck he had borrowed into the garage, so no one on the street could see him. It was a clever move. He wrapped my decaying body in a sleeping bag and tied it with rope, throwing me into the back of the truck.

Benson drove carefully and slowly, avoiding the risk of being noticed by police. It was a smooth, fifteen-minute ride along Shore Drive. I'll never forget the song he played during that drive—"Riders on the Storm." I could hear him humming it. The ease with which he displayed, knowing the body of a man he murdered was in his car, was truly atrocious.

He finally arrived at the distillery; a dark and eerie night awaited him. Three keys jangled from the round key chain—one to unlock the gate at the entrance, one to unlock the main building, and the last key was to my home. Benson made his way through the echoing chambers, dragging my body into the facility. He pulled a hood low over his head and hid his face behind a black ski mask. There was no chance anyone would see him. All the workers were gone, and the next day was Sunday. Luck was on his side. I followed him closely, scraping against the walls, whispering through the crevices, and playing with his mind. And it worked. He jumped with each pound he heard. It gave me such joy.

Inside the distillery, he navigated his way to the back area, where the wooden racks were kept. The dark, damp space was usually bustling with workers. At this hour, the silence was chilling. All he had was a flashlight to guide him through the walkways and endless racks; he refrained from turning on the main switch, in the unlikely event someone would notice the bright lights.

His eyes searched for an empty whiskey barrel, one large enough to fit my body.

With the flashlight, he scanned the aisles of barrels, scouting out the perfect one, and there it was, a 53-gallon barrel. He could manage to fit me inside and roll the barrel into the bed of the pick-up truck with the help of a drum dolly.

There was one caveat. My arms and legs didn't fit.

Benson stood there, debating for a few minutes, but he had to act fast, before the morning light arrived. He wiped the nervous sweat from his forehead, thoughts swirling.

The large barrel couldn't be managed by him alone. The 53-gallon barrel was the only choice, and he had to find a way. An idea came to him.

What he did next was something only the devil himself could do.

CHAPTER 65

BREAKING BONES

It must have taken sheer determination, panic, and ruthlessness to orchestrate what Benson did with my body. He finished off his flask of whiskey to loosen up his inhibitions. The *entire* bottle was enticing to him; however, he needed his wits to complete the task at hand. On the count of three, he bent my limbs in the opposite direction with force, a force so great that my body would be malleable enough to be stuffed into the barrel.

Each time he cracked my bones, he yelled, "For every time you laid your filthy hands on Jane, for every bruise, and for every scar. For every tear..." and a crack would follow. All the anger he harbored for me was unleashed onto my bones; each crack loudly repeated throughout the chamber.

Once my body was forced into the barrel, he secured the lid and toppled it over onto its side. Before he began to push it, I initiated the first few feet, rolling it slowly away from him. When he caught up with the barrel, I rolled it a few feet away again, toying with his mind.

He approached the barrel again, cautiously. As he came close, I began to roll it faster. He chased it down the long corridor, panting, sweating, and out of breath. Sweat dripped down his temples onto his neck, which he wiped with his trembling hands.

I had never seen such fear in another person's eyes until that night. My laughter roared into the night as I rolled the barrel, positioning myself to land directly by the truck, exactly where he wanted me. With quivering hands, he used the dolly to prop up the barrel and secure it in the truck bed.

He missed. The barrel fell and crushed his foot, cracking his left toe. He cursed and shouted in agonizing pain, kicking the barrel with his other foot.

On the second try, it worked. He was intoxicated, scared, angry, and in extreme discomfort—nothing made me happier. He limped back into the driver's seat and turned on the radio, trying to drown out the throbbing pain in his foot.

Driving to the nearest forest, he took the barrel far into the wooded area and left it there; an unknown, deserted wooded area where no one dared venture. It was known as the "Witch's Womb." The solitary, forested land was part of local myths that pagan sacrifices and rituals were held there. The birth of all evil happens in the Witch's Womb, and the community, being highly religious and superstitious, avoided the wooded area like the plague. Children were warned never to set foot in those woods; they may never return. People swore that anyone who entered the dreadful forest never came out alive, and if they did, they weren't the same. It was better to be dead than to come out of there alive.

It really was the perfect plan, carried out with such precision and thought. There in the woods, inside that 53-gallon barrel, my lifeless body would rot, and my presence would be forgotten; a wasted life no one cared about.

But my soul had no intention of resting in peace; it wanted to awaken and disturb the peace of those who wronged me.

I had big plans. I wasn't done yet.

CHAPTER 66

THE CLEAN-UP

When he returned home, Benson found the emerald necklace on the floor of his living room. It must have fallen from Jane's neck during all the chaos.

Jane told me it was a gift from her grandmother, but that was just another lie. She wore that necklace all the time, even when she was with me. Little did I know Benson was always close to her heart. She never took it off. It wasn't just a piece of jewelry; it was a promise.

Benson threw the necklace and the keys to the distillery in an old Puma shoebox. With a bucket full of soapy water and bleach, he scrubbed the walls of the small storage space beneath the stairs. He removed all the boxes and items from the storage room, sprinkled the carpet with a deodorizing powder, and vacuumed it spotless. The door was kept open to air out the room and help it dry. Once the smell of bodily decay had subsided, he began putting the books, blankets, suitcases, and lastly, the Puma box back into the forbidden zone. He was meticulous. There was no trace of a rotting body anymore.

The next morning, Jane mustered up a dramatic saga at the police station. She covered her hair with a scarf and wore sunglasses, gently dabbing her eyes with a handkerchief. It was an Oscar-worthy performance, executed without a single crack. She removed my "final letter" from her purse and handed it to the officer. After reading it, he gave her a sympathetic look and vowed to find me. That was another lie.

The police department began searching for me to prove their commitment to the community and to show they were doing their job, in an effort to display some form of empathy.

The search was immediately interrupted by Father Clemmons. He held a conference with the police department, demanding them to halt the search by the clever use of religious tactics. "Don't waste our valuable resources on a man who abandoned his own family. He's not worth our time. No *real* man leaves his wife and children."

His command turned into a lecture. "Let's not put this man on a pedestal. He deserted his own blood. What kind of example are we setting for the community? Would our savior approve?" The men in uniform nodded in unison. Sheep. They were all sheep. The case was abandoned. What they didn't know was that Clemmons had made a deal with Sheriff Gibson. An envelope was handed over, and the search was stopped.

Clemmons knew I was aware of his transgressions. A sense of relief filled his menacing mind now that he didn't have to deal with me. Missing or dead, it didn't matter to him. I was gone. A thorn was removed from his way. There was no possibility of my exposing his double life—part priest, part gangster.

At least, not yet.

CHAPTER 67

THE HAUNTINGS

The spring air brought the birds back from the south as they gathered by the fountain in the backyard. Helen was watching them from the kitchen window while she kneaded bread and hummed a tune. Benson, at his desk, scanned through pages of a new case at the firm; he had slowly put my demise behind him.

Jane moved on, raising two boys on her own. Her dream of reuniting with Benson remained just that, a dream. It was too risky for them to be seen together, as it would raise suspicion. There was a new Sheriff who would eventually replace Gibson, and he would have the power to reopen the case if he believed there was foul play involved.

That night Helen received a call saying that her mother was sick. She packed her bags and left in a hurry, reciting prayers as she walked down the front steps. Benson offered to drive her, but she insisted on taking a cab.

In the night hours, when he least expected it, when he was all alone, I showed up. Wind passed through his curtains, though the windows were sealed shut. That was me.

His new whiskey bottles were empty before he had the chance to open them. That was me.

Pots and pans clashed in the middle of the night. That was me.

His television would turn on as soon as he shut it off. That was me.

Cabinets would open and close. Faucets would turn on. Appliances would blare through the night. That was all me.

The tricks were endless. His sanity was not. A few nights later, I started the car's engine and put it in reverse. He ran out in his pajamas, screaming. I slammed the car into park and flicked the high beams into his eyes. The music blared, and the disgusting love song he and Jane shared startled his nerves as he cautiously peered through the car window. He was tormented, covering his ears, yelling at the top of his lungs, "Leave me alone!" The Goddards came out of their house warily, tip-toeing onto the front porch. Small faces were glued to the windows, watching the drama unfold as they were awakened from their sleep. After a few of his loony episodes, they eventually stopped associating with him and forbade the kids from playing with Shelby.

It was working. This went on for years. Until one day, he finally cracked and lost his mental capacity to fulfill his duties at his job. Clients complained. His behavior was irrational and odd. They caught him talking to himself during trials, punching the air, sometimes yelling, and other times crying like a child, huddling in the corner. He claimed he was seeing people, hearing voices. His partner at the firm eventually dismissed him.

I broke him. His mental health deteriorated until he was completely homebound.

By that time, Shelby was able to take care of her father. She had to grow up too fast, and as much as I hated her, I realized that she was just a product of his indiscretion. She never asked for any of this. But I had to take my revenge. I wasn't going to allow him to live a normal life. I wanted to torment him until his last breath.

CHAPTER 68

A RECOLLECTION BY HELEN

It was a humid night in July, not a breeze in the air. The trees stood still against the dark skies. And Lord, let me tell you, not a soul came out of their house that night. They stayed put, with their fans on and buckets of ice water close by, towels to soak their feet and heads. The heat had become so intense, and the power had been out for almost 48 hours. Every house was hot and steamy. Folks round here were movin' slow on purpose to save their energy. The devil himself wouldn't be comin' by nobody's place that night. That was one thing we could all be happy about, except Mr. Benson. He ain't believe in all those things. Hell, I don't even think he believed in God, forget the devil. He stopped goin' to service after Chubs died.

I was lyin' about in my bedroom. It was close to midnight. I had a small fan; Mr. Benson loaned me one resting atop my dresser, but it didn't work that night. I just stared at it, wishin' the power to come back on, prayin' to Jesus to save us from that dreadful heat. I liked workin' for Mr. Benson. He was a good man, considerate and kind, and he treated me with respect. I got to thinkin' about the night that woman done threw me out the house—Mrs. Darlene. How could he be her son? She didn't have a kind bone in her body, that woman. Her husband wasn't no better. A snake in disguise. But boy was he a charmin' man. He could sell sand on the beach. Those are the people you gotta stay away from. I'm just glad Mr. Benson ain't turn out like 'em. I got lucky.

The doorbell disturbed my thoughts. At first, I ignored it. Maybe my mind be playin' tricks on me. The heat got me goin' loony. Who's gonna show up here at midnight? Then I heard it again. Mr. Benson must have been down in a deep sleep cause he ain't heard nothin'. As I passed by his bedroom, I heard him snorin' like a damn train whislin' through the night with no intention of stoppin'. No wonder he ain't heard that doorbell. He had been workin' late nights on a new case and he must've just collapsed outta exhaustion.

I tiptoed down the hallway, afraid of who's at the door. Now, what I saw on that doorstep was the last thing I ever expected. It won't no burglar. It won't no mad man. It won't nothin' scary at all.

It was the sweetest little baby girl I'd ever laid my eyes on. She was lyin' in that pink bassinet, makin' all those noises that babies do. My eyes glanced around, but nobody was in sight. They must have left that baby and run off into the night.

I ain't ever had no baby of my own, but I seen' my aunts takin' care of my cousins, and I was the oldest, so I'd always be helpin'. Next to the bassinet was a bag of cloth diapers, some clothing, and homemade formula. That baby came prepared. A small note was hangin' outside the bag. I picked it up and unfolded it.

Please take care of Shelby.

Shelby. What a beautiful name for a little girl with red strands of hair on that cantaloupe-shaped head. But who in their right mind would leave such a sweet pie on this doorstep? And why ours? I brought the baby inside and took her straight to my room. I was so nervous about how Mr. Benson would react in the mornin', but I was excited, too. What a cute little thing to be growin' up in this house, almost like Santa Claus brought us a real-life doll. It would do Mr. Benson some good. Make him smile a little more. He had become so serious lately.

And my prayers were answered. That baby girl brought so much happiness into Mr. Benson's life. I ain't ever seen his big blue eyes light up the way they did when she ran toward him, clappin those stubby little hands together. He took care of that baby like she was his own. I ain't have the courage to ask him nothin', because I knew my place. At the end of the day, I was still his housekeeper. I just helped him with whatever he needed, cause it warmed my heart to see the joy that baby brought to him.

Until one night, when Shelby was a little over three years old, things started to change.

I heard a knockin' on the door. It was loud, and it was an angry knock, and a man had pushed me out of the way. I was told to leave, and I did just that. Ain't come back for another week. Those were Mr. Benson's orders, and I never argued with him.

But I swear on the Lord, things changed after that day.

I've always been able to sense evil. And I could sense it. It was in the house. It lived with us, in every nook and cranny. We were surrounded by it. Mr. Benson would wave me off. I tried so hard to tell him. He ain't ever listen to me. It was the start of somethin' bad. Real bad.

The hair on my arms would stand tall. And it wasn't even cold. That was the first sign.

Many mornings, I'd see the window open in Shelby's room. I asked her if she opened it, and she said no. A nice man in the window opened it every night. She was drawin' on a piece of paper, casually tellin' me about this *man*, who whispered into the night. Mr. Benson said children often have imaginary friends. "It's a psychological phenomenon; a completely normal and healthy part of development that helps with emotional growth. She's a creative child and loves to use her imagination," he would always say. But I knew. That wasn't no imagination. Cause the air in her room would be cold. I'd cover her back up with the blanket and shut the window.

I put a holy cross in her room, on the wall, with Mr. Benson's permission, of course. He just laughed at me, shakin' his head. He ain't believe in all that religious stuff. "Whatever makes you feel comfortable,

Helen. I really don't mind. "Relieved, I got myself a hammer and a nail, hung it right over her bed, and said, "Lord, please protect this child."

The next mornin', I went in to wake her up and get her dressed for breakfast. Again, the window was open. The December chill had made the room feel like an icebox. Her blankets were off, and she was sweatin'. I ain't understand. Why was she so hot? I looked up, above the bed. The cross was still hangin' there, but it had turned itself upside down. And then I just knew. I knew somethin' was in that house. Nobody would believe me, but after that day, I saw objects be movin' around in the kitchen. I would put a pan inside the cupboard, and it would be out in the morning. The milk was out of the fridge, opened. The water faucet would turn on and off before my own eyes. I tried to tell Mr. Benson, and he told me I need to see a doctor. My head wasn't right. I had a "mental condition," and if I didn't stop this behavior, then he'd see me unfit to care for Shelby. It just kept getting worse.

I saw faces in the mirror above my dresser every night at 3 a.m. I couldn't sleep. I was tormented. Sometimes there was a shadow at the beneath the door—walkin' across.

Mr. Benson was already sleepin' in his bed, so it wasn't him. The doorknob would move like somebody was openin' it from the other side. I pulled the blanket up as far as I could and prayed. But nobody ever came in. I barely slept at night and would often doze off on the sofa in the afternoon. I sprinkled salt across all the doors and windows, any opening to the house, and in the corners of each room as a way to cleanse the house of any evil spirit.

I was not losin' my mind. I knew what I saw. I knew what I felt.

Benson had enough of my insisting on this evil in his home. He gave me some money—a good amount—and said he was sorry he had to let me go. Now, I understood from his point of view; he thought I was goin' crazy. This was different than what his mama had done to me. His eyes were swollen up cause I know he cried before he let me go. It wasn't easy for him. But I told him to take care of him, and that precious girl, cause something' was comin' for 'em, *and it wanted me gone.*

Before I left that house for good, I visited the small church I went to as a child and had the minister bless a small vial of water. I threw the holy water from that blessed vile onto the front steps of Mr. Benson's home.

Backing away, with fear in my eyes, I watched that blessed water sizzle into steam, and disappear into the air.

CHAPTER 69

1958 FATHER CLEMMONS' LITTLE SECRET

The 256-pound beast of a man, towering just over six feet tall, was an intimidating figure within the church. Donning his long robe, usually dark green on ordinary days, overlaid by a chasuble, he moved with a slight slouch. A golden stole hung around his neck, stopping just above his ankles. Hairy toes protruded from the leather sandals he wore daily, exposing dry, scaly skin beneath the hem of his robe. Often, he used a pencil to scratch the inflamed flesh of his feet, keeping it tucked behind his ear like a medical device. Clemmons's overweight body hid behind layers of holy fabric; the outer appearance served as a deceitful mask for the malicious activity that festered beneath. His wide, elongated nose, with a slight bump, sat between two round, owl-like eyes, shielded by woolly eyebrows. Scorn usually accompanied his expression, unless he required a favor. Then he could summon a smile and put on a convincing show of warmth to get what he wanted. Those who truly knew him saw through the act, but fear kept them silent.

"How did this happen?" he snarled.

Sister Rosa clutched her rosary, her hands slick with sweat. "I don't know." She did. She knew exactly how they had arrived there. Her skin carried a golden warmth. Almond-shaped brown eyes and black wavy hair were her two most notable features, although her hair was always pulled back and covered in a veil. A large cross hung from Rosa's neck, one that her mother had given her while in Mexico. It was the only memory she had of her mother, who had quickly put it around her neck before she and her sister ventured to Wilshire Pointe.

Clemmons looked at her with disgust. "Stupid woman. Stupid, stupid woman." Spit dribbled along the side of his mouth as he shouted in anger. His coffee-stained canines peered from under his lips. The unusually chiseled daggers protruded even when his mouth was at rest.

Stuttering, Rosa continued, "I th-thought I had the t-t-t-timing of the month right. I'm n-n-not sure how this happened."

Clemmons scoffed, then banged his hand on the desk, causing her small frame to jump.

"Well, fix it. Get rid of it. Go away for some time. We cannot have this child." He stepped closer to her. "And don't you dare tell a soul. This cannot get out. Do you understand me? Look at me when I'm speaking to you." Clemmons towered over her petite body. She could almost feel his warm breath hovering over her, like a swarm of angry bees threatening to sting her if she refused to comply.

"I said, do you understand me?" His low growl created a whirring sensation in her stomach.

"But it wasn't my fault," she said. "I never wanted it. You crept into my room. It's not my fault!" She never forgot the feeling of dread that overcame her each night.

Night after night, she heard his soulless footsteps clunking down the hallway and the door creaking open. To her, that sound was equivalent to the sound of death. Clemmons snuck into her room and had his way with her, clamping his filthy hands over her mouth to keep her quiet. He had no shame, and he smelled like a sealed bag of raw onions that had been opened after a week. It was rumored that Clemmons barely showered, and some would discreetly cover their noses as he walked by them in the halls of the church.

Sister Abigail shared a room with Rosa. She heard everything but pretended to be asleep. In the morning, Rosa woke up in agonizing pain, at times unable to get out of bed, bruised, both mentally and physically. Sister Abigail stared at her with sympathy but was helpless and too afraid to utter a word, carrying on as if nothing were wrong, as shame filled her heart. Rosa never resented her because Clemmons was a man you didn't dare cross. One word against him could land you in the cemetery next door.

Every night, Rosa prayed. She prayed for him to meet the most brutal of deaths; she cursed him in secret. But those desperate prayers went unanswered. Every night, her faith in God kept diminishing until it was completely depleted. It went on for six months, until the nausea awakened her one morning. She knew it wasn't something she ate. It was something far worse.

"Shut up, you foolish woman! Know your place!" Rage flooded his eyes. "I don't want to hear another word from you! Now get out and make sure you have all this figured out before tomorrow. I want a solid plan! And if you don't come up with one by sunrise, I will have you and that dreadful thing growing inside of you forever silenced!" He turned his face away.

Rosa dared not lift her eyes to meet Clemmons's gaze. She kept her eyes on the floor and cautiously moved toward the door. She had been kicked by him before and knew his anger could pounce on her again. She stopped upon hearing footsteps in the hallway.

A man's voice came through from the small crack in the door. "We will adopt the baby and raise it as our own."

CHAPTER 70

THE MAN AT THE DOOR

Father Clemmons and Rosa both jerked toward the man standing in the doorway, his hat pulled low. Their secret was out. Clemmons, now the sheep, stood there with nowhere to hide. There was no way for him to distort the truth.

Edward Smyth removed his hat and walked through the door. "For the last two years, Theresa and I haven't been able to conceive a child, and it's taken a toll on our marriage. Rosa, you may stay in our home in Nantucket. A full-time nurse will care for you while you prepare for the birth and help you navigate the delivery of the child. After the delivery, we'll have our driver pick up the child, and you'll then move to another town and start a new life for yourself. Sufficient funds will be given to you; money won't be an issue for you. We'll make sure of that. *There is your plan, Clemmons. It'll be our little secret,*" he said sarcastically. Rosa couldn't face him. Her back remained turned toward the wall, too afraid, too ashamed.

Edward cleared his throat as he fidgeted with his Rolex watch, "Furthermore, Clemmons, to cover up for your indiscretion, I demand a lump sum of $10,000 in cash." It was the exact amount he planned to give Rosa once the baby was born, minus a few thousand he would quietly keep for himself. Edward Smyth never missed an opportunity to profit.

Clemmons exploded. "Well, that's bribery! How despicable, you dreadful excuse for a man!" His anger quickly dulled, and he shrank to silence, realizing the irony of his statement. Edward shook his head from side to side and clicked his tongue, showing pity toward Clemmons. "Oh? Isn't *that* the perfect example of the pot calling the kettle black? You know, Clemmons, my cousin is the head of *The Bayview Beacon*. They always have an insatiable appetite for such *sensational* stories, waiting for a leak. It will just take one phone call. Thirty seconds, and your life, everything you represent, will be a complete mockery." Edward reached for the phone on Clemmons' desk.

Clemmons stopped him. "No, no, no. There's no need for all that." He slid the phone out of Edward's reach. "We will arrange for Rosa to prepare for her move. She will leave her room at the church grounds when everyone is asleep. The story will be that a family emergency arose, and she had to leave town immediately. As for your payment, you will get it by the end of the week."

Edward scratched the back of his neck. "And I never came here expecting you to be in this predicament. I just came by to deliver this packet." In Edward's hand was an unmarked brown envelope. "But I'll refrain from giving it to you until I receive my funds."

Before Edward left, he turned his face to the side slyly, "Next time, show some respect for the church, or at least be more careful, would you? The community sees you as a holy man. You wouldn't want to break their spirit."

Edward scoffed, then left the room. The door slammed behind him.

Clemmons's face turned red, and with shaking hands, he threw a Bible at the door after Edward left. Rosa stood in shame and silence, quietly weeping.

"Go to your room and pack your belongings!" shouted Clemmons. His pride resurfaced as he stormed out of the room.

Meekly, she scurried to her room, put all her things in a suitcase, and waited in silence. Rosa was sent directly to the Smyths' property in Nantucket, where she was cared for by a home nurse. Nine months later, Rosa gave birth to a baby.

CHAPTER 71

THE BABY

He had the same olive complexion and dark hair as his mother.

Knowing Rosa would never be a part of the boy's life, the Smyths gave her one mercy: the chance to name him. In a world that could be cruel and judgmental, resilience came to her mind. So did fluidity. She imagined him growing into a family where he would look nothing like them, a lion raised among sheep. Frowns and stares would follow him everywhere. Peers might bully him. Others would envy his sudden fortune because of the Smyth name. He would need to rise above it all, and move forward without resistance. To flow.

Rio. No, not Spanish. That would set him apart even more. *What did Rio translate to in English? River.* A strong and beautiful name. River Smyth.

After the birth, Rosa was immediately sent from Nantucket to a town two hours inland with $7,000 to begin her new life. The Smyths wanted her erased. Theresa Smyth never saw the birth mother, and Edward barely had a chance to look at Rosa; her face had been turned away when he overheard everything that night.

The people of Wilshire Pointe knew River had been adopted, but they never knew the real reason why.

Four years later, Edward and Theresa Smyth had a child of their own. His name was Johnny. Once Johnny was born, Edward placed an ad in the paper for a housekeeper who could cook, clean, and care for the children.

In return, she would be given her own living quarters. Theresa Smyth had no interest in domestic matters; she was far too busy expanding the Smyths' jewelry empire. A golden opportunity arrived at Rosa's doorstep.

She had been waiting for an opening—a way to be close to her son.

CHAPTER 72

MARIA ST. CLAIRE

Answering the ad as "Maria St. Claire," she had cut her hair short and lost nearly twenty pounds, unrecognizable from her former life as a nun.

The change wasn't just physical. Rosa had experienced a mental rebirth. The shy, timid nun was replaced by a fierce woman, aware of her worth and her power, and gripped by vengeance. After River was snatched from her arms, Rosa made a promise to herself. No one would ever take advantage of her again. She had taken special classes in home management to prepare for this role.

Rosa rang the doorbell of their towering estate. The fear of being recognized gnawed at her, but Mr. Smyth welcomed her warmly, without any hesitation or doubt. She pleasantly greeted him, dressed in a professional, crisply ironed housemaid's uniform with an apron, hat, white tights, and white shoes. Rosa's hair was up in a net to display her tidiness and concern for hygiene, and her fingernails were perfectly clipped. She was ready.

Wiping her shoes on the mat, Rosa stepped inside the opulent home of her son. It smelled of patchouli with a hint of cigarette smoke. Her first task was to arrange a simple meal, but Rosa was ten steps ahead. She prepared a beautifully seasoned pot roast with scalloped potatoes using the ingredients she found in the kitchen.

The most difficult part was controlling her emotions when seeing

River for the first time in five years. She closed her eyes, said a small prayer, and held back the tears. "Did you wash your hands before dinner, young man?"

Mr. and Mrs. Smyth glanced at one another and nodded with approval.

While the family was at the table relishing their meal, Rosa bathed, changed, fed and rocked Johnny to sleep. He had slept through the night for the first time in three months. She then cleared the table, washed the dishes, and swept the floor, leaving the kitchen spotless and ready for the next morning.

"Alright, River, honey, please go up and change into your pajamas after washing up. Get in your bed, and I will read you a bedtime story." This was the moment she longed for the most, time alone with her son.

Maria St. Claire was the first person they interviewed. She was hired on the spot.

River was her main reason for returning. But she had one more reason. *Revenge.*

CHAPTER 73

WHAT REALLY HAPPENED TO JOHNNY

Fumbling around his father's desk, Johnny was looking for glue and a stapler for his school project. The desk was covered in stacks of papers, folders, and newspaper clippings.

Beneath the mess, a folder caught Johnny's attention. It was labeled *CONFIDENTIAL*. That word itself piqued his curiosity. He hesitated, then slipped it into his backpack and went upstairs to discover what was so confidential.

Johnny locked the door behind him. No one was home, but it served as an extra layer of security. In the folder was a detailed document outlining Clemmons's thievery from the church's patrons and the accounts of where all the money was being transferred. Two of the main families involved were the Smyths and the Whitmans. Some of the funds went to Sheriff Gibson as payoffs for overlooking certain crimes committed by goons. Goons hired by Clemmons.

Though he was a tender teenage boy of fifteen, he had a high regard for morals. Johnny couldn't tolerate any form of corruption or shadiness; he witnessed enough of it at his elite prep school, often resenting his status. To learn that his parents were involved, and through the church, gnawed at what little patience he had left. He made a copy of the documents at the public library and hid the copy under a loose baseboard in his bedroom.

The following day, River dropped him off at school. It was supposed to be the last day of school before summer began. Johnny skipped class, called a cab company from the nearest pay phone, and had it drive him to the church. He bypassed his parents and went straight to the source—Clemmons.

The closer he got to the church, the angrier he became. Once the cab pulled up to the church, Johnny jumped out. Enraged, papers in hand, he marched straight into Father Clemmons's office. Some would call it bravery, others, sheer stupidity.

"What is *this*?" Johnny violently waved the papers in front of his face. Clemmons looked at them briefly. "Now, son...you don't understand what you're holding," Clemmons said quietly, in a calm tone. "Don't call me son, you swine!" Johnny bit back.

"I would suggest you calm down and hand me the papers." Clemmons's tone turned stern, almost threatening.

"What are you going to do, *Father?*" taunted Johnny.

Clemmons knew many people who were willing to do his dirty work for a price. He saw the rage in that boy's face and knew it was a matter of time before the news got out. Clemmons would do anything to save face. "You will pay for this!" Johnny exclaimed as he ran out with the papers in his hand.

Clemmons made one phone call. "Handle it immediately. And no evidence."

Johnny took his usual route back home from the church. Footsteps followed him, but he paid no attention until they got louder and closer. Pretty soon, he felt himself running. The four guys behind him had their faces covered in black ski masks and chased him into a deserted alley. They began to beat him to a pulp. The main goon held a gun to Johnny's head and forced him to snort cocaine–a first for Johnny; the remaining bags were then planted in his backpack.

It was more than his body could take. Johnny went into cardiac arrest and collapsed..

PART 3

CHAPTER 74

THE RECKONING

The moon has assumed Nolan's face, illuminating the sky, as his voice trumpets through the atmosphere.

"You have been living under the shadow of lies. All of you. The entire town of Wilshire Pointe. The injustice can't go on. It's high time you open your eyes to the monsters who walk amongst you. This town needs an awakening, and I am here to give it to them. Now, listen carefully. In three days, if my body is not found and a proper funeral is not given to me, the entire community will go under. The earth will swallow everything in sight. The truth needs to be told. Let them know. Expose them! You have three days, otherwise—"

The dream shifts to a scene where the earth engulfs the town. Flames erupt. People are screaming; there are landslides, floods, power outages, and finally, a massive earthquake swallows Wilshire Pointe, leaving no trace of the people or the town.

Shelby, River, and Jared were jolted awake by a loud, harsh *CAW!*

Seated at the window was a large, black crow, looking inside. It tapped on the glass three times before flying away, disappearing into the dusky clouds.

CHAPTER 75

THE LAST RESORT

It was up to us.

Without any time to waste, River, Jared, and I showed up at the police station. With no plan or script, we asked to speak with Sheriff Ramsey. Luck was on our side. Gibson retired last year as his health didn't allow him to continue. Ramsey had taken over, and the difference was immediate. Petty crime dropped. Traffic stops slowed. Kids straightened up—no longer bashing in mailboxes or pestering their neighbors. There were occasional flare-ups, but far fewer than before.

People trusted him. He was what the town needed: honesty and reliability. The question wasn't whether he was capable; it was whether he'd believe a word we were about to say. But we were out of options. This was our last resort.

We waited in the sitting area until the secretary called our names and motioned us to follow her to Ramsey's office. It wasn't too long ago that we filed the complaint about the bloody knife in Jared's home—the one the cops never found. We were already on their radar. Officer Leonard saw us walking by his desk and muttered something under his breath along the lines of "these kids, again?" Our reputation wasn't so great.

We stood in front of a door with a simple nameplate screwed into the front: *SHERIFF SEAN RAMSEY.* The secretary gave two knocks. "Come in," he shouted from behind the door. He cleared his throat in preparation.

The room was sparse. A desk. A leather chair. Two metal chairs that looked intentionally uncomfortable. No clutter. No warmth. Just business. Fit, tall, and serious, he had no time for games. Ramsey studied us as we entered. He was calm, yet watchful, attentive to our movements, twitches, and expressions. "You kids look like you've got somethin' serious to say," he said, fingers steepled. A straight shooter. We'd heard he had no patience for wasting time.

He sensed our anxiety. "Go on. Take the floor."

I inhaled slowly. "There's no easy way to explain this," I said, "But Nolan Mitchell, the case from 1963, he didn't simply disappear. He was murdered."

Ramsey leaned back. A minute-long pause heightened our anxiety. He knew about the case of Nolan Mitchell's disappearance; it was all over the local news and became quite a story in Wilshire Pointe at the time. Ramsey squinted at me. "And where exactly are you getting this information from?"

Jared closed the blinds and leaned forward. He wiped his palms on his jeans. This caught Ramsey's attention.

With desperation in his eyes, Jared continued. "Sheriff, we wouldn't be here if we didn't think you could help us. The church fire. The flood. Alice Whitman. None of it was random. It's all connected. We have information. That's why we're here."

Silence filled the room. Ramsey looked at the floor, then looked up at us.

"Ya'll been smokin' some grass?" Ramsey asked in all sincerity. "I won't tell your parents. It would just be a warning this time around." Jared interrupted. "My father, Nolan Mitchell—he wants his body found. He was murdered, then put inside a barrel and dumped somewhere in the Witch's Womb."

Ramsey's jaw tightened. His green eyes pierced straight through Jared. With great intensity, he asked, "And who killed him?"

The room went still. Jared looked to Shelby for help.

"My father," Shelby stated matter-of-factly. "And Jane Mitchell helped cover it up."

Ramsey took a deep breath, almost uncertain of what to do with that information. Shelby didn't know what else to confess. They waited.

Something in River stirred. He had been quiet for too long. "Sheriff Ramsey, with all due respect, we came here seeking your help. Give us twelve hours. Cadaver dogs. A police unit. If you find nothing, we'll accept whatever consequences you see fit. But if we're right—"

Ramsey raised his hand, motioning him to stay silent. He studied us. Really studied us. His silence was torturous. Finally, he spoke.

"You get twelve hours. Tomorrow. I will bring four officers and two dogs. This stays quiet. If this is a stunt, every one of you will regret it."

We nodded. A nervous excitement rushed through our bones. It was hard to believe that Ramsey was on board with our mission.

"7:30," he said. "Be ready. We're gonna do this fast so word doesn't leak. My position is at stake here."

River and I made our way to the door, but Jared stood still, refusing to leave just yet.

"Can I help you, son?" Ramsey asked, tapping the tip of his pen on the desk.

"Sheriff Ramsey, why did you agree to help us, especially after our false alarm with the knife?" Jared genuinely wanted to know, especially since he was the one who called the cops last time.

Ramsey shifted uncomfortably in his chair, then stretched out his shoulders. "I was a young man during the case of your father's disappearance, new to the police force. I overheard a conversation Gibson had with Clemmons. Let's say it didn't sit well with me. But at that time, I had to put my head down. Not anymore."

We left his office unable to speak—terrified, relieved, and painfully aware that by this time tomorrow, everything would change.

CHAPTER 76

THE WITCH'S WOMB

The alarm rang at 6:00 a.m. sharp. We stayed at Jared's house. Our movements were quiet as we got ready for our mission. Boots, jackets, and backpacks were already packed. River cooked without speaking—eggs, toast, bacon, and a side of anxiety.

From my peripheral vision, I caught Jared peering into his mother's bedroom. I asked him about it. "I look in there every morning, hoping she dropped in overnight. I just need her back, for me, for Mathew. He's gonna be home from camp in the next few days. I don't even know what I'm gonna tell him." His eyes swelled.

There's not much I can say to console him. She's my mother, too.

By 7:25 a.m., we were seated in the station's waiting area. The building felt hollow. The break room was empty. The coffee pot was off. Ramsey had planned it that way. He wanted us gone before the rest of the department arrived. The officers on this mission walked in, reluctant and annoyed. We interrupted their usual schedule.

Two dispatch Jeeps carried us toward the Witch's Womb. No radio or conversation. Complete silence until we arrived.

The Witch's Womb boasted thirty acres of dense forest that had fed the town's legends for generations, and we were about to enter it, the most forbidden area in Wilshire Pointe. In the daylight, it looked ordinary. Almost welcoming. Birds darted through the trees. The air smelled clean. It was scenic; nothing we would have expected. That somehow made it worse. Ramsey split us into two teams. River and I went with Officers Warren and Duncan, and the cadaver dog, King. Jared went with Ramsey and the second team, Hunter pulling ahead on the leash.

By 9:00 a.m., we were moving swiftly through the forest. We worked from opposite ends, pushing inward. The forest was quiet in a way that felt almost too cooperative. Red maples stretched overhead and towered into the sky. Thorns snagged our pants as we trudged through high shrubbery. Sweat soon soaked through our shirts, leaving damp spots. A clear day was on our side. No wind, no beating sun, and no rain. It was ideal and comfortable. Almost *too* ideal, as if Nolan had carefully orchestrated the perfect conditions to lure us in.

Three hours passed. We regrouped briefly to eat. No one spoke. Ramsey wiped his forehead and didn't look at us. By late afternoon, irritation turned into resignation. Flashlights clicked on as the daylight began to fade. When the teams met again at the center, there was still no evidence of Nolan. I couldn't bring myself to look at Ramsey. Jared and River wore expressions of defeat. The Witch's Womb felt harmless now. Just trees. Just another story the town told itself and believed. Maybe it was too boring here, and people needed a juicy story for entertainment.

We were preparing to apologize. The three of us huddled together, rehearsing the shameful speech we would give to Ramsey and his team.

"You kids may have a lot of explaining to do," taunted one of the officers. It was at that point when his flashlight flickered.

Once.

Twice.

It wasn't just his flashlight. All of them flickered in unison.

The officers cursed the batteries.

But we knew.

CHAPTER 77

DREAD IN THE AIR

We felt a wild gust of air. It was speaking to us, warning us to be prepared for what was to come. It wasn't a question of *if* it was coming, but when.

The atmosphere mirrored that dark day in the university courtyard. The day Alice was taken from us. The air was the same. The temperature was the same. The feeling we had was the same. King and Hunter whimpered, tails tucked between their legs, refusing to budge any farther. The officers snuck glances at one another, confused. They had never seen this kind of strange behavior in the dogs before. They were always in protection mode, but tonight things were different. The canines felt a pulse. Something alive beneath the ground. They no longer wanted to be there, and for good reason.

The temperature dropped rapidly by at least 30 degrees, and a chill laced the air. We weren't prepared for it. I clutched my elbows, my teeth chattering—not just from the cold, but from fear. River wrapped his arms around me, rubbing them to create warmth. I knew he was just as scared, if not more. In the distance, wolves howled. The moon was full tonight, its beauty masking an omen.

The officers attempted to maintain their strong façade, but deep down, they knew something wasn't right.

A faint sound of crunching leaves interrupted the silence and compounded our fears. Hunter and King pulled hard at their leashes, desperate to move back toward the Jeeps, whimpering as they strained against us. They pulled so hard that they almost dragged one of the officers through the leaves.

Then they stopped. Their furry bodies went into submission. They stared toward the noise, almost becoming statues, their bodies quivering. The sound of crunching leaves grew louder as it approached, something heavy moving along with it. The darkness clouded our vision. The flashlights began to flicker uncontrollably, and the officers shook them in hopes they'd adjust, but instead, they went completely out. Darkness.

The noise paused. A brief silence followed.

We sighed in relief. A part of us hoped the mission would fail because the fear had become too intense to bear. The bargaining began in our minds: community service, jail time, anything. We'd take it. Just let us get out of here alive and in one piece.

But the Witch's Womb had other plans. It wanted us to stay.

After about a minute, the flashlights snapped back on. They didn't just turn on, but shone even brighter than before, as if they wanted a full audience.

Hunter and King collapsed to the ground, paws covering their eyes, trembling.

Then it appeared.

A massive barrel rolled toward us, slow at first, then faster with every second. There was no wind pushing it. No slope.

It rolled with a mind of its own.

CHAPTER 78

THE FINAL CONFRONTATION

The mist cleared to make way as the barrel rolled violently, and its contents slammed against the wood in a rhythmic beat. We were so engrossed in the barrel while we watched it roll on its own, until we realized that it wasn't alone.

Close behind it, trailed a tall, feminine figure with disheveled hair. The figure appeared to be in torn and tattered clothing, floating off the ground. The disfigured body, with limbs bent backwards in nearly impossible angles, possessed a demonic grace while swiftly moving toward us. Bony feet protruded from under her long dress; not an ordinary dress, but a wedding gown with streaks of blood soaked across the front. Our breathing stopped. No one moved. The figure hovered a few feet in front of us.

River grabbed my hand as I let out a scream.

Hanging around her neck, glowing as bright as ever, was the necklace with the oval green pendant. It was unmistakably Jane. But a warped version of her, with hollow eyes that rolled back into her skull. A dirt-smeared face peered through the netted veil, cut, bruised, and barely human. Fingerprints faintly stamped the center of her neck.

One of the officers fainted, and the others were huddled together with the three of us, horrified. They looked to us for answers, but we had none. Ramsey was unable to speak; his eyes locked onto the figure. A cigarette hung helplessly between his lips, on the verge of collapsing.

Officer Stanley tried to flee the scene, but as he lifted his leg, the air became so thick that it made it difficult for him to move; his body froze in midair.

No one was going anywhere. It wouldn't let us.

The witch-like figure presented herself from behind the barrel, "Looks like I brought everyone together." Her hideous eyes stared directly at River, Jared, and me. "You three did well. YOU DID WELL. You listened," she screamed and broke into an evil laughter. The despicable voice coming from her mouth was not hers—it belonged to Nolan. Jane's lips moved, but the words were his.

I covered my ears. Flame erupted from her mouth along with the stench of whisky.

Circling us slowly, Nolan spoke through Jane's body, "You're wondering why Jane's body is here. Well, I called her, and like an obedient wife, she came to me. She walked all the way here. Barefoot and wearing nothing but her wedding gown, she returned to her loyal and faithful husband. The voice turned darker. "Where she belongs."

"What did you do to her?" Jared roared. Shedding his fear, he demanded to know where his mother was. The ghastly figure shot a look at Jared. Smiling, the voice of Nolan addressed Jared with sarcastic sympathy, "She looked so beautiful, but her beauty would never mask what she and that Benson did to me; I will never forgive them for that. A disgrace. That's all your mother ever was! She got what she deserved. Now she's with me, forever. Didn't you find it strange that your mother was missing for so many days, Jared?"

His tone turned melancholic, and the hideous figure donned a drooping face, "Oh, my son, Jared, you have grown into a young man." She took her long, rotten hand and placed it on his head, causing Jared to flinch in disgust. Her nails were filled with dirt and grime, and one of her bony fingers fell to the ground, next to River's foot.

Slowly, she moved in River's direction, who, in unyielding terror, was now paralyzed as he stared at the fallen finger by his feet. Without any warning, the ghost-like figure pulled a whisky bottle from under the tattered dress and slammed it across River's head, knocking him out cold. "I never liked your pretentious father, Mr. Edward Smyth. Always thought he was such a hotshot. Son of a bitch." She spat on the ground next to River.

"And you!" She pointed at me. "You wretched girl! I hated you since the day I saw you. You ruined my life. It was perfect before you came along." Her hollow eyes fixated on my entire being, running an electric current through my body, as her lips pressed together in fierce anger. "And tonight, you're finally going to be with your mother," she snarled.

You're not my mother. You're not my mother, my mind began to chant. She somehow read my mind and chimed in, "Oh, but I *am*." Charging forward, the figure grabbed me by the throat, and a guttural growl exited her mouth, a gaping black hole. It was the sound of hell.

The officers acted quickly and motioned toward me, but a violent force pulled them away and smashed each body against a tree trunk. Pinned midair against the trees, the officers froze, breath locked, eyes wide, suspended like insects in amber. It made sure that no one could save me.

My consciousness was falling, pouring out of my ears, nose, and mouth, until I could barely breathe or hear. With heavy eyes, my body slipped away from underneath, and it felt almost weightless. A puffy cloud held my body. My father's face flashed across my mind. In another world, I heard Jared scream. "Dad, you don't have to do this. Please. We know. It's not your fault. Let go of her!" He sounded desperate, pleading with his father.

Bravery came over him. It was now him versus his father in his mother's form. The figure began to move backward, dragging my limp body along with it.

"I'm sorry. I'm sorry for what you went through—all the lies. Trust me, you'll be given a proper burial, and I'll be sure the town knows the truth. No more lies, I promise. Just let her go." Jared's bargaining morphed into an uncontrollable rage, "You weren't perfect, and I don't blame Mama for what she did! I would have done the same! I hated you! Mama hated you, too! Let her go now, you coward! I command you!"

Jane's tortured face turned to agony, and she let out a crying moan as she fell to the ground; her bones knocked on top of one another in a heaped pile.

The officers collapsed from the trees with a thud. Ramsey watched the entire scene unfold. He didn't move an inch. Nor did his cigarette. We splashed water from our thermos onto Ramsey's face to relieve him from the shock. From a few feet away, we heard River moan. He rolled to the side, groaning in pain. His hand touched the spot where his forehead was cut open by the bottle.

The bones of Jane disappeared, and all that was left was the wedding dress and the necklace with the emerald pendant, lying in a puddle on the ground. Something squirmed underneath the gown, attempting to emerge, but it was tangled in the fabric. We stepped in closer with caution. Jared flashed his light on it and poked it with a stick. Out of the clothing appeared a black crow. It flew up to the barrel, knocked its beak three times, and vanished into the night sky.

We proceeded to head back the same way we started the journey: in silence. The officers rolled the barrel as they walked back to the Jeeps. This time, it didn't roll by itself.

It was true. The Witch's Womb left a mark on those who survived it. For those who were initially skeptical and didn't believe in the afterlife, or in the evil that lurked in the shadows, their lives were forever changed.

I could now accept the fact that my mother was dead. And she was never coming back.

CHAPTER 79

MOTHER AND SON

Maria mindlessly gazed at her reflection in the kitchen window while she washed the last pot. A tired, defeated, and dismal woman stared back at her. A woman who arrived at the Smyth home with a purpose, ready to reclaim what was always hers. She tucked the fallen strands of hair back into the hairnet and washed her hands—hands that had become hard and leathery from the daily work of washing dishes and scrubbing the bathrooms. She wiped them on the stained apron tied gently behind her back. They carried the permanent scent of garlic and onions, which she chopped finely almost every day.

She didn't come all this way for nothing.

Bang! She cut a fish's head off with a butcher's knife. The menu for that evening: almond-crusted salmon with leek cream sauce and lemon risotto for the main course. A house salad with Italian dressing for the appetizer, and bread pudding for dessert.

Her patience was now wearing down; she was mentally exhausted from harboring so many secrets. How much longer was she supposed to live under a false identity? The kitchen window now caught River's reflection as she walked towards her. He had grown into a man before her eyes, with chiseled features, stubble on his chin, and masculine arms.

Standing by her side, he began cutting the lemons and squeezing the juice into a bowl. Maria looked at him curiously, wondering why he was there, preparing food with her. He had never done that before. River only acknowledged her presence to inquire about where his belongings were or what his next meal would be.

He wiped his hands and took a small pad and pen from the drawer. On it, he wrote *Rosa Elena Alvarez*. He then gave her the paper. She hadn't seen those words in decades, ever since she stopped being Rosa. Her eyes widened, and she grabbed the paper, burning it with a match. River sensed her anxiety and fear of getting caught by Mr. and Mrs. Smyth.

Taking her hands and kissing them, he calmed her nerves. "I know everything. Don't worry. You are safe now, *mama*." Tears streamed down her cheeks. He wiped them away.

She had been yearning to hear those words for so long. It only took those few words from River to make her realize all the heartache and pain she had been through was well worth it.

"Does Clemmons have any allergies?" he asked his mother.

CHAPTER 80

FREEDOM IS NEAR

Edward and Theresa Smyth were scheduled to go to New York City for the International Diamond Council and would return after two days. "Bye, sweetheart. Take good care. Just let Maria know what you would like for your meals; you can use the intercom system to connect with her. We'll be back on Monday evening. Stay out of trouble!"

River rolled his eyes while half acknowledging Mrs. Smyth. He offered to carry their luggage to the car, performing politeness as if it were a well-rehearsed role. Dutiful son. Grateful heir. He hated every minute in that house, but his time there was temporary. He was making plans.

River called from across the foyer to his mother, "Where will you be staying? You know, just in case I need to reach you for any reason." Theresa paused, delighted to know her son was so responsible.

"Oh, that's a great point. Why did I not remember to give you that information? Here, I'll jot it down." She pulled out a Mont Blanc pen and began scribbling the hotel name and phone number.

The St. Regis New York

Two E 55th St, New York, NY

(212) 753-4500

"Your father and I will be staying in the Dior Suite, isn't that correct, honey? Or was it the Bentley? Oh, I can't remember. Just ask them to connect you with us. They'll know. We're on their VIP list, so there should be no problem. You should come along with us next time, River. We can teach you the ropes of the business. I think it's time, don't you, honey?"

Edward Smyth shut his leather briefcase and entered the code to lock it. "Yes, darling, that's a fantastic idea. We'll be going again in six months. River, it's set. You'll be joining us."

Theresa Smyth smiled, pleased with herself. The pretentious behavior of his parents was something he once overlooked, but nowadays, it gave him acid reflux. He was physically sickened by their ways, their actions, and their associations. The ease with which they moved through a world built on silence and complicity was disturbing.

Six months from now, he hoped to be as far away from this life as possible. *It's just a matter of time. This will soon be an episode I can put behind me.*

River knocked on the car's roof three times to signal that the luggage had been placed in the trunk, and the driver was free to move along. As the car turned out of the driveway, a sense of ease overcame him. Freedom felt close enough to touch.

CHAPTER 81

MEXICAN WEDDING COOKIES

Now that River was by her side, Rosa felt empowered. The sense of wasted time was lifted. This woman had teeth. What she didn't have was mercy.

River took triumphant strides away from the crescent-shaped driveway and flashed her a smile. One step closer to their plan.

He slipped the Santana record from its cover, blowing dust off the surface. The vinyl settled onto the turntable's platter, and the needle dropped. His favorite song—Oye Como Va. No one was there to tell him to lower the volume.

In the kitchen, Rosa began to sway; her hips moved gently with the rhythm. In the adjoining room, River performed his own dance, circling the room freely, completely lost in the beat of freedom. She pulled an apron from the drawer and slipped it over her neck, rolling her shoulders as the music carried her. So much time had been lost. But now it was her turn. She was in control of her present and her future. No regrets, because this was what it had all been leading to.

Butter and powdered sugar creamed together into something light, almost innocent. She then dropped a measured amount of vanilla into the deceitful mix.

River joined her in the kitchen and watched as she created the sweet kryptonite. He crushed the pecans in a plastic bag with a rolling pin, then tipped them into the bowl. Next came the final ingredient. The one that would do the job.

Rosa reached beneath the sink and retrieved a small pouch she'd hidden there—shrimp tails saved from lunch, dried and brittle. She ground them into a fine powder and blended them with sweetener and vanilla, until there was no trace of a shrimp smell. The powder disappeared into the dough.

They watched in silence as the cookies baked to perfection.

CHAPTER 82

JOHNNY'S LAST WISH

The copies were exactly where the dream had shown them—beneath the loose floorboard in his bedroom. Johnny had hidden the evidence. River crouched on the ground, fingers brushing the warped wood, imagining his little brother in that room, panicked yet determined to expose the lies.

If only he had told me. I could've helped him. We could've done this together. The thoughts came fast and merciless, but it was too late. River had to finish the job. He had to do it for Johnny.

By nearly midnight, he'd already stolen the keys to his father's office just a few blocks away. The staff room inside the jewelry store had a mimeograph machine. It was old and loud, but reliable. Thirty copies later, his hands were stained with ink. He drove straight to the church. River almost switched the radio off, but the song "Somebody to Love" began. That's when he knew—Johnny was with him.

Shelby and Jared waited by the church playground.

"I got 'em," River said, pulling the papers from his canvas bag. His voice was steady and calm. "Right here, all thirty copies." Their heads were covered with hoods. He handed ten copies to Shelby, ten to Jared. The rest stayed with him.

They slipped in through the back door of the newly reconstructed St. Theresa Church. One by one, they tucked the documents into the hymnals, secured behind the first page where every worshipper would find them, working in silence.

By 4:00 a.m., the last book was finished.

Before leaving, River placed a plate of Mexican wedding cookies on the podium, right where Father Clemmons would stand to deliver his sermon the next day. That night, they went home and slept peacefully for the first time in a long while. It gave them great comfort to know that the people of Wilshire Pointe would finally see through the lies.

CHAPTER 83

SWEET REVENGE

It was a cloudy Resurrection Sunday morning, and the town of Wilshire Pointe was in celebration. Families arrived in good spirits, full of faith and gratitude. A long picnic table in the courtyard was set for a luncheon, packed with homemade casseroles and pies.

Children performed a short play dramatizing the Easter story, followed by an egg hunt in the playground. They came well dressed and equipped with tiny baskets. When the festivities ended, the congregation filed inside and took their seats.

Father Clemmons positioned himself center stage for his special Easter sermon. A long, gold stole draped over his shoulders and stopped at his hips, one he wore only on important religious ceremonies. His wrinkled fingers guided him through the passage as he read through round spectacles perched on the bridge of his long nose. He cleared the phlegm from his throat.

"Christ is Risen! He is Risen indeed. If Christ is not raised, faith is futile, but because He is raised, believers have a living hope..."

River felt his acid reflux flare as Clemmons continued. His fists tightened. "Murderous maggot. You have some gall standing behind that podium." Clemmons paused. He looked straight at River. "What was that, son?"

"Nothing, Father. I was commending your joyful sermon," River answered with a twinkle of deceit in his eyes. Father Clemmons removed his spectacles to find his place in the book and continued the sermon.

After the sermon ended, his eyes drifted to the plate of Mexican wedding cookies resting on the podium. They were his favorite. Assuming it was made by one of the parishioners, he raised a woolly eyebrow, selected one, and placed it in his mouth. River watched carefully as Clemmons chewed slowly, savoring each bite. Clemmons selected another cookie, followed by another, until nothing but crumbs were left on the plate. Rubbing his fingers together quickly to dust off the powdered sugar, he then continued, "Those were delightful. Shall we begin?"

The congregation opened their hymnals, but the first page was not a hymn. It read:

FATHER CLEMMONS IS A FRAUD AND HAS BEEN LYING TO YOU ALL.

The words were printed in bold letters. Beneath them were detailed financial records—amounts stolen from parishioners and transferred to hidden accounts.

Names followed.

Clemmons. The Whitmans. The Smyths. Sheriff Gibson.

The energy in the room shifted. From disbelief to disgust to anger. Clemmons swayed, gripping the podium as dizziness overtook him. Gasps rippled through the pews. Women covered their mouths with gloved hands. Men gathered their families without speaking.

One by one, the congregation stood, collected their belongings, and walked out. No accusations or questions. Just pure disgust.

Clemmons reached for a hymnal with curious eyes. As he read, the words turned blurry. "No, no," Clemmons croaked. "This isn't what it seems. Someone is trying to destroy me..." No one heard him. The church was emptied, except for one other person, River.

He used his gold stole to wipe the sweat dripping from his forehead and clutched his chest as the bells began to ring relentlessly. Pain seized him and he collapsed to the floor in a fit of violent coughs, followed by gags.

River stood over Clemmons, calm, almost amused. "You're not looking so well, *Father*. Rosa sends her love," River added quietly. "Oh—and the cookies, too."

He stepped over Clemmons and walked out of the church as the towering arched doors slammed behind him. Sprawled on the floor, Clemmons could hardly move. Through his cloudy vision, he saw a crow appear at the window. It flapped its wings and disappeared into the sky.

And that was the end of Father Clemmons.

CHAPTER 84

CLOSURE

River stood in his brother's old bedroom and inhaled what was left of Johnny's scent. No one ever went inside. It was left just as it was. A jacket hung on his desk chair, his soccer uniform in a puddle on the closet floor. All the memories flooded in. The late-night ghost story sessions while their parents were asleep, conversations about girls they crushed on, and the exotic locations they would travel to one day.

It was all a distant memory. Johnny's laughter was deep from his stomach. River would tease him just so he could hear the roaring sound of his brother's laughter blasting through the halls. The tent they camped in was intact, still in the corner of the large room. They'd set it up in the bedroom and lined it up with sleeping bags and Christmas lights. On Friday nights, they'd lie in the tent and browse the latest issues of Playboy. When their parents were out, the boys stuck their heads out the window to enjoy a smoke, sometimes saying nothing at all, just a rebellious exchange between two brothers.

River snapped back into the present moment and wiped away longing tears with his sleeve. On the desk was Johnny's favorite figurine, the Incredible Hulk. River slipped it into his pocket. "We did it, Johnny." He turned the light off and closed the door.

It was time to go now.

River's entire life now fits into two large suitcases. Mr. and Mrs. Smyth stood in the foyer, emotionally distraught over the recent events.

Their own son had smeared their name. River dragged his suitcases behind him and stopped for a moment. "Are you upset because you both were exposed?" he asked them coolly. "Or are you upset because you've lost another son?" They couldn't meet his eyes. Shame filled the space between them.

"River, please don't leave us. We never meant for any of this to happen. All we wanted was to give you and Johnny a good life." Theresa burst into tears while Edward put his arm around her, and questioned his son, "Why are you hurting your mother, River? Hasn't she been through enough?"

He snapped back angrily, "She's not my mother, and she never will be. She's not fit for that title." River shook his head and proceeded through the large French doors for the last time. Before exiting, he took a framed photo of Johnny that was sitting on the console.

River rolled his suitcases to the curbside, where Rosa waited for him in a taxi.

Together they drove into the night, without looking back, and with no regrets.

CHAPTER 85

TIME TO GO

"Will you be coming to the funeral?" I asked River, hoping to see him.

"Who's funeral?"

"Nolan's." The name sheepishly escaped my lips.

The other side of the call went quiet. Maybe I should have asked him this question in person. It was too intimate, not something to inquire over the phone. Immediately, I regretted asking. Of course, it was awkward. He'd been possessed by Nolan's spirit not too long ago. *What a stupid question*, I thought. "I'm sorry, that was... I mean, I don't expect you to. That would just be weird."

My mouth felt like it was stuffed with marshmallows as I fumbled through the words. The truth was, I just wanted to see River. It had been a long few weeks since I last saw him; he needed time to process everything.

"It's okay, Shelby," he said gently. "I'll be out of town for a while. Mama and I are traveling to Mexico. I'm finally meeting my biological grandparents and cousins. She's excited for me to meet the rest of the family."

"That's incredible, River! Why didn't you tell me? How long will you be going for?" He was quiet again. I knew that kind of quiet. It was the kind that made me queasy.

"River, let's go. We are getting late for the airport!" I heard his mother calling from a different room.

"You're leaving today?" I asked, my disappointment slipped through the line. *He could have at least told me.*

"Shelby, I wanted to tell you in person, trust me, but the timing... it was never right. We have a one-way ticket. Not sure exactly when we'll be back. All I know is that I need to get out of here. Especially after...after all this." His voice trailed off.

The words hit hard. I wasn't sure how to respond. We had been taking a break for some time, but I always expected we'd make our way back to each other. I wanted to be angry with him. I hated finding out about this over the phone. But I couldn't hate him. Not after everything we'd gone through. But it still hurt. Only because a part of me had started to love him, and now he was leaving.

"I'll miss you. You'd better write to me and send me photos from Mexico."

"I will, Shelby. This is just temporary. My first home will always be Wilshire Pointe." His voice faded, thick with emotion.

We both put the receivers down. And just like that, he was gone.

CHAPTER 86

¡BIENVENIDO!

Greeted by sights and smells all foreign to him, River thanked the cab driver with a generous tip and reached for the suitcases from the trunk.

They stopped in front of a bustling market filled with dozens of street vendors selling colorful textiles, handmade crafts, and fresh produce. Each stall was uniquely decorated according to the owner's tastes. Shopping here wasn't a mundane chore; it was an experience that tickled all five senses. People weren't there just to buy and sell goods; they wanted to connect. They wanted to hear about one another's families, their hardships, their achievements, and their fears. What River noticed the most was the pride they carried for their heritage. For the first time, he felt like he belonged.

"Eh, that's too much of a tip. Eso es demasiado dinero," Rosa said affectionately. "And let the driver get the suitcases for you. That's the least he can do with the big tip you just gave him." Rosa lovingly scolded him, knowing it would take time to learn the ways of the city. Living such a sheltered life in that mansion, his street skills were dull.

She thought River felt out of place in a land she once called home a long, long time ago. But he didn't. He soaked it all in—everything he had missed, everything he had been denied, was now tangible, and he wanted to consume it.

They finally arrived at their ancestral home after a forty-minute drive from the airport. The bright blue concrete bungalow, surrounded by patches of yellow and red flowers, was something out of a storybook. River had never seen anything like it before. It was a sharp contrast from the bland houses at Wilshire Pointe. The arched windows, framed by ornate tiles in yellow and orange patterns, stood out against the blue facade.

The door was what fascinated him the most. The grand, arched French doors at the entrance featured square inlays with carved flowers in each; two-foot-long, antiqued brass handles gripped the doors. It wasn't only this home, but every door in the neighborhood was unique, like a piece of art.

A sensuous salsa tune blared throughout the courtyard, rattling the windows of the house. The entire family waited at the entrance–about twenty people piled along the front, tiled veranda. In the central courtyard, a cookout had begun, with enough food to feed the entire neighborhood. This wasn't just a gathering. It was a celebration.

"¡Bienvenido!" they cried. They kissed him. Hugged him. Touch his face in disbelief. River was taken aback by the warmth. He thought of the pin-drop silence of his old home. His parents were rarely there, and when they were, they sat stiffly, reading a novel or playing solitaire beneath a single dim lamp. The Smyth house always felt cold. Stoic.

Here, it was the complete opposite. These people were carefree, in love with life and its simplest pleasures. Happiness filled the air. Gratitude. A raw love for living. These people were his family. This was his home now.

For the first time, River felt at ease, absorbing the celebration, the joy, and the fact that all the excitement existed partly because *he* existed.

As for Rosa, it was a fantasy she never thought would be real. She stepped into this house after twenty-one years, twenty-one years of separation. Rosa once lived like a princess here, until her older sister, Vera, took her to Wilshire Pointe and left her at the church with nowhere to turn.

CHAPTER 87

VERA

Vera was never considered marriage material by the locals.

It started the day she was born. That very day, the region was struck by its worst earthquake in history. Hundreds died, and that was all it took. That single coincidence sealed her entire fate.

The locals were deeply superstitious, and words spread like wildfire. People came by to sprinkle holy water on her from a distance, pretending to be concerned while feeding their curiosities.

What kind of devil baby could cause such destruction?

The family was forever viewed with suspicion. As she grew into a young woman, the curse grew along with her. No man from town would marry Vera. She became the subject of dares. Men challenged their friends to date her or to spend one night with her just to see if they'd survive. It was cruel. Ruthless. Desperate for affection, Vera went along with it. Again and again. Used, discarded, and passed around until she lost count.

At her wits' end, she waded into the lake near her house while her family was asleep, but she didn't know how to swim, and she didn't care. She wanted to disappear. No one wanted her. She would only be a burden to her parents, who were already struggling to survive. But her plan failed.

A young sailor saw her thrashing in the water. He jumped in and saved her.

And that wasn't the last time she saw him.

CHAPTER 88

THE FATE OF TWO SISTERS

Vera had fallen in love with this sailor from Wilshire Pointe. For two weeks, they spent much of their time together, but he soon left town and travelled back to his home, promising to marry her and to build a life together if she followed him there. The false promise was an easy way for him to escape without the emotional baggage, as the thought of her going to Wilshire Pointe seemed impossible to him.

By then, Vera was in her mid-thirties.

Unmarried and childless, her parents gave their reluctant blessing out of desperation. They agreed to let her travel to Wilshire Pointe, using their entire life's savings for the expensive journey. She had no future in this small city. Their only condition: she had to take her younger sister, Rosa, with her.

Vera resented the responsibility. To her, Rosa was a burden.

Once they arrived at Wilshire Pointe, she left Rosa outside St. Theresa Church and told her to wait inside while she ran to the store for necessities. Vera never returned. Devastated, afraid and alone in a new town where she barely spoke the language, Rosa sat at the steps of the church for hours. The Reverend Mother found her at the steps and took her in. The sisters welcomed her with warmth and kindness, guiding her into a life she never chose. A life Rosa would later wish to bury deep in an eternal abyss. That day marked the beginning of her misery.

Vera had one mission: to find the Navy officer who had made poetic promises to her. His name was Nolan Mitchell. The Navy unit was deployed along the Pacific coast for 4 weeks at a port stop in Mazatlán, Mexico. To Nolan, Vera was temporary entertainment. A distraction. A body. He humored her with false promises of life in Wilshire Pointe, never intending to keep them.

"You planning on bringing her home to meet the wife?" his fellow shipmates would joke.

"Oh yeah, I'm sure she'd be thrilled to meet your new Mexican doll," another would laugh.

Nolan laughed along with them.

Vera wasn't aware of his marriage. She hung on every word he fed her. Every lie. She imagined a future with children, a home, a place where she was finally chosen and accepted.

The hope in her eyes died the day she finally spotted him at the market with his wife hanging on his arm. That lie sealed her suffering. Too ashamed to return home, too broken to face her family, and too afraid of being seen as the fool she had become, she vanished. No one ever heard from her again.

CHAPTER 89

THE GIFT

Rosa sat with her parents through the night, holding their hands, kissing their worn fingers. "I'm so sorry I left," she whispered. "I never should have gone."

They looked at her with tender eyes. "Don't be silly, mija," her mother said softly. "If you never left, how would we be welcoming this handsome grandson home?" She squeezed Rosa's hand and gave her a wink. Rosa never imagined this moment would exist. Sitting with them and speaking freely. She was finally home. She was finally free.

Hector, Rosa's older brother, though younger than Vera, clapped his hands as his round belly bounced to the beat of the music. A thick mustache rested proudly above his upper lip, the ends twirling upward, joyful, just like him. He had an important announcement, so he climbed onto a chair in the center of the courtyard. "Familia!" he announced. "Friends! Tonight, we celebrate the return of my beloved sister, Rosa, and her son, River!"

Cheers erupted from the joyous crowd. "Words cannot express our gratitude to the Lord for bringing them back to us. This day will never be forgotten." Hector wiped his tears with a napkin and then stuffed the damp napkin into his pocket. His somber face shifted to an expression of delight within seconds. "And we have a small gift. We all pitched in so that River can feel at home." He hopped down and gestured for everyone to follow his lead.

They crowded into the house, funneling into a modest sitting room. Too many bodies, too much excitement. Some pressed into the doorway, others leaned over shoulders, all straining to see.

A large object sat on the floor, hidden beneath a sheet with a shiny, red bow perched on top. Hector grinned. "Uno! Dos! Tres!" The guests echoed after him, counting down.

He pulled the sheet away to reveal a brand-new television. The room exploded with applause, laughter, tears, and embraces. River understood immediately what this meant. A television here wasn't casual—it was a sacrifice. At the Smyth house, they had three. One was in his bedroom. Being a housekeeper for so many years at the Smyth residence, Rosa knew he was accustomed to the luxuries. But this gift, this *gesture,* shattered her. One month's wages gone, to welcome him.

River hugged his uncle tightly, crying into his shoulder, wishing he had known these people sooner. As the emotions ran high, a reflection appeared on the dark screen of the television. River was the first to see it. The memories flood his mind. She stepped closer. The room's noise faded into a dull hum as River turned.

Hector wiped his eyes and smiled. "Ah—this is our new neighbor. Alicia. She moved here last week." He elbowed River playfully. "Perfect timing, mijo. She's your age."

Then Hector's smile softened. "Her parents passed away in a terrible car accident last year. She now lives next door with her grandmother. God bless them." He kissed the cross on his neck.

River couldn't breathe. Gruesome images flashed through his mind. The ones that scarred him. She was a replica of Alice Whitman—same eyes, same lips, same cheekbones, the same nose that tilted ever so slightly upward—the same thick brows. River's left eye began to twitch.

Alicia shook his hand, smiling, almost warm and a bit flirtatious. "Nice to meet you, River," she said. "I feel like we've met before." She handed him a tin that was still warm to the touch. Inside it was freshly baked banana bread.

Before River could process what was in his hands, the television turned on, but the remote wasn't nearby; it was on a stool by the window. A small lamp in the corner of the room began to flicker, unsettling River's nerves.

A silence took over the room, replacing the joy that had filled it just moments before. Hector finally broke the tension, "Debe ser un fantastma!" and laughed as he threw his hands up in the air, and waved them around, signaling something paranormal. "Must be a ghost!"

Everyone laughed—everyone except River.

CHAPTER 90

SHELBY'S NEW NEIGHBORS

Moving trucks and squealing young children disturbed my train of thought as I attempted to study for my LSATs. Each time the large moving truck backed out, it was accompanied by a beeping sound too shrill for the human ear to absorb, and I had to reread the paragraph.

Three houses down, movers unloaded furniture and boxes from a sixteen-foot truck, while a family watched and directed where the boxes should go. I counted the number of children—one, two, three, four, five, six—a family of eight, four girls and two boys, twins maybe.

But that was Wesley's home.

After reading the same paragraph four times, I closed my book and went for a walk, mainly to inquire about these new neighbors. *And what happened to Wesley?* I slowed down at the top of their driveway and waved. "Hello. You have quite a family. My name is Shelby. I live over there." I pointed to my house. "Welcome to the neighborhood."

"Hi, Shelby. Kids, can you say hello to Ms. Shelby? I'm Grace and that's my husband over there, Porter." Grace's arms carried a large box, so she used her head to point to Porter, who was busy directing the movers. He gave me a nod as he pulled up his sleeves.

The younger kids began asking me all sorts of questions about fun things for kids to do around Wilshire Pointe, and the two older siblings shot me an uncomfortable gaze, half-smiling. They sat at the curb browsing *Teen Magazine*, irritated by the interruption.

"I'm sorry, Shelby. It's been a long day. Please excuse me. I'm gonna run to the Chinese restaurant and grab some take-out. We hope to be all moved in by this evening and would love to have you over once settled in."

"Oh, it's okay, I understand. Unpacking boxes is never fun. I wanted to stop by to say hello, and um, I, uh...I also had a question." Fidgeting with the bandana in my hair, I asked in a quiet tone, "Do you, by any chance, know the previous owner or where he went? His name was Wesley."

The couple glanced at one another, perplexed. Grace cleared her throat, tightening the shawl around her as a breeze came through. "Previous owner? Our realtor told us this house has been empty for the last five years. It was an impossible sell for some reason. But we just moved here from Utah and fell in love with the property. We can't imagine anyone not wanting this home." Porter lovingly put his arms around her; the teenagers groaned in the background.

At that moment, bird shot through the sky and swooped by the large oak tree in their front yard, smashing into the second-floor window; it then fell onto the front porch. The younger kids ran to the porch, crowding around the bird, hunched over. After careful examination, one of the boys yelled, "It's dead!" A chill ran up my spine.

"Oh, for heaven's sake! Porter, could you please take care of that? What a way to start our first night here. Shelby, are you alright? Shelby?" She caught me in a daze.

"Yes, I'm fine. Sorry to disturb you all. Well, I hope you enjoy this neighborhood. It was nice to meet you." As I began to walk away, their front porch light flickered, struggling to stay on. Eventually, it shut off.

I continued my walk, though I had no destination in mind.

CHAPTER 91

THE FUNERAL

The tombstone read:
NOLAN LEE MITCHELL
PO2 U.S. NAVY
September 2, 1934 - March 31, 1963
"SOMEWHERE BEYOND THE TIDE."

Whatever was left of his remains in the barrel was placed into the casket and lowered into the ground. Father Francis, a noble and humble priest, had assumed Clemmons's position and conducted the burial ceremony for Nolan Mitchell. I went in support of Jared and Mathew. They were my family now. As uncomfortable as I felt there, knowing the sheer hatred Nolan once harbored toward me, I couldn't abandon them.

"We gather here today to celebrate the life of Nolan..."

The Father's ceremonial words fade into the background as my mind wanders to Jane—my mother. I had lost my mother twice. The first loss was completely fabricated, and when I found out the truth, it was too late. She was gone again. And this time, for good. A part of me hated Papa for keeping me away from her. Another part of me resented her for not fighting harder to be in my life. I was cheated out of having a mother.

Caroline was a bit late, but Jared's face softened the moment he saw her. She offered an apologetic smile and took her place beside him, with Mathew standing on his other side. Jared surprised everyone by holding on to Caroline. She may have entered his life when he needed her the most. She broke through Jared's concrete exterior and became his first real relationship. For the first time, he no longer felt the need to arm himself against the world. There was nothing left to hide. Nothing left to fear.

We all stood there hoping for the same thing, for Nolan's soul to finally be at peace.

Jared was in full uniform. He started training under Sheriff Ramsey's mentorship the day after our trip to the Witch's Womb. Impressed by his bravery, Ramsey took Jared under his wing. Jared stood tall, hand in hand with Caroline. Mathew pressed close to Jared's other side. He had been too young to remember Nolan, but he stood quietly, wiping away the tears. I assumed they were for his mother. I gave his hand a tight squeeze. A small smile formed at the corner of his lips.

Next to Nolan's gravesite, a tombstone for Jane had been placed. Because there was no body to bury, the wedding gown was used in its place. It was still stained with her blood.

CHAPTER 92

PAPA

Papa was taken to a hospital for the criminally insane after he was formally convicted of Nolan's murder. After they placed him in handcuffs, a glazed look washed over his eyes, and he mumbled words that no one could understand.

Then he looked straight into my eyes. "I saw the boogeyman last night," he whispered. "He's back!" He then laughed hysterically, throwing his fists up in the air as a sign of victory. My heart stopped. The guards shook their head, but I knew exactly what he meant. Only I knew.

That was the last time I saw Papa. It was all too disturbing for me to revisit that part of my life. They were taking good care of him there, more than I was physically and mentally able to do. I just wanted my life back again. I had to move forward, and being around Papa dragged me back into the haunting memories. The trauma. The memories I wanted to forget.

A few months later, I received a phone call from Wilshire Pointe Psychiatric Institute. They asked me to come immediately. There had been an incident.

"Are you Shelby Jones, daughter of Benson Ray Jones?"

"Yes, that's me, and he is my father," anxiety filled my body. The tone on the other line was stoic, yet urgent.

Upon arriving at the facility, I barely put my car into park and jumped out. The woman at the front desk didn't look up at me when she asked for my information.

"Could you please show us your driver's license, honey?" Her tone was sympathetic, which caused me to worry as I pulled out my ID. She verified my photo with my face, and sighed, handing me my card. "Please step into that room over there, and one of our staff members will be with you shortly?" I wished someone would hurry up and tell me what was happening. My head spun with questions as I nervously tapped my foot. A woman in a white uniform stepped in and closed the door behind her. "Hello, Shelby. Please have a seat. This isn't easy to say, but I'm afraid something terrible has happened to your father. We don't know exactly what happened," she began softly. Then she held my hand. I felt my teeth sink into the corner of my lip. "But it appears as though your father met with an awful accident. It's a mystery how he managed to escape his room and get up to the top floor, but he was last seen by one of the janitors." I looked at her, hopeful. "What do you mean by *last seen*?"

She hesitated before continuing.

"One of our janitors reported seeing him on the terrace. He was sweeping when he noticed your father yelling at a large black crow perched on the ledge. Your father appeared agitated, calling it names, trying to strike it."

I could barely breathe.

"He climbed onto the ledge and shouted at the crow, '*She never loved you. She was always mine!*'"

Her voice softened. "In trying to reach the bird, he lost his balance and fell fifteen stories. He was pronounced dead at the scene. He's been taken to the Wilshire Pointe Morgue. I'm so sorry, Shelby."

I knew in my heart that this was no accident.

Down at the morgue, I saw his body covered in a white sheet in room 003.

The anatomical pathology technician ushered me inside and drew the curtain. Pacing the room, the technician began to speak quickly, almost frenetically; his movements were abrupt, matching his nervous energy.

"We've never seen anything like this before. I think you need to have a look. Please, brace yourself. This is going to be difficult for you, Shelby." He put a hand on my shoulder and removed the sheet. Papa's face was completely distorted, yet a wide smile appeared across it.

No child should ever have to see their parents in this condition. I wanted to remember him as he once was—handsome, intelligent, a respected lawyer. The father who used to lift me onto his lap, pumping his fists and shouting, "Education is power!"

"It shouldn't be possible," the technician interrupted my memory. "Facial muscles can't remain in that position after death. A smile requires active muscle control." He moved the sheet further down. Branded on my father's chest was the word L-I-E-S.

"What can you tell us about this? It seems to have been done recently, within the last two weeks. Is it all right if we preserve his body for research purposes?"

"Absolutely not," I said immediately. "Please prepare for a cremation. You may give me the ashes once it's complete. I want no further discussion." My face was stern, and my shoulders were stiff. I had no other words for the pathologist; he was stunned at my robotic response, but he had no idea, and I wasn't going to retell the story. I wanted it to be over.

No amount of research on his body would explain what happened. I wanted a cremation. If Papa turned to ashes, then maybe he could rest in peace. I wanted him completely gone, even his skeleton, so that no evil could harm him anymore.

But who was the evil one, my father or Nolan? The lines were blurred and my thoughts began to unravel.

After the cremation, I carried the ashes to the church and asked Father Francis to dispose of them. It just seemed like the right thing to do. Father

Francis gave me a solemn look of empathy and blessed me, placing his hands on my head as a small prayer escaped his lips. Tears streamed down my cheeks. It was over. I could finally let it out, and I felt safe.

A week later, I received a call from Father Francis.

"Shelby, dear child, how are you? I wanted you to know that your father's ashes have been dispersed into the wooded area behind the church. Your father is now free. Please know that his soul is at rest. We said a special prayer for him early this morning."

I listened to him, staring blankly across the room at nothing. The wooded area behind the church. The Witch's Womb. It was the last place we saw Jane's physical body.

Together at last—Benson and Jane. The way it was always meant to be.

"Shelby, my child, are you alright?"

"I'm not sure, Father," I said quietly.

"But I will be."

CHAPTER 93

ONE LAST ENCOUNTER

The familiar aroma of sweet hazelnut coffee filled the air. Morning had officially begun once I stepped foot in Pearl Café, where the locals were getting the headlines for the week, quietly sipping their coffee and enjoying breakfast. The comforting sound of sizzling bacon put me into a trance. And the smell. It felt like home—the home I chose to remember, with Moses and Papa, who sang while cooking buttered scrambled eggs with bacon on Sundays.

A long bar with round stools sat parallel to the chef's cooking range, for the people who needed to eat and run. Square tables filled out the main area for those needing a moment to themselves, savoring their morning coffee and breakfast while perusing the paper.

I always chose a table by the window and pretended River was sitting across from me. I sent him a few letters, but they were returned to my mailbox. I relied on the postcards and letters, which stopped suddenly over the last month. A part of me wondered if he'd met someone new there. Or if he wanted to forget Wilshire Pointe altogether, leaving all the suffering behind him.

Pearl Café was the heart of the town. Everyone here knew each other's names. And everyone knew me. My name was associated with all things paranormal around here. My reputation followed me wherever I went; some found me interesting, and others chose to keep their distance. But I had managed to gain the trust of a handful of people who were able to see me for being an ambitious woman, despite the recent events and family history—a woman who would one day be partner at Lambert & Blyth, where Papa used to work.

Ravi looked at me from behind the counter, smiled, and called out my order, which hadn't changed in six months. "One medium dark roast coffee with an egg croissant coming right up for Ms. Jones!" Ravi used to work with Jared at Moody's. No one would have ever expected him to rebel against his parents and quit Harvard Medical School, but that's exactly what he did. He was the lead guitarist of a rock band popular with the locals and spent the day at Pearl Café, serving them.

"Thank you." I gave him a nod and took my seat. It was my thirty minutes of calm before I began my paralegal job at the firm. I pulled out some notes to review for the day. Someone was watching me.

Mrs. Baker. The town's gossip queen was staring at me so intensely that her left eye had begun to twitch. Her curly brown hair was tucked neatly under a beige hat with two silk flowers on the side. She was the catalyst behind the rumor that identified me as a Satan worshipper. One would think that after surviving the horrific fire at the church, she would gain some perspective on life. Her world remained the same, absorbed in useless gossip. She was the initial match that lit a candle, which eventually lit another, and before you knew it, the town was on fire with her entertaining stories—always concerning the lives of others, but never hers. Fed up with her nonsense, I abruptly turned around in my chair, let out a hiss and flicked my tongue at her. I knew it was wildly inappropriate, but I couldn't help myself. Slowly, I stood up, my eyes fixed on her, giving her the impression I was walking towards her. Mrs. Baker jolted upright in a huff, attempting to mask her fear, and waddled out of the café in horror. She mumbled some religious jargon and used her new Japanese sensu to fan her sweaty, red face, as she clutched her rosary in the other hand.

I could resume my morning in peace.

As she exited the French doors, an older woman in elegant, poised attire caught my eye. Her wardrobe was from an entirely different era, as if time moved on but she hadn't. Her perfectly pressed skirt was accompanied by a matching hat and a leather handbag that hung delicately off her shoulder. A light coat of makeup blanketed her frail skin, and a black silk Dior scarf with a damask print hid her neck.

With beady eyes, she looked around, removed her gloves, and set her gaze on me. Immediately, I became aware of my posture and attire, hoping they were suitable for this stranger. "Is this seat taken?" she asked, pointing to the empty seat at my table. Opium by Yves Saint Laurent clouded my nose as she moved around—a classic fragrance used by the upper class.

"No, ma'am, it's not." I don't know what possessed me to say "ma'am", but her presence demanded that kind of respect. I pushed the chair back and made way for her to sit.

"I'm so sorry, but I'm not sure I know you," I said. The woman sat gracefully across the table, and folded her hands across her lap, "Don't be sorry. And you're right, you don't know me. But you will soon. I'm Darlene. My, what a beautiful necklace you have on there." She looked at it with a stiff smile. I was wearing the necklace with the emerald pendant; it had become my signature symbol.

Darlene. I knew that name. This couldn't be the *same* Darlene. Where did she suddenly come from, and how did she know I was here? A strange feeling of unease with a hint of excitement filled my heart, as if I were meeting someone from a story I'd read. *Darlene Jones*. Oh, Papa would have a fit!

Maybe she came back for her necklace. That's why she commented on it right away. I shifted uncomfortably in my seat, unable to make eye contact with her. Should I take it off and give it to her? Or would it be awkward? I clutched it, unsure, feeling like an accused thief. The memory of how she treated Helen after losing this very necklace flashed across my mind.

Darlene calmly reached inside her purse and pulled out a small wooden box. Constructed of intricately carved wood, perhaps with some ivory inlay, and featuring a small lock and a key, it looked like something made centuries ago. She handed me the box, "I thought you may want to have these."

When I turned the key in the lock, the box opened. Inside were the most beautiful oval-shaped emerald earrings. I looked at the earrings with great admiration. The necklace was part of a set. I was missing the earrings, and Darlene was missing the necklace.

"They pair with the necklace. It belongs to you now. I hope you like it."

There was something about her that was kind, opposite to what I was shown. Maybe all these years had softened her, and she realized she had ruined her son's life. It's possible she's here to make amends, since she could never do so with Papa. I wasn't sure, but my curiosity was at its highest peak. I wanted to know more. I wanted to be around her and ask so many questions. What poise she carried about her, what grace, what a woman she was. I was both starstruck and upset that Papa had kept me away from her for so long.

"I wish you could have met my other son, your father's younger brother. He was Benny's favorite—Benny called him Chubs. That little boy always looked up to Benny for everything, but he left us too soon. It was so sudden. He couldn't handle the pressures of living in New York and sadly took his own life." She patted her dry eyes with a handkerchief. "Your father was devastated. He never mentioned Wesley's name again. His name was Wesley Jones. I don't think Benny told you about any of this, did he?"

I shook my head no, but I knew.

His face appeared before my eyes. Three houses down. The initials WJ around his neck. It all flashed quickly into my mind. It was all too much to absorb.

"Well, we have much to catch up on, dear." She began to shift in her chair, signaling that her time with me was coming to an end. Nervously,

I blurted out, wanting to see her again, "Would you like to come over to my house for tea one of these days?"

"I would love that, Shelby. I would really love to meet you again."

I gave her my notebook so she could write down her contact information. Her movements were so composed, so calculated, as if she had taught a class in etiquette. I felt my shoulders slouching and instantly straightened up.

After jotting down her information, she closed the notebook, slid it across the table, and gave me a playful wink. She put her black gloves back on her frail, perfectly manicured fingers.

As she stood up, she straightened her dress. "I hope to be hearing from you soon, dear."

"Yes, ma'am, it would be wonderful to see you again." I stood up, not knowing if I was supposed to shake her hand or hug her. She abruptly turned away and sauntered out of the coffee shop, barely making a sound as she left. I couldn't believe it. A visitor from the past suddenly entered my life, in this café, and presented me with a gift.

Giddy with excitement, I grabbed my notebook and opened it to the page she had written on. The bitter taste of whisky crept into my mouth.

Next to her name was her address and a short note:

"Don't be fooled. I'm still here, you wretched girl."

-The Boogie Man

EPILOGUE

It was the perfect evening. The melodic sound of ocean waves gently hit the pier as calm waters reflected the glint of the moon. October evenings introduced a new chill in the air, replacing the warm days that now ran short. Caroline wore her ring with pride as it sparkled in the candlelight of the dinner. She clinked her glass of champagne with Jared's glass, celebrating the moment she said "yes." It was earlier that day when Jared surprised her at the yoga studio as she wrapped up the last class. He took her out for ice cream, where they had their first date, and popped the question.

They were now dining at Wilshire Pointe's finest restaurant by the shore, The Grande Wilshire, where they relished filet mignon with a side of house salad and fondant potatoes. Cutting into her meat, Caroline looked up at Jared, "So, when can we tell Shelby? I want her to be the first to know." He smiled and sipped his champagne. "How about tonight? After dinner. We can swing by her place."

Jared pulled into Shelby's neighborhood. The crisp October evening showcased front porches with glowing pumpkins, while fallen leaves puddled across front lawns. The lights were still on inside the house, which meant Shelby was awake. He parked his van and opened the door for Caroline.

A light wind caused the mailbox door to swing open. It was old and rusty, and creaked as it gently swayed in the wind. Jared jogged over to close it. It seemed as though Shelby hadn't bothered to check it in days, if not weeks, so the door wouldn't fully close. Jared removed the overflowing stack of mail from the box. As he was about to close the door, he saw a thick piece of paper that was left inside. It was a postcard—torn along one corner, as though it had struggled through the journey to arrive at its final destination. The front displayed a serene photograph of a Mexican beach at sunset. There was no name, nor was there a return address.

"Jared, honey, it's chilly out. Let's go in," Caroline called out to him. He didn't look up; he just stared at the mystery postcard. "Yeah, I'll be there in a sec."

A slow unease prickled his arms as the hair rose along the surface. Four words were written in rushed ink, almost as if afraid to be caught.

Help me. She's here.

A gust of wind picked up, blowing leaves across the front yard, and three houses down, a porch light flickered and eventually shut off.

ABOUT THE AUTHOR

Work is play and play is work. As Maslow said, to be self-actualized, you must not only do work you find important, you must do it well and enjoy it.

Wilshire Pointe is my debut gothic horror novel. A love for horror began early—when I was seven years old and my dad accidentally rented The Exorcist for a room full of kids during a party. While all the other kids were horrified, I was fascinated.

I keep my head down and my heart focused. I love discussing the development of the self and the mind with people. I'll probably run the other direction if someone attempts to gossip with me—or complain.

I love anything that makes me laugh. My partner is guilty of doing just that. Laughter, to me, is an essential vitamin—the kind of laugh where you can't see straight or breathe for a few seconds.

If I hear a favorite tune in a store, I'll dance. My kids will be mortified. But hopefully they'll learn that what people think about them is none of their business. Fame by David Bowie is an all-time favorite.

Good news and good people are what I aim to be surrounded by. Some might say I'm a bit of a vibrational snob. And I wouldn't doubt that one bit.

Cover design by cheriefox.com

E-book – 978-1-970853-55-1

Paperback – 978-1-970853-56-8

Hardcover – 978-1-970853-57-5